PENGUIN BOOKS
DESERT SHADOWS

Anand (P. Sachidanandan), a civil engineer by profession, is known for his serious and thought-provoking works of fiction in Malayalam. Though he writes in Malayalam, his novels are pan-Indian in setting. *Desert Shadows (Marubhoomikal Untakunnatu)* was published in Malayalam in 1989 and has already gone through twelve editions. His later works, *Travels of Govardhan* (an intertextual work taking off from Bharatendu Harishchandra's *Andher Nagari Choupat Raja)* and *Vyasa and Vighneswara* (which moves between writers and readers), have been acclaimed as pathfinders in modern fiction writing. Now retired from service, Anand lives in Delhi.

*

K.M. Sherrif was born in 1962 in Calicut and completed his Masters in English from the University of Calicut. His translations from Malayalam, Gujarati and English have been published in several journals and magazines. His translation of Gujarati Dalit writing appeared in a special edition of *Indian Literature,* the bimonthly journal of the Sahitya Academy, in January 1994, and won the Katha award for translation in 1993. At present he teaches English at Aringar Anna Government Arts College, Karaikal, Pondicherry and is also working on his doctoral thesis. He is married with two children.

Anand

Desert Shadows

*Translated from the Malayalam
by K.M. Sherrif*

PENGUIN BOOKS

Penguin Books India (P) Ltd, 210 Chiranjiv Tower, 43 Nehru Place,
New Delhi-110 019, India
Penguin Books Ltd., 27 Wrights Lane, London W8 5TZ, UK
Penguin Books USA Inc., 375 Hudson Street, New York, NY 10014, USA
Penguin Books Australia Ltd., Ringwood, Victoria, Australia
Penguin Books Canada Ltd., 10 Alcorn Avenue, Suite 300, Toronto, Ontario, M4V
3B2, Canada
Penguin Books (NZ) Ltd., 182–190 Wairau Road, Auckland 10, New Zealand

First published in Malayalam by DC Books 1989

Copyright © P. Sachidanandan 1989

First published in English by Penguin Books India (P) Ltd. 1998
This translation copyright © Penguin Books India (P) Ltd. 1998

10 9 8 7 6 5 4 3 2 1

Typeset in Palatino by Eleven Arts, Delhi-35

Printed at Chaman Enterprises, New Delhi

This is a work of fiction. Names, characters, places and incidents are either the
product of the author's imagination or are used fictitiously, and any resemblance to
actual persons, living or dead, events, or locales is entirely coincidental.

Desert Shadows

12/11/'99

To

Dear Two in California

A book about the present civilization
— Surrounded by deserts, so about
Man who seek Shadows in
deserts. With Love

T. S. Saba

Saba

Chapter One

'Makhan Singh,' the Project Jail warder called out, straightening his back once again on the uncomfortable folding stool, and peering with his long-sighted eyes at the paper he was holding at arm's length. 'Height: one hundred and eighty, weight: seventy-eight, a deep scar on the right cheek.'

A man with a long moustache and a defiant expression on his face got up from the group of men squatting before the pointed rifles of the policemen who had accompanied them from the City Jail. He walked up to Kundan as fast as the shackles around his knees allowed him, and turned his face to show him the scar on his cheek. Kundan glanced at him first and then shifted his gaze to the photograph on the card before him. Suppressing a yawn he nodded, and the man walked across to join another group of men sitting hunched up before the rifles of the security guards of the Project at the other end of the platform.

The new batch of prisoners sent from the City Jail to work in the sensitive areas of the Rambhagarh Strategic Installations Project were being handed over by the warder of the City Jail to Kundan, the Project labour officer, who, after duly identifying and certifying them, had to hand them over to the warder of the Project Jail. It was a tedious exercise, lasting several hours, conducted on the only platform that the railway station of Rambhagarh boasted. A solitary tree, which had already started withering, provided the only patch of shade there.

Rambhagarh was a small town in the desert which got its name from a fort built on top of a huge rock which stood out prominently in the otherwise flat terrain. The king who had built it was all but forgotten now. The sheer height of the fort, its strong and still undamaged walls, and the vast space it enclosed, could have been the factors that influenced the selection of this place for the Strategic Installations.

There was a brief tea break when the camp staff served tea to everyone. The prisoners raised the mugs to their lips with both their hands, which were manacled together. Even while drinking tea they did not talk or try to look at one another.

Beyond the railway tracks lay the sprawling sandstone quarries, blurred by the cloud of dust that hung in the air. The perfect silence that reigned in the platform, where no train was expected till late at night, was broken only by the sound of the quarry workers' hammers falling on the stone blocks, muffled by the distance that separated the platform from the quarries. There were no vertical objects around to cast lengthening shadows. Yet the approach of the night could easily be discerned by the dying noises, the glow of freshly lighted hearths and the cooling of the air. Though it was only the beginning of April, days were already considerably hot. It would be a year of severe drought, the old people of Rambhagarh said. They had their own way of predicting such things.

The warder of the Project Jail, his throat cleared by the hot tea, called out the next name: 'Pasupati Singh. Height: one hundred and seventy, weight: seventy-five.'

The man who rose from the group of prisoners looked

2

meek and servile. He had a pathetic expression on his face, unlike the other prisoners who appeared to be unruffled. And he was thin and short.

'Wait a minute. Read that again,' Kundan stopped the warder who had started reading out the identification marks too: '. . . half of the little finger on the left hand missing.'

The man who stood before Kundan looked pleadingly at the warder and made no attempt to show his fingers to Kundan. But Kundan managed to see that all his fingers were intact. It was evident that the hefty Pasupati Singh staring at him resentfully from the photograph on the paper in his hand could not even be mistaken for the feeble creature who stood cowering before him.

'Get back there,' the warder sent him back to the group of prisoners waiting to be identified and handed over.

Except for the warder from the City Jail, nobody, not even the Project Jail warder, seemed to have noticed anything odd in the discrepancy.

'Sir, we can come back to this case later,' the warder from the City Jail quickly turned to Kundan and said. 'Let us dispose of the others.'

The thin, stooping man with round, metal-framed glasses looked more like a railway clerk than a jail warder, who usually conjures up the image of a tough, no-nonsense official. The pathetic expression on his face matched that of the prisoner who now stood before him.

Though slightly unnerved by the mystery of identity, Kundan conceded his request.

'All right, send the next.'

No sooner had Kundan finished identifying the rest of the prisoners than the sun disappeared behind the unbroken line of the desert horizon. A dry wind blew across the platform and the air suddenly turned cold.

The security guards led the prisoners to the vehicles kept ready for them. Soon, only the prisoner who went by the name Pasupati Singh and the warder from the City Jail were left with Kundan on the platform.

3

'We can't do anything with this man,' Kundan told the warder, 'you can take him back.'

The warder's face fell. His stoop became more pronounced.

'Please, sir, let him stay here for a couple of days. It is my humble request, sir. We can find a way out by then, sir.'

'A way out?' Kundan frowned at the warder. 'Look, mister, I can't issue him a pass. They won't let anybody into the jail without a pass. What prevents you from taking him back? You know he is not the right man. Surely there has been some mistake. You can get it checked there.'

'I can't do that, sir.' The warder was now the embodiment of humility. 'There will be trouble, sir, really bad trouble. Trouble for everybody—for him, for me and even for you. Just two days, sir. We will find a way out by then.'

'Trouble for me too?' Kundan found it strange.

'Please save us, sir!'

The warder stood expectantly before Kundan without looking at his face.

Kundan sat down on the chair again. It was obvious that this man and the prisoner about whom he was making his fervent pleas were in some sort of serious trouble, about which neither of them had so far been forthcoming. Whatever the problem was, it was Kundan who had to take the decision. They were now trying to leave everything in his hands by appealing to his generosity. Kundan, on his part, could have firmly asked them to do what he told them. But he did not want to do that.

It was one of those occasions when duty and necessity do not speak in the same voice. Kundan was forced to make a choice. He always felt miserably alone on such occasions. He was usually slow in taking decisions. Even after taking one, he was not content to leave it at that and kept arguing with himself whether it was the right decision or not.

Kundan's eyes wandered to the camp of the quarry workers. Though the quarries lay across the railway tracks

4

in the distance, the workers, out of their desire for staying closer to human habitation, had pitched their tents on this side of the tracks, beside the road from the railway station that led to the town, under the shade of the few trees that had managed to survive. The workers were now back in their camps. The men were relaxing or smoking beedis. The women were lighting fires while the children played around them.

What were the conflicts and choices that confronted these people, Kundan wondered. He was sure that their life too was riven by conflicts. In the city it was the monotony of his job and the feeling that nothing was going to happen that had driven him to seek a change. That was how he ended up accepting this extraordinary, outlandish job in the middle of the forlorn desert.

Kundan summoned the warder of the Project Jail. They talked the matter over and the Project Jail warder agreed to keep the problem prisoner in the Project Jail on a temporary basis for two days.

Kundan was not sure whether his feeling at the conclusion of the incident could be called relief.

Chapter Two

Back home, Kundan went straight to the bathroom. Fortunately there was water in the tap which was still warm, though the atmosphere had cooled down considerably. Taking off his clothes and turning on the shower lightly, Kundan stretched himself under it on the stone-paved floor.

This was something he loved to do when he was exhausted or lonely. He would then remove all thoughts from his mind and concentrate on his body and the jets of water that fell on it. It was a therapy which almost always restored his flagging spirits.

Stepping out of the bathroom and into kurta-pyjamas, Kundan climbed the stairs to the terrace. The walls, the roof and the stairs of the house were all made of sandstone. The days when the artisans were keen on leaving the mark of their craftsmanship on every piece of stone was gone. But, perhaps as a ritual, they still exhibited a bit of their art somewhere on their works. Here, leaving the walls, the windows and the balcony, they had chosen the staircase for the purpose. Perhaps the artisans were trying to convey a message by this strange choice of theirs: that art had managed to survive not at the top or the bottom, but somewhere on the way up—in the interfaces, passages and junctions in our busy world. Nevertheless, the lotuses they had carved on the banisters only made it difficult to run one's hands along them smoothly.

As soon as Kundan sat down on a cane chair on the terrace, Gulshan brought him a whisky. Seeing Kundan head straight for the bathroom without waiting for his tea, Gulshan had assumed that he needed a shot of whisky more than tea. But Kundan had no taste for anything. He just twirled the glass in his hand.

The shower therapy did not seem to have worked today. Something lingered like a bad taste in Kundan's mouth. Neither the lights and sounds from the nearby houses built in the modern style nor the faraway look of the havelis whose lights and sounds had long died down helped him get rid of it. The huge, sombre shadow of the Rambhagarh fort brought no solace either.

It was not just the incident of mistaken identity that depressed him. This was the first time he had been assigned to receive a batch of prisoners. Soon he would have to hand over the prisoners now working in the Project to the City Jail authorities. During the last five months since his arrival, such new assignments kept cropping up one after the other. Strange jobs which labour officers working in factories in the city could not even imagine. The jobs in the Project were indeed extraordinary. Its work force came from two sources. The men for the first group, which was called the Pioneer Force, were recruited from the market on a contract basis for a fixed period. The rules governing them included certain provisions of the Army Act. Kundan's primary duty was the recruitment of this work force. The Prisoner Force was the second group of workers on the Project. The prisoners were picked up for the job from the jails in the city. A new batch would arrive every six or eight months and the old batch would go back to where it came from. The routine supervision of the two forces was the responsibility of the respective commanders, while the construction wing regulated their work on the Project. But Kundan, as the labour officer, had to be omnipresent. Every single member of both the forces was inducted into the Project by him. Again, when they were relieved on completion of their term, or when they deserted the lines or overstayed their leave, it was Kundan who had to set things right.

The incident at the railway station refused to leave his mind. He could foresee how the warder from the City Jail would argue his case: what if a Rahim was taken in instead of a Ram? Both were prisoners after all. While Kundan was very particular about checking the height, weight and identification marks of each prisoner, for the others they constituted a mere molten mass with a common name: prisoner. Even the Pioneers, whose particulars and history he so meticulously recorded at the recruiting centre, instantly turned into a similar mass the moment they were enrolled. No one, not even their commanders or the engineers at the site, seemed to have any interest in learning even their names.

Kundan was the only person vested with the exclusive privilege of knowing these people as individuals with names, height and weight, and moles and scars on their bodies. Of course, it was his duty. But was his duty now crossing its ordained limits, he wondered. Was he now delving dangerously into the amorphous mass lying at the bottom of the Project? He tried to recall the hateful eyes of Pasupati Singh staring at him from the photograph in the dossier and the scared look of the meek prisoner, whose real name was still unknown to him. What did the warder mean when he said there would be trouble for the prisoner, for himself and for Kundan?

The air on the terrace began to shimmer. It was a sign of the advent of summer. As the night advanced, a sudden gust of wind would blow in from somewhere in the depths of the desert. It would last for about an hour. When the wind begins to stir, the people of Rambhagarh rise from their sleep, open the doors of their houses and come out into the streets. Those who cannot come out stand at the windows to welcome it. The deserted roads come alive. As the wind dies down, the air becomes cooler, the doors are closed and the roads become deserted again.

Kundan sat on the terrace, waiting for the summer the wind was ushering in. The summer which, as the elders in the community had predicted, was to bring drought, suffering and death in its wake.

Chapter Three

When we call something unique, we usually mean it is extraordinary or incredible. Yet, it is real too. Here 'real' is something that·can happen and does happen. Thus, when we call something unique, it only shows that we lack the knowledge or experience to accept it as real. In other words, the frequency with which the word 'unique' occurs in our expressions is also a measure of our ignorance or inexperience. This world which we describe as elusive or mysterious is in fact concrete and ordinary. We describe it as elusive or mysterious because we live in a self-created situation which leaves us ignorant and muddled when exposed to realities. As ignorant and innocent as Alice was before she entered wonderland or got behind the looking glass.

Take, for instance, the two events that befell Kundan one after the other on a single day.

First, Daniel.

Daniel appeared before him in a pair of baggy blue trousers, a soiled white shirt and a cotton summer cap. The white cap had turned brown with dirt. His clothes, his face and his body all looked worn out. He did not carry anything in his hands, not even a bag. Above his greying beard and sunken cheeks, the eyes that preferred to stay immobile looked distant and vacant.

Kundan was in the middle of the morning's hustle at the recruiting centre. Every morning he had to spend three to four hours there till the sun came directly overhead and everything became as hot as the inside of the furnace of a glass factory. The recruiting centre and the Pioneer Force camps were on the rear side of the hill on which the fort stood, on the poromboke* which stretched out into the desert. Apart from them, there were only a few garbage dumps and a growing patch of slums there. The entire town lay in front of the fort. There were two radial roads starting from the hill which separated the town from the stretch of poromboke, one leading to the railway station and to the distant green lands beyond, and the other to another town lying deep in the desert.

Every morning as he drove to the recruiting centre, Kundan would think of the residents of the town who enjoyed the comforts of modern civilization, of the Pioneers who were trapped within the barbed-wire enclosures guarded by the security police, of the slum-dwellers who had only the mounds of garbage around them for fencing, of the huge yawning mouth of the desert which loomed before them all, and of the people who had made it their home. As he sat down in his chair at the recruiting centre, Kundan faced a long line of people who came from the wilderness of the desert seeking admittance within the barbed-wire fences of the Rambhagarh Fort. Daniel's case was rather unusual. He had once slipped through the fence and was now coming back voluntarily.

---

*Poromboke: literally means 'outskirts' or 'no-man's land' in Malayalam. It would, in an extended sense, mean the unaccounted section of society, which does not figure in the urban and elite thinking, which lies beyond and abuts its civilized nucleus.

It had happened two years ago. Daniel, who was a Pioneer in the Project then, had gone on leave to his hometown far away from the desert, watered by a river and endowed with lush greenery. A dam upstream on the river collapsed and the whole town was submerged. Daniel's entire family—his wife, children, brothers and sisters—was washed away by the rushing waters.

On examining the file brought from the records office, Kundan came upon the report of the death of Pioneer Daniel. He did not know how the report had entered the file. But as far as the Project was concerned, Daniel was dead.

'What do you want now?' Kundan asked Daniel, trying to decipher the expression on his face.

'I want to join duty, sir,' Daniel's voice came out in a hoarse whisper through his pursed lips.

'Why didn't you think of it in the last two years?'

'Think of my situation, sir. Perched precariously on a branch above the swirling waters . . . watching my wife and children being washed away . . .'

Kundan stopped him. It was a terrible situation that Daniel had asked him to imagine, especially in the desert where not a drop of water was to be seen and where a friend, let alone close relatives, was as elusive as a mirage to him. Kundan felt a lump in his throat.

Shaking off the feeling that had overcome him , Kundan looked up at Daniel again. 'But Daniel, according to the records that we have here, you are dead. You are no longer on the Project's rolls. So you are free. You can live now as you please.'

Daniel said nothing.

'Why Daniel, don't you believe me?'

Daniel's eyes were still vacant and dry. He whispered again through pursed lips, as if he was speaking for somebody else.

'I have nothing with me except the clothes I have on

12

myself. There is not a single rupee in my pocket. There is nobody to wait for me. Even if I have the freedom you are talking about, God knows I can't go about in the open with it. They will get me.'

'Who?'

'The police.'

A desertion report and an apprehension memo dispatched to the police from the Project·challenged Kundan from the file before him. For two years, the man who now stood wearily before him had been moving about stealthily, with nothing but a shirt on his back to dodge the police. He had now realized that his freedom, the freedom he had taken so much pains to guard, was of no use to him at all.

Kundan shut the file. He put a paperweight on it and rotated it. He was feeling all alone again.

'What if I give you a death certificate?'

The moment Kundan uttered the words, he realized the absurdity of the remark.

'They know I am not dead, sir,' Daniel's lips curled in a mock smile.

Kundan shook his head. 'There is a death certificate here. I am sorry, I don't think I can help you in any way, Daniel.'

Some day the police would bring this man before him. This wretched man with no feelings, his hands tied with a rope . . . What would he do then? He might not be able to set him free on the plea that he was dead.

And then Sulaiman.

After finishing his job at the recruiting centre, Kundan drove to the prisoner's camp in the Project Jail inside the fort. As the road climbed the hill, negotiating several hairpin curves on the way, the town below grew smaller and looked more and more alienated. When the road reached the gateway of the fort, the town was not even visible. Only the fort remained, its imposing walls and huge portals with exquisite engravings on yellow sandstone captivating visitors.

Inside the portals, close to the walls on the right, stood the palace which had been converted into the Project's office. On the left, the hospital came first, followed by the jail in which the Prisoner Force was lodged. Beyond them was the construction site.

The first piece of news that greeted Kundan on reaching the jail was that the City Jail warder who had brought the last batch of prisoners had fallen ill the previous night and was lying unconscious in the intensive care unit of the hospital. The solution he had promised to find in the case of Pasupati Singh had melted into thin air.

The second bit of news concerned the prisoner who had been brought to the Project as Pasupati Singh. Kundan got it from the Project Jail warder.

'Sir, Pasupati Singh has been making a ruckus, screaming and shouting that he wants to see you.'

'Warder, he is not Pasupati Singh,' there was a touch of annoyance in Kundan's voice. 'They made a mistake. He is someone else. The solution, plain and simple, was to send him back with the papers. My fault was that I didn't do it. And now it has become a problem.'

'That is why I say sir, let him be Pasupati . . .'

Their eyes met and the warder paused.

'Where is he?'

The warder took him to one of the prison cells. Most of the cells were empty as the prisoners were out on work. The man who had been brought under the name Pasupati Singh squatted on the floor in the cell, his eyes popping out with the same fear and anxiety on his face which Kundan had observed on the platform of the railway station.

When he saw Kundan, the prisoner rushed to the grilled door of the cell. He stretched out his arms through the iron bars and went down on his knees. Kundan stepped back hastily before the prisoner's hands could touch his feet.

'Don't send me back, saheb. They . . . they won't leave me alone. They will arrest me.'

'Arrest you?' Kundan stared at him incredulously. 'Aren't you a prisoner?'

14

The prisoner rose to his feet and began to sob.

'I am not Pasupati Singh, saheb. I am Sulaiman. I am not a convict, sir. I am serving a sentence for Pasupati Singh, saheb. Pasupati Singh has promised to pay my wife and children five hundred rupees a month. If you send me back, they will arrest me and put me in jail. Or Pasupati Singh's people will kill me. My wife and children . . .'

Kundan froze. He glanced uneasily at the warder and then at the policeman standing apart. They had certainly heard everything the prisoner had said. Yet their faces revealed nothing, as if they didn't find anything unusual in it.

Why is it that all these things appear strange to me alone, Kundan asked himself. And why was it that everything looked like an insoluble problem only to him? The City Jail warder, now lying in a coma in the hospital, had no doubt about Kundan's ability to find a solution for the problem. As for the Project Jail warder, he would have liked Kundan to let the prisoner go by the name Pasupati Singh, if he wanted to. Why should Kundan break his head over a trifle like that, they seemed to ask him. Gradually, it began to dawn on Kundan that it was not their insensitivity but his ignorance that was getting exposed in such situations.

Meanwhile, a change came over Sulaiman's expression. Now there was no fear or anxiety on his face, only grief. Tears rolled down his cheeks and his lips quivered as a new sensation seized him—the consolation a man feels after opening his heart out to someone, when he leaves everything to the listener, who, he thinks, understands him. Kundan was taking over all the worries this man was relieving himself of, whether he liked it or not. It took a few moments for Kundan to come to terms with what he had taken over. He had to decide the fate of this sickly man who had chosen to undergo the rigours of prison life in order to save his wife and children from starvation. He was also bearing on his back the sins of a criminal, every gram of whose seventy-five kilograms oozed hatred towards his fellow-beings, who was, perhaps, at that very moment sitting smugly in his cosy bungalow, swallowing one whisky after another.

As an official appointed by the Sarkar to see that its laws were implemented, as the labour officer responsible for the orderly execution of a sensitive defence project, as a human being who should not allow injustice to prevail, what Kundan should do was to expose the truth, the absolute truth, without hesitating. But he was faltering and buckling under pressure.

What was weakening him? Those thin hands stretching out through the iron bars of the prison? He took another look at the man. He should have been terribly angry with this man who was no less than an enemy who sought to destroy whatever he valued, an adversary he should crush under his feet.

But Kundan did nothing of the kind. He turned and walked away, stopping for a moment to turn and mutter to the warder, 'Enter Pasupati Singh's name on the register and send him to the site. Send the papers to the office for my signature.'

Chapter Four

Kundan tried to persuade himself that he had solved, or at least found an answer to, the vexing problem of Pasupati Singh and Sulaiman. Still, at times it appeared like an apparition and stalked the corridors of his mind. Why did the human mind have such corridors which had no defence against these disquieting apparitions? Why did they come out like snakes from their holes—under the hanging balconies in the narrow lanes, in the dark corners of bushy backyards, everywhere man treaded—as they liked, with no end and no rule?

Kundan had been handing over the batch of prisoners relieved from the Project to the new warder who had arrived from the City Jail at the railway station. Throughout the proceedings his nerves were on edge. Every time a prisoner's name was called out, he shuddered. Would the details of the prisoner given in the paper tally with those of the man who was being handed over? He wondered if a Pasupati Singh or a Sulaiman would raise his ugly head again. Fortunately for Kundan, every prisoner who passed through his hands matched the descriptions in his folio—

height, weight, wart and mole. When the last man was identified, Kundan heaved a sigh of relief and was ready to forget the heat of the day and the spoiled Sunday.

Then, as the Project security police lowered their guns and retreated to their barracks, and as the policemen from the city marched the prisoners off with their guns pointed at them, one of the prisoners suddenly started screaming. Hitting his fettered hands against his head and swaying from side to side, he sobbed and wailed. Tears from his eyes and mucus from his nostrils mingled with the frothing saliva from his mouth and streamed down his chest. After watching the scene for some time, one of the policemen decided that enough was enough. He caught the man by the collar of his shirt and slapped him repeatedly on each cheek. The man's cheeks crunched against his teeth and began to bleed profusely, the blood mingling with the other fluids streaming down his chest. Though the blows could not shut out his anguish, they did bring down the pitch of his screams. Satisfied that he had achieved that much, the policeman flung him down with both hands as though he was bouncing a ball. As the man fell, he kicked him in the back with his boot.

Kundan stood stunned, unable to stop what was happening before his eyes or even to utter a word against it. His lips had gone dry. It took him a few moments to discover that everyone else there, officials and prisoners alike, were dazed like him, watching the scene with dry lips and dead tongues.

However hard he tried these days, to moisten his lips and activate his salivary glands, the dryness persisted. The stories about the drying streams and aquifers in the desert were becoming a horrifying reality for him.

Kundan did not go straight home from the railway station. He called at the house of a friend to whom he usually turned to share his feelings—Hassan, Commander of the Pioneer Force.

It was difficult to imagine two individuals with such diametrically opposite characters and temperaments as Hassan and Yogeshwar, the Commander of the Prisoner Force. Most people kept their distance from Yogeshwar. He had erected a barbed-wire fence of isolation around himself, and held everything close to his chest. It was not for nothing that everybody called him 'jailer saheb'.

Hassan was just the opposite, and his wife Waheeda was as amiable as her husband. She soon joined Hassan and Kundan in conversation.

'Hassan, have you ever had this problem? My mouth has gone dry, so dry that it hurts when I speak,' Kundan said.

Waheeda promptly placed her palm on his forehead.

'No, he has no temperature,' she said to Hassan with a mischievous smile.

'Did you have to go yourself for this job, Kundan, on such a hot day, and that too on a holiday?' Hassan gently rebuked Kundan. 'Couldn't someone else, that assistant of yours, Jaswant, for instance, have done it? To be frank, he is a far more suitable person for this job than you.'

Kundan smiled in assent.

'But it couldn't be just the heat. Something must have happened. Why don't you tell me about it?'

Kundan narrated the incident he had witnessed in the morning at the railway station. He also referred to the strange case of Pasupati Singh and Sulaiman. He had been longing to unburden the secret to somebody. Who else could be more eligible for that than Hassan?

'Don't you think something is wrong somewhere?' Kundan asked Hassan after concluding his account, feeling more encouraged to be frank with him. 'If "wrong" is too strong a word, say "lacking" or "deficient", or "absent"— the lack or deficiency or absence of links between men and events. It could be a weakness too. Look, I didn't ask the man what troubled him. Perhaps I had become wiser— after another man's tears landed me in trouble. But . . .'

'Kundan, the trouble with you is that you insist that everything should always be perfectly logical and rational, that there should be no suffering or injustice anywhere, that there should be no drought or famine, that the same amount of rain should fall on every spot on the earth. Of course, there is nothing wrong in entertaining such wishes. I too would wish the same. But to insist is not the same as to wish.'

Hassan rose abruptly, a dark shadow falling on his face. He emerged out of it with a short laugh. Waheeda went in on the pretext of fetching something to drink.

Hassan and Waheeda had a ten-year-old son. Mentally and physically retarded, he was a mere mass of flesh which could only crawl around the room on its own. He was unable to express his needs or respond to questions. When he was ill or in pain, only the tears that rolled down his cheeks would show it. Hassan and Waheeda loved him dearly as all parents love their children, though he in turn could not express his feelings or complain if he was neglected. They carried him with them from the hills to the plains, from forests to deserts, wherever Hassan's job took him. Afraid that their affection for him would be divided, they decided not to have another child.

When Waheeda brought some cool drinks on a tray and they allowed their minds to relax, Kundan resumed the conversation. 'It is not a question of wishing or insisting, Hassan, but of reacting. People do react to things which they can't reconcile themselves to, don't they? If reaction comes from application of reason or logic, rather than emotion, should it be deprecated? I have not refuted the system, in spite of its oddities. And yet, at moments, it mystifies . . .'

'Kundan, if you admit that the state is necessary—a necessary evil, if you like—you must also grant it the right to demand its pound of flesh from its citizens for its existence. The Pioneer Force was first raised by the British

Army during the last war to build roads at the war front. As for the convicts, every government employs them for some work or the other as a matter of course. Do you think everyone who fought on the side of the Unionists in the American Civil War was opposed to slavery? We have to concede that we are all, at some level, like those soldiers.'

'You see, Hassan, man has created countless laws, customs and conventions over the last ten thousand years since he began to live in societies. Although almost all of them were intended for ensuring justice for the members of the community, in course of time they became instruments to perpetrate injustice. If you always stick to laws and conventions, you may in fact be acquiescing in things which these laws and conventions were intended to prevent. In every age, there should be some people who could look at things not through the eyes of the law alone. You might call them laterally entered people, those who don't have anybody's mantle to inherit, while the others, the vast majority of the people, are only links in the endless chain of succeeding generations. They are the ones who separate things into black and white in the light of the situations ·existing at the moment without being influenced by history, backgrounds or obligations. In the absence of such men, Sulaimans will be punished for the deeds of Pasupatis and that would be reckoned as the course of the law.'

'Whoever knew there was such a rebel in you!'

Hassan and Kundan went out together for a stroll in the evening. Hassan took Kundan through the narrow streets hemmed in by walls, which were by turns yellow in the slanting rays of the evening sun or grey in the shadows. As they walked on and on, Kundan for the first time became aware of the fact that the town was big enough to accommodate such long walks. At last Hassan stopped at the open courtyard of an old haveli which appeared to be standing at the end of the town.

The haveli, neglected for long, was now a dilapidated,

21

tottering structure. Tattered clothes were strung up to dry across its balconies, windows and doors. Out of its gaping holes, emerged, at times, an old woman, a sickly man or a child. In the courtyard squatted a group of children with dusty eyes and darkened faces. Their strange silence and passivity frightened Kundan.

'It is said that when Sultan Alam Khan's forces entered the Rambhagarh Fort, one of Raja Mansingh's wives hid herself in a corner of the harem to escape the fires of the jauhar kund into which the other wives had jumped *en masse*.' Hassan began to narrate an old episode in the history of Rambhagarh. 'While plundering the fort, Alam Khan's soldiers combed every nook and cranny and finally caught her. On learning that she was one of the ranis, the sultan made her his property. Later, when he and his men abandoned the fort and went away, she refused to follow them. As she came out of the lonely fort into the town, a mob tried to stone her to death. She escaped the crowd and spent the rest of her life as a dancing girl. Some of those who threw stones at her became her customers and begat children by her. One of her sons became a prosperous merchant. Another raised a well-trained army which served the chieftains of the various principalities in the desert who were perpetually at war with one another. The haveli was built by these two sons from the wealth they had amassed. It came to be known as the sultana's haveli. In course of time, the family line came to an end and no one was left to inherit the haveli. Homeless people made it their dwelling— people of all sorts and kinds, from beggars and prostitutes to artists and scholars.'

After a pause, Hassan resumed: 'I brought you here because this haveli was built by people who were mavericks, those who had no family line to perpetuate, as you said. Those who made their entry into society laterally. Like cyclops, each one of them followed his own law and lived in his own den. Being one-eyed they couldn't see things in depth. They lived in a two-dimensional world, seeing everything only in lengths and breadths . . .'

Hassan was getting carried away by his own words. He gestured like a man possessed. It seemed he was pouring out all his indignation at those lone tuskers among men. Or was it only a show to cover up the admiration he really had for them?

Hassan who pleaded for pragmatism, Hassan who accepted his cruel fate as something natural, was himself a lone tusker. There was a cyclops in him, following his own laws. Living in his own den, he saw only the lengths and breadths. Pasupati Singh was a loner. Sulaiman too. The prisoner who screamed, hitting his fettered hands against his head, tears, spittle and mucus streaming down his face, was also all alone.

And yet the society they all lived in was in the same state as the sultana's haveli—a polyps colony, a coral reef. The things they exuded or excreted formed accretions to their dwelling, adding endless rooms and cells to it. Darkness stared through its holes and disquieting apparitions stalked its corridors.

Chapter Five

Kundan could have easily passed on work to Jaswant, his assistant. As Hassan had remarked, Jaswant was far better than Kundan at such jobs. In fact, it was Jaswant who had taken up the job on a similar case some time back. Even today, when he rang up Kundan in the morning, Jaswant had been planning to go himself. Bhola, a Pioneer who had deserted, had been apprehended by the police in a village about fifty kilometres away and he had to be collected. But Kundan told him to look after the recruiting for the day and took up the job himself.

It was a trifling event that influenced Kundan's decision. As he was speaking to Jaswant, he was gazing through the window at the long, narrow street that stretched into the distance. Bounded by the rows of houses, the road led to the promontory of the town from where the poromboke took over. A group of people were moving along the road, some mounted on camels and some on foot, towards the barren desert beyond. This scene along with Jaswant's description of the village where Bhola was being held, and the picture of the world outside the Project taking shape in his mind from which mysterious creatures like Sulaiman and Daniel emerged, made the decision for him.

But as Kundan put down the receiver and sat down to eat his breakfast, it struck him that he was not going to the poromboke on a picnic, but to arrest and bring back a man from his home and dear ones. It was from the same poromboke that Bhola had emerged to get himself recruited as a Pioneer. And it was now two weeks since he had run away. Recruits joined the Pioneer Force on a four-year contract and were governed by the provisions of the Army Act. Once recruited they were required to live in the barracks surrounded by barbed-wire fencing and to eat the rationed food prepared in the langar. They could go out only after securing an out-pass and were to return promptly at the stipulated time. Bhola went home on two days' leave, but did not return. The Commander of the Pioneer Force had, according to procedure, dispatched an order to the local police to apprehend the deserter and to send him back to the Force. The police had subsequently informed the Project authorities that Bhola had been arrested and was being held in the chowki of a village fifty kilometres away.

Gulshan had put together a delicious breakfast of parantha, cheese and a kind of chutney made from dried chillies and jaggery, the result of a combination of his own expertise and the culinary skills of the villagers: the parantha was his preparation, while the cheese and the chutney were bought from the market. There was a weekly bazaar on Saturday, when the villagers would bring whatever they produced—food, clothes, furniture and handicrafts—to sell to the townspeople. They would then linger in the town for a day or two more. Those were heady days for Gulshan. He would get lost among the villagers, no matter if they were total strangers to him. If there were girls of his age in the crowd, Kundan would not see Gulshan at home for the whole weekend.

Sitting in the jeep, on his way to the village where Bhola was held, Kundan had forgotten all about the spicy breakfast he had eaten within half an hour. He found that the only thing on his mind was Bhola's desertion and arrest. He was not sure whether he had caught hold of the problem or whether the problem had taken possession of him. It was often the case that when a man thought he was doing something it was, in fact, being done to him. The driver sat on Kundan's right. Behind him sat two security policemen with rifles and a pair of handcuffs. To an onlooker, Kundan might very well have appeared to be a prisoner in custody, on his way to a prison.

As they left behind the narrow lanes of the town, passing the Pioneer camp and the recruiting centre, and reached the road which stretched straight into the desert, the driver stepped up on the accelerator. Looking smart in his perfectly fitting uniform, seated upright in his seat, he drove the jeep without taking his eyes off the road even for a moment. He was also a Pioneer. The stiffening starch of his uniform seemed to have seeped into his body—even into his mind, perhaps.

While living in the city, Kundan had to commute every day for an hour to reach his office. Sitting cooped up in the bus for an hour was exhausting. He used to relieve himself of the tedium by studying everything that his eyes fell on. One such object was the bus driver. Boarding the bus at the terminus, Kundan used to occupy the seat immediately behind the driver's. The thin, emaciated man would never be seen in presentable clothes. He always wore the same soiled, tattered khaki shirt. The unshaven face with dishevelled hair reflected in the mirror in front of him had a tortured look. His eyes appeared feverish all the time. It used to be late when Kundan returned, and quite often he happened to board the same bus—with the same driver. Ten or twelve hours at a stretch on such a job! Then one day he was no longer there. Another driver whom Kundan had never seen before was at the steering wheel.

Was the driver dismissed from service on account of his poor health? Was he dead? Or did he just vanish without a trace, leaving no explanations for his disappearance? Kundan did not ask the conductor or anyone else these questions, for he was sure of being scoffed at if he did. Kundan thought it very odd that, after all those days, he was now on a journey through the desert with policemen, guns and handcuffs to apprehend a missing man.

After a long drive, a camel appeared with a rider on its back as a sign of life on the roads. And then some rocky outcrops came into view, followed by a few houses, which appeared to have sprouted from the road like the outcrops.

It was a small village of about fifteen houses. Stone slabs fixed vertically on the ground formed their walls. The roofs too were made of stone slabs. Some khejri trees stood around them, their stunted branches looking like the afflicted limbs of lepers. There were also some shrubs which had no chance of growing any higher.

'Looks like a deserted village,' Kundan remarked.

'No sir, there are people inside,' the driver seemed to know better. 'Don't you see the camels near the trees, sir?'

'How do these people live?' Kundan wondered aloud, surveying the expanse of barren land around.

'You won't believe it, sir,' the driver's eyes narrowed in a smile. 'These people are carpenters, traditionally—expert carpenters!'

'Carpenters!' Kundan was surprised. 'Where do they use their skill?'

'Almost all the men have left for towns where wood is available. Two of us didn't go: Bhola and myself. We belong to this village, saheb. We too are carpenters!'

Of course, carpenters they were! One of them an offender who had broken his contract with the government and run away, the other a faithful servant of the government on his way to arrest his friend. Was there any wood, or even a little sprout of green that could bind the two again as friends?

The jeep pulled up before a house. The driver went in and was back in a few minutes with a pot of camel milk. They resumed their journey after drinking the milk.

The next village was bigger, a cluster of little hovels around a water tank. The exquisitely cut flights of steps at different parts of the tank showed that it once had water. There was also a small temple-like structure supported by four carved stone pillars in the middle of the tank. Remains of a dried-up garden on one side and the ruins of a covered platform in the centre of it could still be been. Though there was not a drop of water in the tank, a few trees still grew around it.

'The tank began drying up years ago. There was no rain last year. If it fails this year too, many of these people and their animals will die.' The driver's voice was mournful. He was talking about his own people.

The desert too had its share of rainfall. The precious rainwater was preserved in tanks and in baolis dug around the houses. They lived on this water for a year. Survival was a problem only if this share of rainfall failed to arrive the next year. The driver was saying that this was one of those years.

It was noon when they reached the police chowki. The village was large enough to have one. The chowki was a stately structure that had been built by one of the rajas who had held sway over the area. With its arches and domes, it resembled a temple or a tomb. It might well have been one before the police took it over. Time made prisons out of castles and shrines out of tombs. It was not unusual for dancing halls where mehfils used to assemble to be turned into hangman's blocks.

It was not easy for Kundan to see Bhola as a prisoner. He did not know how this man's face, out of the faces of the hundreds of Pioneers who passed through the recruiting centre, had stuck in his mind. There was nothing remarkable about the features of this carpenter-turned-Pioneer whose hands were now bound with a length of rope.

One end of the rope was tied around Bhola's waist and the other was held by a policeman. Kundan signed a register at the chowki and the free end of the rope was taken over by one of the security policemen who had accompanied him. The return journey began.

No one spoke in the jeep. Bhola and the driver hailed from the same village and knew each other well. Yet they did not even cast a glance at each other as the vehicle sped back to Rambhagarh.

They stopped before a small kiosk and bought kachories and lassi. Bhola held the glass with his bound hands and emptied it in a gulp. Kundan wanted to speak to him. With the glass in his hand he approached Bhola.

'Why did you run away, Bhola?'

Bhola did not reply. His eyes were downcast. His thick moustache drooped down the sides of his lips and his huge turban was wound several times around his head. If he had been in better clothes and free from the ropes that bound him, he would have passed for a small-time raja.

But today he could not even claim to be a commoner. His body was bent as if he had been kicked in the belly. There were blood stains on his arm, one of his cheeks was swollen and he walked with a limp.

'Did they beat you up?'

Again Bhola was silent. The sparkle in his eyes was not that of the agility of a king, but the beginning of tears.

The Sarkar's two lengths of rope now bound this man who had the audacity to break through the barbed-wire fence around the Rambhagarh Project. Not content with apprehending him, the Sarkar poured its wrath on him through the policemen for violating his contract with it. Who broke the contract and how were certainly things to be resolved legally and decided in a court of law. The issues were, of course, more complex in cases like those of Daniel's and Sulaiman's. But in all these cases there was never any attempt to analyse the rights and wrongs, only a mindless outpouring of sheer rage, contempt and apathy at the first instance. Who adopted what attitude was not a reflection of the person's sense of justice or reason, but of the power, the authority or just the physical strength at his disposal at that point of time.

The round jal shrubs sprouting sporadically from the expanse of sand looked like heads of men buried to the neck. It was a horrifying illusion in the lengthening shadows of the evening—as if the victims were entering the darkness of night, with no companion other than their hopeless fate. Everything else had receded into the distance: the day, Time, Justice and the State.

The sight of the approaching town with the tall majestic fort at its centre was a mystifying experience. It grew in size and its details became more striking as the jeep hurtled towards it. How would Sulaiman, Daniel or Bhola, all of them belonging to the vast poromboke, have approached this structure which was to be their bread-giver, master, adversary and oppressor? With apprehension, awe or admiration? As for Kundan, the experience was only visual. At least for the moment, he was not interested in making it anything more than that.

A rocky cliff on the left side of the road was the first signpost on the way to the fort. It was almost as high as the cliff on which the fort stood. The radar towers built on it were visible from quite far. It was a barren hill with just those skeleton-towers on it. Not far from it two more cliffs appeared to the right. Both were small and lay close to the road. On top of the first lay the ruins of a fort, or rather the unfinished parts of a forsaken fort. Before the Rambhagarh fort was built, some king had, perhaps, tried to build on it and had later given up the attempt. On top of the other were a number of pagoda-like structures. Those were the chhatris of kings who ruled Rambhagarh at various times. Wherever he died, every king had to be cremated on this hill. A chhatri was built at the place of cremation for him by his successor. After these hills appeared the town, looking like a massive sculpture with its solid rock-like fort, the clusters of houses and the evening sun throwing weird patterns of light and shadows on them. The festering slums of the town laid on one side in sharp contrast to the neatly planned barracks on the other. Then the fort suddenly loomed large. Before a visitor in a vehicle got a chance to contemplate it, he could have pierced it, or got buried in it—like a missile. Launched from the poromboke with all its violent anger compressed in it, the missile was destined to be buried and lost in the massive body of its adversary.

Chapter Six

Long ago, when Kundan was a young boy, a friend of his told him that a mirror did not give a true image, only an inverted one. Kundan went to the attic of his house, picked up a dusty, corroded mirror which had been dumped there, and spent a long time before it to test the theory. He couldn't find anything wrong with the image. When he said this to his friend, his friend laughed. Look carefully, he said, the right side of your body will appear to be on the left and the left side on the right. That took him to the attic again. The hand holding a ball was holding it in the image too, he observed, and the one gesticulating at the image was gesticulating back at him. Exasperated, but determined to prove his point, his friend held an open book in front of the mirror and asked him to read from the image. Suddenly, Kundan lost all his faith in the mirror. Had it been deceiving him all along, he wondered. Was his face really different from what the mirror had always been showing him? The incident set him asking a number of questions of himself.

But then, Kundan needed the mirror only to see his face. He could see his arms, his legs, chest and belly without the help of a mirror. And they all looked exactly the same in the mirror, as he could easily verify. As for the face, Kundan could see that the image of his friend's face was no different from his real face. Was it possible that the mirror was playing a trick on him with the written page in the book, and perhaps with his face too?

Even if he were to accept his friend's theory of the left-right reversal of the image, why was it only from side to side? Why not from top to bottom? Here Kundan's friend had no answer. After pondering over it for some time, he suggested that the eyes were set horizontally, not vertically, to each other on the face. Though Kundan granted him that much, he went on to ask what would happen if human beings had only one eye and if it was set on the chest or the belly instead of on the face.

Kundan's friend, who was not so learned as to come up with an answer to that one, deftly shifted the focus of the discussion a little and remarked that the human body was horizontally oriented, not vertically.

But this led Kundan to another problem. What if the symmetry of the human body were vertically oriented? Two legs, heads and hands to the left and the right . . . What would the image of such a grotesque figure look like? It was scary even to imagine it!

Kundan did not get satisfactory answers to his questions. And one day his sisters spied upon his antics before the mirror. They surprised him in the act with cries of 'Coquette! Coquette!' which put an end to his communion with the mirror. As he grew up, such curiosities were replaced by others. Questions about mirror images were antiquated now. But Kundan still had no answers to them, though he could now declare, without a moment's hesitation, that mirrors gave inverted images. The doubts that vex us in childhood are seldom cleared up, but are merely forgotten in course of time. As we grow up, we cultivate a habit of raising only practical questions instead of fundamentally theoretical ones. The pursuits of life allow certain beliefs—call them knowledge, if you like—to grow upon us, which insulates us from many of our childhood curiosities.

Back in his house, as he dressed to go to dinner with Yogeshwar, the Commander of the Prisoner Force, Kundan, ruminating over his childhood encounter with the mirror, glanced at the one before him with a rueful smile. For a fleeting moment he imagined that it was the young boy that looked back at him from the mirror. He smoothened the twist at the corner of his lips, averted his eyes in a pang of regret and went out.

It was mid-summer and it took longer for the air to cool down after sunset. The pleasant, cool breeze which brought relief from the sweltering heat of the day now arrived only after midnight.

Yogeshwar's house lay five blocks away from Kundan's. It was only a short walk. In fact, it was a short walk to any part of the town. It was fun to walk along the narrow streets lined by closely packed houses which almost touched one another. Many of them were old havelis and some of them were still in good condition. They stood majestically, their facades and balconies carved in yellow sandstone. Thriving merchants and affluent Brahmins had once lived in them. Some had been occupied by dancing girls and a few by mercenary bands who held kings at their mercy, but were also sometimes manipulated by them. Many power struggles had been played out in the dark corridors of the havelis. The rotting smell of blood mingled with the strains of the ghunghru and the jingling of coins.

Sitting across Yogeshwar and his wife, Kundan became conscious of the strained atmosphere in the room. Yogeshwar, too, looked uneasy. He said something about the climate of the desert being healthy and broke off.

'I don't know,' Kundan said, merely to join him in conversation. 'I think the weather cycle is completed only when the water evaporating from the surface of the earth comes back to it as rain. As this does not happen here, the desert leaves a feeling of incompleteness in me.'

'I agree with you there,' Yogeshwar admitted hastily, showing his characteristic fear of contradicting anyone. 'There is that incompleteness about the desert climate.'

The topic did not make any further progress. Silence reigned till Yogeshwar's wife brought some drinks on a tray.

Amala—that was her name—placed a chair between the two men and sat on it. Suddenly Yogeshwar launched into a speech about his wife, about her temperament and proclivities, her charms, her changing moods and her love for him. He declared that he was proud of getting her as his wife. Till that moment, Kundan had not known that it was possible for a man to talk about his wife to another man so freely in her presence. He began to feel it was outrageous on Yogeshwar's part to do so. He could have chosen to speak about the articles of furniture, the pictures on the wall, or the curios on the shelves, for such costly and attractive things were displayed in plenty everywhere. Or he could have talked about the wealth he had amassed or the high positions he had occupied in his career. But not about his wife.

Amala said nothing. She was keeping herself aloof from the conversation with an effort. The expression on her face became more and more mournful and she struggled to keep her face from drooping. With some women you can talk about their beauty and charms and they won't demur. In fact, most women—men too—like to hear they are attractive. Obviously Amala was not one of them. There was something beneath her assumed impassiveness, something vast and deep. Perhaps one could talk to her about the endless dimensions of human life, about experiencing a poem, or even about God, but never about the shade of her eyes or the curve of her nose. How could Yogeshwar bring himself to do it? How could he dare?

Perhaps that was not what Yogeshwar really wanted to

say, Kundan realized a few moments later. There was something on his mind that was agitating him. He had invited Kundan to dinner to tell him something, but could not make up his mind how to put it across. So he spoke at random, reaching out to odd topics. Amala incidentally happened to be one of them. His clumsy gestures and the way he shifted uneasily on the sofa were sure signs of it.

Yogeshwar's troubles continued at the dinner table. There he left his wife and grappled with the dishes. Then he abandoned conversation altogether. Finally, dispensing even with table manners, he attacked the dishes with a feigned gluttonous impatience, breaking pieces of chappatis, dipping them in chicken curry and thrusting them into his mouth. Amala merely made a show of eating. There was nobody else in the house but for the three of them—a jailer, his wife, who to all appearances was his prisoner, and Kundan. What exactly was this man aiming for, Kundan asked himself. So far he had been shooting wildly at sips of whisky, pieces of chicken and chappati, and Amala's beauty.

Kundan got the answer soon enough. When they finished their dinner and went back into the living room, Yogeshwar abruptly broke the silence and launched into a long speech:

'Kundan, what drew my attention to you, what made me almost an admirer of yours, was your order to accept the prisoner. What was his name? Ah, Sulaiman. I will be frank with you. We have a system of keeping new officers under observation for some time. Call it a kind of probation. You have handled the problem that confronted you wonderfully. You have used the authority vested in you with great tact and understanding. You have given to the government what is expected from you. In fact, Amala and I have invited you for dinner today to congratulate you on your achievement.'

Kundan noticed two things at the end of this burst of adulation. There was no trace of any appreciation for what he had done on Amala's face. What he saw instead was distress. Secondly, all the embarrassment and hesitation which had characterized Yogeshwar's earlier digression had disappeared. He was transformed into another person. Now that he was on his tracks, he steamed ahead, unambiguously, clearly and confidently. He no longer fidgeted and his voice was firm.

'It just happened as it did,' Kundan replied. 'Realizing his predicament, I had to help him.'

Yogeshwar, who was pacing the room, suddenly stopped and looked menacingly at Kundan. 'Your inference is wrong there, Kundan. Who is this Sulaiman? A miserable, starving man born in some dirty hole and destined to end his life there. What is his life worth? He became Sulaiman because his mother thought it was a good name for him. Do you think you were helping that non-entity? No, it was the Sarkar you helped. Rescued, I should say.'

'What has the Sarkar to do with it?'

Yogeshwar gently placed his hand on Kundan's shoulder—like a doting grandfather. 'Kundan, you have absolutely no idea who Pasupati is. His is not a life to be wasted in the dingy cells of a prison. He may be a shrewd manipulator accumulating his millions. He may be a law-breaker and a murderer, but he performs certain services which you and I cannot. It is not for you to ask what they are. Do you ever ask what type of machines are required in this Project and when and where they are to be installed? Do you ever insist that you will recruit Pioneers only after you make sure which beam is to be of what length and which nut is to be placed where at the site? Wisdom is something which tells you where to ask questions and where not to. When we are told that public interest demands that Pasupati remain a free man, you and I have to accept it without any questions.'

'You mean to say it is part of a well-laid scheme of the Sarkar?'

The tenderness vanished from Yogeshwar's face. From a

doting grandfather he was recast into a sententious patriarch. His eyes glared at Kundan from behind the glasses—in fact it was only then that Kundan became aware he was wearing glasses.

'Need I tell you how long the Sarkar's arms are and how they move?'

A shudder passed through Kundan. The City Jail warder's warning, his taking ill suddenly, the Project Jail warder's advice, the indifference of the security policemen . . . What came as hints, subdued or camouflaged, were now raining on him like bullets. Why did this man take it upon himself to pass on all this information? Surely these were not the words of Yogeshwar, the timid Prisoner Force Commander. Somebody else was speaking through him. Who had decided that Kundan, the labour officer, had passed the stages of soft signals and veiled threats and now had to face direct bombardment? Perhaps there was a Grand Design which was omnipresent and which worked through everyone—Sulaiman, Bhola, Daniel, Kundan, perhaps even Yogeshwar—a Grand Design nobody could see or comprehend. Uniforms, caps, designations, vehicles, pens, shovels, axes, brands of liquor—these were all like dyes or paints. The threads on a fabric have no way of knowing why certain portions of their lengths are given certain colours. Then, as the carpet comes out of the loom, the colours take the form of a tiger snarling at the world, or a huge Kali with blood dripping from her mouth. Who was this Grand Designer? He used to be called God. Today, perhaps, the Grand Designer went by the name Yogeshwar seemed to be fond of invoking frequently: the Sarkar

'Yogeshwar, if Pasupati is so indispensable for the Sarkar, why couldn't it pardon him on its own, instead of leaving such important jobs to the discretion of such dispensable men like us?'

'The law and authority are two different things, Kundan. The law takes, must take, its own course. To protect its interests, the Sarkar uses not the law, but authority. Authority is not concentrated in a single place or person. It lies distributed among the Sarkar's officials. The Sarkar has, therefore, to depend on its officials to exercise its authority. They should, in their turn, bear in mind that whenever authority has to be exercised, it has to be exercised in favour of the Sarkar which vested them with it.'

The patriarch was exhausted after his long exercise of showering tenderness and gilded threats. Yogeshwar stopped pacing the room and sank wearily into a sofa. What he said next was more agonizing. Kundan then knew the way the samurais, after stabbing themselves with a dagger in the stomach, kept churning it till the intestines came out.

'I remember the police bringing Pasupati to the jail,' Yogeshwar was wearily losing himself in memories. A weak smile appeared on·his lips and his eyes swept the walls from one end to the other. His voice kept faltering. 'I was then the jailer there. In fact, I joined the service at the age of twenty-two. Now I am forty-two. Well, it was a sight which jailers rarely see in their careers; but not something they are surprised at. We had to arrange a separate room, not a cell, for Pasupati to live in. We had to pay special attention to his needs. He had endless streams of visitors. He had been booked on the charge of murdering a foolish young man who had thought of investigating into his business affairs. Later his body was found in a disfigured condition. His fingers had been chopped off and his eyes gouged. He was Amala's brother.'

Kundan got up from the chair involuntarily. He walked to the window and looked out into the night. He could see nothing except a long stone wall across the narrow path. He did not know whether Yogeshwar was still speaking. He had heard enough.

Before Kundan left, Yogeshwar had a parting shot for him. He reminded Kundan of the fact that it was he, Kundan, who had identified and certified Pasupati as a prisoner. But Kundan had no time to go over that fresh warning. He was gazing at Amala who had come with Yogeshwar to the door to see him off. Though she still tried to control herself, it was not difficult to see that her eyes were moist. Kundan felt a terrible sense of loss that he had not tried to engage her in conversation even once during the evening.

The summer evening storm had already blown itself out. The night was cool. There were no lights in most of the houses. An aged camel stood on the side of the road, leaning against the wall of a house. Though it did not turn its head, its eyes followed him as he walked down the road.

Kundan stopped at the turning. The path to the left would take him home. The path that branched off right led to the bazaar. Instead of turning left or right, Kundan walked straight ahead towards the slums that lay on the fringe of the town. Soon the rows of houses were left behind. Now, on either side of the path lay rows of garbage heaps which gave out a piercing stench. This was the dumping ground for all the garbage in the town. Kundan heard the grunts of pigs rummaging among the garbage heaps. Though there was no light in any of the hovels in the slums, Kundan heard voices drifting out from them into the air, breaking the silence of the night. Beyond the slums, in the vast open spaces of the desert moonlight was shimmering.

As Kundan stared into the desolate terrain that stretched before him, two images appeared before his eyes. One was of himself as a boy. The child was too far away for him to talk to, though his face brimmed with questions he would have liked to ask the grown-up Kundan. The other face was Amala's. It was as sad and taciturn—though quietly eloquent—as he had seen it when he took leave of Yogeshwar and her. Not a word came from her lips.

It was well past midnight when Kundan reached home. The desert sand had lost all its warmth and was now as cool as the stone-paved roads in winter.

Chapter Seven

A letter from Ruth came as a complete surprise. Kundan took some time to reconcile himself to it, to accept it as real. Not that he had forgotten Ruth. In the intellectual vacuum in which he felt himself suspended, he always thought of Ruth whenever there was something on his mind which he wanted to share with someone. It was not as if Kundan moved in intellectual circles in the town he lived in before he came to Rambhagarh. In fact, Kundan could never really qualify himself as an intellectual. Things that occupied a common man's life—films, plays, restaurants, cricket, friends—occupied his too. But after reading a book or when an idea suddenly struck his mind, he wanted to talk about it to someone, and Ruth used to be the obvious choice. Besides, a discussion with his friends on any subject of common interest, a news item, a film or a popular story, used to become lively if Ruth was around.

They had studied together in the University. In those days they used to meet frequently in groups. Though Kundan had often felt that he shared some common characteristics with her, neither he nor Ruth had tried to develop their relationship into something special then. Later she discontinued her studies and took to journalism, while he stayed back to get his degree in Law. They stopped seeing each other after that.

After his graduation, Kundan got a job in the city. He began a life in which weeks were divided into days and days into hours with mathematical precision. His life fell into a groove—a bus leaving at a particular time, a particular table in the canteen, a standard menu, the same set of faces in the bus, the office and the canteen, the same sets of clothes. It was at this time that Kundan started seeing Ruth again. He could not recollect how or when their meetings resumed. Ruth had grown into a mellowed woman. She stuck to her profession, having developed a passionate interest in it. As for Kundan, his life after the university days had made him more aware of the world, though his concerns and interests had not gone much beyond the stage of ideas. It was then that Kundan got this break—the job in the Project. He immediately jumped for it. Ruth too had disappeared. They had not even had time to note down each other's address.

The envelope bore only his name, the name of the Project and the name of the town, Rambhagarh. Perhaps she remembered that much from what he had told her of his assignment. The letter spoke of an incident which had suddenly reminded her of him and the Project.

'It seems that the Department of Culture is taking a keen interest in your project. They had a workshop here a month back on how to organize cultural programmes for the benefit of the patriotic workers serving in defence establishments. "We should not give them a chance to feel that we do not remember them," the secretary remarked. They specifically mentioned the name of your project and also the type of programmes they wanted to organize. The mention of patriotism and culture was interesting. The State gives everything its own set of meanings. Knocking down

42

everything else, it keeps its version aloft on a pedestal and then builds a pagoda around it . . . A few of us forming a small group have been on the move for a few weeks. Our next trip begins tomorrow—to the desert.'

She had said nothing about her programme. Kundan knew little about the activities of her group. How much did he know about what he himself did, for that matter, Kundan wondered. What was he doing, except acquiring one problem after another day after day? All the same, her letter brought some badly needed solace to his confused mind.

There was no way he could send a reply to the letter. The address she had given was 'Ruth, Desert'! There was also no hint that she would write to him again. But he noted that her letter ended with a question, whatever her intention in posing a question to one who had no means of replying:

'You said you were going to the Project in search of new, untrodden pastures. You have already become familiar with a part of it. What will you do when the rest too is revealed to you?'

Chapter Eight

Kundan saw the woman standing outside in the veranda in the mirror while he was shaving. Half of her face was veiled by the tip of her red sari. She had just got back the can in which she brought milk.

But for some reason, she was lingering. Gulshan, after a brief conversation with her, came into the room.

'Saheb, it is the woman who brings the milk.'

'So I see,' Kundan replied without glancing at him.

'She wants to have a word with you.'

Kundan washed his face and came out into the veranda.

'Huzur, there is no grass for the cows because of the drought,' the woman said hesitantly.

'Want some money? I can give you some.' Kundan turned to fetch the money.

'No, it is not that, huzur,' she stopped him hastily. 'The cows don't give us much milk. There is hardly any to sell.'

'All right, you can give me just one measure, instead of two from tomorrow.'

'No, huzur, that is not what I meant. I won't give you less. I won't think of giving milk to anybody else before I bring you what you need.'

'As you like. If you want me to pay more for the milk I can do that too.'

'No, huzur, that is not . . .' she paused.

Kundan was puzzled. He felt the rays of the sun—already quite hot so early in the morning—beating down on his face. Soon, the insides of the houses would be as hot as the rocky outcrops in the desert, he thought.

'Huzur, my husband . . .'

'Yes, your husband. What is the matter with him?'

'Huzur, you arrested him and took him away?'

Kundan frowned at her for a moment. Then he remembered.

'Is Bhola your husband?'

Without replying, she looked down at the ground. Kundan realized that she was sobbing behind the edge of her sari which now covered her face. Kundan walked up to her and, in a consoling tone, invited her to sit on the parapet of the veranda. But she would not.

'Bhola should not have deserted his work,' Kundan tried to explain the situation to her. 'It was the wrong thing to do, against the laws. Why didn't you try to make him understand that?'

'Huzur, we are poor people. We have only three cows, and the land is no good. We do all sorts of jobs to make both ends meet. Last year there were no rains. We were helpless. We moved to the town with our cattle. Someone tricked my husband into joining the Project. Now he will never come back . . .'

She sobbed violently now. Kundan was astounded.

'Who told you he will not come back? Just because he has been arrested, it doesn't follow that he will be hanged or exiled. He has been brought back to work in the Project again. He will get a month's leave every year. And after he completes his term, he can leave the Project permanently if he wishes.'

'No, huzur, no,' she shook her head. 'We know he won't

come back. Those who go to work in the Project never come back. When the work is over they will kill him.'

Kundan was startled. Who could have put such ideas into the minds of these people?

'Look, somebody has been scaring you with stories. This is a government job like any other.'

'No, huzur. In our village there is a man called Balbir who used to work in a sarkari office. When he didn't want the job he left it. My chacha's son also worked for the Sarkar. Once, when he came home on leave, he did not go back. Nobody came to arrest him. My husband, after coming home on leave was visiting some relatives with our little son when the police pounced on him. They hit him all over his body with lathis. They kicked him in the belly. Our son tried to put his arms around him. They punched him away. Balbir said the Project workers would be shot after the work is finished.'

Kundan did not know what to say. But his silence would only confirm her suspicions. She was still sobbing, wiping her eyes and her running nose.

'They are poor people, saheb,' Gulshan, who had been watching the scene quietly, thought it fit to intervene at this stage. 'If that man goes . . .'

'Gulshan, do you believe such canards too?' Kundan was visibly irritated.

'I did not mean that, saheb. You have the authority. If you think it is all right, you can perhaps let him off . . .'

Here it comes again, authority! Kundan grimaced. After Yogeshwar's long discourse, it was now Gulshan's turn. Kundan was amused to imagine himself in the role of a great dispenser of justice with authority before whom a long line of people queued up devotedly.

'Well, sister, I shall take care of Bhola,' Kundan told her by way of consolation. 'Nothing will happen to him. And he will certainly come back to you, perhaps even before his term is completed. All right?'

'God bless you, huzur.' She looked satisfied as she picked up the milk can and turned to go.

Kundan went back to the room. He took the towel and was about to go to the bathroom when the woman appeared again at the window.

'Huzur,' she spoke in a low voice. 'Shall I send my daughter again from tomorrow?'

Kundan was as stunned as Bhola must have been when the police lathis fell on his head. They had hit Bhola in front of his son, his relatives and neighbours just to show them they could do it. This woman was the embodiment of civility and amiability, a study in contrast to the roughshod policemen. She was powerless to inflict such a crushing blow. She had only learned to entreat and beg and to make offerings to people who mattered. Here she was doing precisely that—something that people like her had been doing for centuries to save their lives or to appease their hunger. But for Kundan it was a stunning blow all the same.

Her daughter was a mischievous, frolicsome girl. After delivering the milk, she would linger for a while chattering or cooking up some prank. On lonely mornings with only dull, uneventful days to look forward to, her presence used to be a welcome diversion for Kundan too. It was this intimacy between the two that had made the girl's mother decide to take on the delivery of the milk herself, Gulshan had once told him. Kundan had laughed at it then. But it was no longer a joke.

'Look here, sister,' Kundan went up to the window and, unlike the woman, shouted at the top of his voice so that the whole world could hear him. 'I don't care who brings the milk. You can decide that. But it certainly does not matter to me who I buy milk from. The whole lot of you mean nothing to me—you, your husband and your daughter. I could chase the whole lot of you away if I wanted to. What do you people take me for?'

The frightened woman slunk away. As her figure receded

into the distance, she was reduced to the red sari she wore.
Only two naked feet with thick silver anklets jutted out of
it.

Kundan should have felt exhilarated at having made a
point and emerging out of the encounter with his character
unblemished. But as he watched the staggering steps taken
by the two naked feet on the sand, he felt that it was he
who had been defeated. She was returning to the poromboke
after coming out of it for a moment to tell an unadorned
human tale, to remind people like Kundan that it was not
all sand out there. Suddenly a thought struck him like a
blow on his head: What did the people of the poromboke
think of him and his like? To think of others was, of course,
not a privilege enjoyed exclusively by a select band of people
like him.

Chapter Nine

An army unit had arrived in the town. The soldiers came in about a dozen jeeps and trucks in the small hours of the morning. They pitched their tents in the open space between the railway station and the town. Soon a kitchen and a row of latrines appeared and a parade ground was set up. Vehicles were lined up and stores were laid out. They had come from beyond the hills and were on their way to a border outpost.

The unit Commander, soon after his arrival, visited the fort and exchanged pleasantries with the Project Commander. The officers on both sides made friends with one another. The ranks in their battledress marched along the main streets in the morning. In the evening they came into the town with out-passes and wandered in the streets and in the market, glancing around with curiosity and chatting with one another.

The people of the town did not remember anything like this happening before. Though the Project too was basically an army affair, no one had noticed its installation or its getting established. The Project personnel had no flag-cars, shining belts, epaulets or guns. Besides, they did not march in the streets. The army unit, however, made the town's residents apprehensive. The stiff, bright uniforms of the soldiers, their very uniformity and the hammering of their boots on the cobbled streets aroused their curiosity. People came out of their houses and shops to watch the morning drill and the orderly movement of the army vehicles. The presence of the army, of course, did not bring any fear of an impending war. In fact they did not associate the army unit with war. It was the unit itself that made them apprehensive.

As the sun went down, their curiosity turned to anxiety and alarm. The soldiers did not march in squads then. They appeared in twos and threes and moved about shooting glances in every direction. The lustre of their epaulets and the stiffness of their uniforms now presented them in another light, and the discordant sound of their boots introduced a kind of uncertainty in the air. When they entered a shop, the shopkeeper immediately attended to them, keeping the other customers waiting. When the price was mentioned, they would remark, 'Why do you need so much money, boss?' put whatever coins they liked into the shopkeeper's hands, pat him on his back and walk out merrily. The shopkeeper, not daring to pick a quarrel, would just watch them with a sheepish grin as they walked away.

As they roamed the streets, the soldiers stared at terraces, peered through windows and occasionally let out shrill whistles. The same soldiers who in the morning marched in files like one man without a wrong step, did not hesitate to make offensive remarks to passers-by or even to start a fight with them. People began to close their doors and windows tightly and chose to remain indoors as soon as night fell. The streets were deserted even before the sun went down.

On the next market day after the army unit arrived in the town, there was no sign of Gulshan even after nightfall.

Though he would be late on occasion, he had never failed to turn up. But this time he did not appear even on the next day or the day after. Kundan was worried.

Then, on the third day, Gulshan turned up suddenly with a girl. He was as agitated as the girl and they held each other's arms tightly. Swift and watchful in every movement, clad in dresses of deep, contrasting colours, they represented the innocence and helplessness of the desert people who always appeared like the hunted rather than the hunter. Gulshan seemed to have shaken off all his impishness and his craze for the city's charms. He had suddenly become a matured, elderly man, wounded and defeated by the reality that confronted him. Kundan noticed he was crying only when he raised his hands to wipe his eyes.

The girl had come to the weekly market from her village with her merchandise. She and Gulshan had been on the lookout for each other, but without success. It took two days of hectic search for Gulshan to locate her—in one of the dark cells of a dilapidated haveli. In tears, she told Gulshan what had happened. Some soldiers had caught hold of her in a lonely lane. She had somehow managed to free herself from their clutches and take refuge in the haveli. For two days she hid herself in the cell, not daring to come out.

'Please, saheb,' Gulshan was repressing his tears and trying to sound normal. 'Please let this girl stay here till the next bazaar day. And please tell her folks that she had been staying here all these days. I shall bring them here next marketing day.'

Lies were heading his way again, Kundan thought with amusement.

If the girl's people came to know that the soldiers had tried to molest her, they would throw her out of the house—that much was obvious.

'Don't worry about that, Gulshan,' Kundan said. Then he added as an afterthought, 'But the girl . . .'

Gulshan drew the girl to him and held her tightly. 'She is mine, saheb. I will marry her.'

'Very good,' Kundan put his hands on their shoulders. 'What about the soldiers who tried to molest her?' he asked Gulshan a moment later. 'Can she recognize them?'

'Who can fight the Sarkar, saheb? Let us not think about it.'

Sarkar! The Sarkar was the monster that let a man like Pasupati, who cut an innocent young man to pieces, go scot-free and made Sulaiman pay for it. Kundan had acquiesced in it then. He had just now agreed to cover up what the soldiers had done to the girl with a few well-chosen lies. He had forfeited his right to be enraged at Gulshan for refusing to fight with the Sarkar.

Kundan went in and came out with some money which he handed to Gulshan. 'Go and buy the girl some clothes. After that you two can fix up a good meal. The three of us will have a small celebration!'

Yet, in spite of having acquiesed with Gulshan, when the jeep came the next day, Kundan got into it and drove straight to where the army unit had been camping. He had with him his green identity card which gave him the authority to approach the Commander directly, as well as the letterhead bearing the seal of the Project. But when he reached the maidan adjoining the railway station, he found the place empty. There were only the markings left behind by the tents and kitchens and the covered-up bore-hole latrines. The army unit had moved the previous night.

Chapter Ten

'Two more have deserted today,' Jaswant remarked, half to himself, his eyes skimming the papers in the folder. 'No company is different when it comes to desertion.'

Kundan had once conducted a brief survey on the pattern of the incidence of offences of various types among the Pioneers. Desertion, drunkenness, violent squabbles, insubordination, sexual offences—that was how he started classifying them. Jaswant had suggested then that offences could be broadly classified into just two groups: desertions and other offences. Jaswant's logic was that while desertions had an external dimension, all the other offences were internal in nature. Internal offences were to be controlled by severe punishments. Desertion had to be tackled differently. It was at this time that cases of the latter had started rising. Now their number was so alarmingly high that it had become a topic of discussion in the administrative circles.

It is typical of bureaucracy to react straightaway with stringent measures when there is a rise in incidents of indiscipline without inquiring into the causes. It was not any different at the Rambhagarh Project. The hunt for deserters was intensified and security men were employed in great numbers on the roads, at the railway station and at the bus stands. They pounced upon every suspect, many of whom were not even remotely connected with the Project.

Sitting in the record room, which had once been the horse-stable of the old palace inside the fort, Kundan and his assistant entered everything in the files: the names and numbers of the deserters, the companies they were attached to, the names of those who were later apprehended and those who were still at large, the time taken by the civil police to catch each deserter, whether the company commanders were following instructions to raise the period of imprisonment for desertion from fourteen to twenty-one days . . .

In the horse-stable-turned-record-room, the smell of horse dung had given way to the musty smell of stacks of paper. The floor was clean, but air circulation was restricted, owing to the partitions that divided the room into several cubicles. The record office was a protected place and it was only natural that it did not have more openings in it than were absolutely necessary.

In the dimly lit room, Kundan and Jaswant battled like two old warhorses in the little time they could find after attending to the routine duty at the recruiting desk, the medical examination centre and the store rooms where kits were issued to the new recruits.

The record office was a strange phantom world where human beings existed like shadows or ghosts in their physical measurements, photographs and identification marks; in the particulars of their ancestors and children; in the offences they committed and the punishments they received for these; in the history of their ailments and in the assessments their superiors made of them. The record folder of a man was a sort of negative print of his life. A man like Daniel actually died in those pages! Think of the positive of a man in one of these folders, a man rising from this table of life . . . He is now pausing a moment before lifting a stone at the workplace to gaze at the walls of the fort around him, or he is lying on his back in the barracks, staring at the ceiling . . . No, his mind is breaking open the walls and the barbed-wire fence and even his physical body to wander into the green pastures beyond, in a world of his own imagination . . . he is dancing on the green grass on an autumn afternoon with a lilting song on his lips . . . he is lying on soft haystacks listening to the sweet nothings his girl is whispering in his ears . . . or, who knows, he is standing stunned at the anguished cries of a little child who came running to rescue him from the clutches of a bunch of hefty policemen . . .

It was only three years since the recruitment of the Pioneers began. Their period of contract was four years. Hence a case of someone discharged after completion of his term was yet to be recorded in any of the folders. Bhola's wife was right in that regard: no one had yet returned home from the Project, not even a labour officer. Kundan's predecessor had died in harness.

The last three years had seen the Project being literally flooded with recruits. According to Jaswant, there were no men left in the villages nearby. But desert villages normally had not more than thirty or forty inhabitants. It was natural that they ran away from the Project, particularly after the rains. Each shower of rain was precious. The opportunity to raise whatever little amounts of food crops or fodder with the water was not to be missed.

As Kundan and Jaswant were digging out the records, the door of the office was rudely pushed open and Jagtap, the security officer, walked in.

He went straight to Kundan's desk, pulled a chair and sat down. Then he removed his peaked cap and laid it on the table along with his polished cane. His clean-shaven face, chubby nose, thick lips and dark eyelashes gave his round face a feminine touch. Above his well-starched uniform, its edges as sharp as a knife's, beneath the peaked cap that menacingly pointed forward, his handsome face always wore a transparent veil of gravity. Beauty did not always mean syrupy smiles or coquetishness, Kundan would remind himself whenever he saw Jagtap; there was beauty in gravity, anger, spite and even cruelty.

'Welcome, Jagtap. You have come to my stable for the first time.'

Without acknowledging the greeting, without even pretending to have heard it, Jagtap came straight to the point. 'Look here, Mister Labour Officer, Bhola is yet to complete a year. He has a long way to go.'

Kundan now understood the purpose of Jagtap's rude intrusion into the records room. He had obtained an application for premature release from Bhola who was undergoing his twenty-one days' imprisonment for desertion and had forwarded it to the Station Commander.

Swallowing the insult, Kundan too came to the point. 'So that is what brought you here. All right. But you should also get the facts clear. Bhola's request for release is on compassionate grounds, and that is perfectly within the rules.'

'Rules?' Jagtap raised his eyebrows. 'Has the Station Commander allowed him to put in such an application?'

'Well, the Station Commander can allow or disallow the request only *after* getting the application, not *before*, can he?' Kundan smiled.

Either Jagtap couldn't follow Kundan's reasoning, or he was beyond any reasoning. He merely repeated his argument. 'Look here, Mr Kundan, you should not have forwarded such a petition without the Station Commander's consent.'

Kundan did not smile this time. Though irrational to the very core, he watched the security officer's argument taking the shape of a reality which he was getting to apprehend every day: the reality of Pasupati Singhs and Sulaimans, of nature showering its blessings on some lands and forsaking others, of an Almighty who created some people handicapped and others strong and able-bodied.

'Secondly,' interpreting Kundan's silence as assent, Jagtap went on, 'you should also have remembered that only the Company Commander of the petitioner has the authority to forward such petitions.'

'Look, Jagtap, you are pretending to be ignorant of all rules,' Kundan protested. 'When he wrote the petition, Bhola was undergoing his punishment in the quarter guard. He will be posted back to the company only after the expiry of the term. Till then his commander is the labour officer.'

'Bhola has now come back to the company. So the petition you so kindly forwarded stands cancelled.' Jagtap put down his palm on the table and pressed it as if all arguments had been laid to rest under it.

Kundan rose, shaking his head in disgust. 'Why do you have to get so worked up over such a small issue? And what is your business in it, anyway? A Pioneer petitions for discharge on compassionate grounds, the Station Commander can dismiss it if he finds it not worth considering.'

'You don't understand,' Jagtap shook his head. 'I don't have to tell you that the Project had to resume recruitment after work on the second unit started. Then came this spate of desertions. In such a situation, if the labour officer himself goes about with petitions for discharge from Pioneers who had deserted earlier . . . One doesn't need much wit to understand that it will only encourage others to take to the same course.'

The security officer pulled out Bhola's petition from his pocket and handed it to Kundan. Kundan could not stand this from a man who had nothing to do with his department. 'I sent this to the Station Commander, not to you.'

'Well, I am returning it to you now.'

Jagtap picked up his cap and placed it on his head. He then bent towards Kundan as if to whisper in his ears. But it was not in a whisper that he spoke. 'By the way, everyone knows about your interest in the girl. I mean Bhola's daughter, the one who brings you milk every day.'

Kundan could not imagine that an officer's impudence would stoop to that level. He stood speechless at this outrage.

Jagtap walked out stiffly. The door closed after him with a bang.

Kundan felt angry and sad at the same time. Jaswant had been watching and listening to everything that had been said. Kundan did not know how to face him now. He knew he had nothing to be ashamed of. Yet, in certain situations one does not know how to look others in the face.

Both of them worked in silence for the rest of the day. In the evening, when they locked the room and came out, Jaswant, as if to change the subject that had been occupying their minds, said: 'Two more deserters have been caught, sir. The police are doing some good work at last.'

'H'm,' Kundan nodded.

They dismissed the jeep and walked down the hill.

'It is time for the villagers who had migrated with their cattle to return,' Jaswant was analysing the motives behind the desertions. 'Now they will be around for six months. The few rains they get during these months will help them raise some fodder. In November, they will leave the place again. It is their life cycle. Last year, there were not many migrations. The drought forced them to join the Project instead. But their cattle migrated by themselves. Many of them perished. Now they have no cattle left, and no crops either. Even if the rains are good this year, there will be a famine. The remaining men too will line up for recruitment this year. So we needn't worry about the desertions, sir.'

Kundan said nothing.

When they reached the hill, Kundan took leave of Jaswant and entered a small restaurant which stood beside the road to the bazaar. It was an ancient haveli which belonged to a family of merchants who had gone bankrupt. An enterprising young man with an eye for the good life bought it and fashioned it into a restaurant. There was a large rampart just behind the fort-like gate. Putting up a shamiana and spreading carpets under it, he converted it into an open air restaurant and called it Dewan-e-aam. A raised platform stood on one end facing the row of tables. It was covered with bright and colourful carpets which gave glimpses of the glory and splendour of the past. In the evenings, banjara groups of the desert put up their shows there, singing folk songs and playing flutes and drums. The customers, who included some tourists, gave them baksheesh. Kundan liked to spend some time there in the evenings, listening to the songs while sipping a cup of tea or a glass of beer.

As the minstrels began to sing, the annoying altercation, with the security officer and the disturbing question of how he came to know of Bhola's daughter bringing milk to him faded from Kundan's mind. His attention was arrested by the colourful turn-out of the singers with their huge, princely headgears and long moustaches. The meaning of the song eluded him, but its quickening rhythm and rising pitch fascinated him. As the minstrels sang in gay abandon, the other men from their villages who had wandered into the Project were spending their time staring at the walls and ceilings of the barracks or the quarter guard. The small coins thrown to them by the tourists as baksheesh sustained these free birds. Some day they too might sell their freedom and their songs and find their way into the barracks.

As Kundan walked towards his house leaving behind the narrow lanes where the shadows of the buildings criss-crossed, he noticed that the sun had not set as yet. This was of no particular consequence to him. Nevertheless, he was somehow happy to see the shadows of different objects separately—before they joined forces to form an impenetrable mass of darkness.

A swarm of dragonflies flying recklessly collided with Kundan. The first shower of the season, a couple of days before, had released them from their slumber in the soil. They buzzed about, hit against each other and mated in the air—as if they were at a carnival.

Chapter Eleven

'Running with the hares and hunting with the hounds' is a well-known idiom. Supporting opposite positions alternately according to convenience and saving one's own skin in the process is the usual meaning accorded to it. But if you leave the idiom and come to the real world, where hounds and hares do not remain the same eternally, and where hunting and running are not very clearly defined, the smile that the idiom brings automatically to your lips disappears. It then becomes an expression of the human predicament with all its ruthlessness, cruelty and helplessness.

It is the law of nature that some animals prey upon others and in turn become prey to other predators—a law carefully followed by nature till it comes to humans. It is only when human beings fall ill or die that worms and microbes can prey on them. The phenomenon of hunting, and fleeing from the hunters, relates largely to the confused area of human relationships.

A man may at times find himself playing the role of a hound and a hare simultaneously. Or he may find himself switching from the role of a hunter to that of the hunted in a shockingly small period of time when his prey turns on him or a new hound appears behind him. Theologians call it retribution. The scriptures say that God carefully takes care of the details of every individual in his dispensation of justice. But the fact is that however much the scriptures may preach and moralize on the sin of violence against fellow-creatures, they have not been able to stop man from his hunting expeditions. Interestingly, the scriptures have not in any way asked man to desist from becoming a prey or a victim. On the contrary, they profusely extol the virtue of remaining silent and guiltless victims of oppression.

One of the things that characterizes a hunter is his belief in his superiority. He need not actually be stronger than his victim; in fact, the victim may quite often be the stronger of the two. But as long as the victim continues to run and the hunter keeps up his chase, the equation does not change. A hunter pursues his prey for a variety of reasons—for food, for fun, or just to satisfy a sense of superiority. An emperor, a zamindar, an industrialist, a gang leader, a superior officer in a department, a scholar, a teacher, a jailer, a doctor, a womanizer—anybody who occupies a higher rung in a social hierarchy starts looking at those on the lower rungs as his prey the moment he feels himself to be superior. It does not mean that the prey is immediately set upon with fangs or paws, or knives and guns. Every glance, every smile of the hunter, each furrow that appears on his forehead, each word of approval or disapproval he utters, is an attack on the prey. The hunter becomes a surrogate cannibal, eating his prey mentally, and as the cannibalism fills his mind, he almost becomes the prey himself.

The prey, on the other hand, is self-obsessed. He becomes increasingly conscious of, and concerned with, those qualities in him which attract the hunter. In a woman, it is her body; in a worker, his physical strength; in a patient, his weakness. There are a variety of factors which make one a prey: ignorance, helplessness, inferior social position.

Faced with the hunter, the prime concern of the prey is to save himself. As he begins to walk faster, as he breaks into a run, as the chances of escape vanish one by one, he gets rapidly reduced to his body. He starts imagining that his body is in the clutches of the pursuer who can now do anything with him: disrobe him, laugh at him, play with his helplessness like a rapist. If the prey is the hunter's food, his insides are pulled out and the organs are ground to pulp in the hunter's mouth; he becomes the flesh and blood of the hunter. The rest becomes his excrement, foul smelling, detestable stuff to be thrown out of the rectum. This is the mental world of a victim, stretching from the agony of being insulted and the apprehensions about being stalked, to the identification with the excrement of the hunter.

All men live in two worlds at the same time, the world of the hunter and the world of the prey. It is man's fate, not only to live and express himself in both as the occasion demands, but also to be flung from one to the other, nursing the bruises he gets from each fall. He penetrates the nakedness of others while also striving to protect his own modesty. He gnaws at others' bodies even as he feels somebody's teeth sinking into his flesh. While he feeds on others, he cannot but visualize himself as somebody's food.

Starting as a small-time village muscleman, growing up as a bandit, plundering and killing, betraying, appeasing and again betraying people, showering favours on the trusted few, sticking knives and swords into them the very next moment, ascending the rungs of the ladder of power, a man becomes a king. He collects heaps of men and weapons, builds a palace, and stores his wealth in it. He constructs a harem and fills it with women. But what forms the pinnacle of his achievements, what defines the long history of his hunt, is the fort he builds around his palace. Building a fort is the final point in the long history of hunting by a king, for the fort is meant to defend, not to attack. With that the history of hunting comes to an end and the history of the hunted begins. A fort is the abode of the hunted, not of the hunter.

From the fort, the king continues to rule over the people living outside it in the poromboke, making them work, extracting taxes and allegiance from them, making them fight his wars and kill their own kin, slighting them, humiliating and enslaving them, whipping and raping them—always reminding them that they are his subjects and he their king. But the king is haunted by the fear that these emaciated and emasculated subjects of his might at any time rise against him and invade his fort. The armies of other kings are only an occasional threat. But these people in rags with their rickety limbs and punctured lungs are, in fact, on a permanent siege around the palace and the fort. The hunted themselves may not know that they too can become hounds. The hounds who are always aware of this fact, live in perpetual dread of the hunted.

While apparently relaxing in his palace inside the fort, erected with the choicest golden sandstone blocks, accompanied by his queens, entertained by wine and dancing girls, Raja Mansingh of Rambhagarh never enjoyed peace of mind. In every watchtower of the fort stood vigilant sentinels watching every movement in the vast desert that surrounded it, their weapons ready for action. Huge cauldrons filled with oil simmered on fires, and large heaps of firewood were piled up beside them. The raja's long wait ended on a cold autumn evening four hundred years ago. On the horizon of the starlit night a thin line of cavalry appeared. Thus began the historic siege of Rambhagarh fort, a siege that lasted the whole of the winter and the summer that followed.

Sultan Alam Khan was attracted by the challenging beauty and invincibility of the fort and the fabulous wealth amassed by Raja Mansingh. Prepared for a long war, the sultan pitched his tents around the fort. His camp with its soldiers, courtiers, horses, workers, servants and dancing girls resembled a small town. Alam Khan knew that strangling the fort through a siege, though time consuming, was a better strategy than storming it. Each day his men attacked a part of the fort and retreated in the evening. Months passed in this way. Mansingh began to run out of arms, ammunition, food and water. Yet he refused to give in and Alam Khan refused to retreat. After the winter the desert grew hotter. But despite the fatigue and dreariness that tormented both sides, the battle went on.

In the midst of the war, in the shadows of death and destruction, a strange kind of understanding and recognition began to develop between the hunter and the hunted. A kind of detached sense of worldly wisdom transcending the conflict compelled them to accept and respect each other, without compromising their positions. Every evening, when the bugle sounded to announce the end of the day's hostilities, Raja Mansingh would come out of the fort alone, through a secret passage and reach the appointed place under a tree between the withered outcrops of the maidan, where Sultan Alam Khan waited for him. They would greet each other and sit cross-legged on the ground for a game of chess over a glass of wine. They did not say a word to each other. Only the mumblings, grunts or whoops of joy normally emitted by chess players came from them. The game took them deep into the night. When it was over they returned to their original positions in battle, Mansingh to the fort and Alam Khan to his camp, to plan the next day's operations.

The conditions inside the fort were driving the raja to the brink. People were dying of hunger. Outside the fort, Alam Khan's men were becoming impatient and irritable, while the sultan himself was almost at his wit's end as to how to break Raja Mansingh's indomitable resistance. But Mansingh and Alam Khan continued their rendezvous under the tree in the maidan every evening. At last, one day at the peak of the summer heat, events overtook the raja and he decided to take the final plunge. A fire was lit in the jauhar kund inside the fort. The women jumped into it and the men threw firewood over them. Alam Khan and his soldiers watched the rising flames in the fort with awe. When the screams of the last woman died out, the massive gates of the fort were thrown open with a terrible grating sound. The saffron-clad soldiers rushed out to pounce upon Sultan Alam Khan's men. The fierce battle that followed lasted till late in the evening. By then, the last of Mansingh's men, and Mansingh himself, had fallen to the swords of the enemy. With blazing torches, the sultan's soldiers marched into the fort, where only the smell of burning human flesh greeted them.

The sultan stayed in the fort for a few months, wondering all the time what he was doing there and why he had captured it in the first place. The wilderness and the eerie white of the desert sand almost drove his soldiers mad. Finally, on a moonlit night in winter, Sultan Alam Khan and his men marched out of the fort quietly.

The Rambhagarh fort remained empty for a long time after that.

Nobody knows how many rajas and sultans went in and out of it afterwards. None of them could make it their permanent abode. Years later, the British, who had occupied the country by then, repaired it and made it a military camp. And when they left the country, it became a tourist attraction. The tourists too had to abandon it when the government decided to build the Strategic Installations Project in it.

Kundan wondered who was holding the fort in siege now. A small town had sprung up around it, a town with water supply, electricity, roads, a bazaar and a railway station. A Municipal Commissioner and the members of the Municipal Council elected by the residents of the town looked after the town's affairs. The residents of the town were engaged in a variety of occupations which included quarrying sandstone, petty trades, government service, theft and prostitution. They had nothing to do with the fort that stood at the centre of the town and the Sarkar that functioned from it. They had not laid siege to the fort. Or had they?

Kundan, in his lonely and terrifying moments, thought that they had. The barracks lying at the foot of the hill, the prisoners he brought from the railway station, their hands bound like slaves, the lives of the men, women and children scattered on the poromboke which evaded or belied his understanding . . . Why should there be such a large security wing in the fort? Why did the officials at the fort behave so arrogantly? Wasn't the fear of the hunted reflected clearly in their eyes? What would Ruth say if he advanced a theory that the modern states which entrenched their power structure with the help of the police, the army, espionage agencies and a faithful bureaucracy are, in fact, always, and even without their knowledge, under a siege laid by their people who have been emasculated, raped, humiliated and deceived by them. What would she say if he told her that Mohammed Bin Tughlak used to keep the bodies of the men he had executed for public view outside the gates of his fort for three days. He was reminding his subjects that they were mere rotting corpses to him. There had never been a happier moment in his life than when he stood in triumph on the ramparts of his fort and surveyed the panoramic view of Delhi, and later Daulatabad, where he could see no moving object, no smoke rising up from any chimney, nor hear a single sound which indicated human activity. The people are my enemy, therefore I punish them, Tughlak had said. Tughlak's subjects did not revolt against him. Some of them occasionally scribbled some remarks against him on a piece of paper without identifying themselves, and dropped it in a box kept at the palace gates for receiving complaints and suggestions. The slaves of Rome waged a war against the emperor for three years and finally lost it. After subduing the slaves, Pompey hung six thousand of them on crosses erected on either side of the highway from Kapua to Rome till they died, their flesh rotted and their bones crumbled. Like Tughlak, Pompey too was reminding the slaves what they were to him. Isphahan, which was considered a city with no parallel in the world, was also destroyed in the end. Do you know how it happened? The uncultured Afghan brigands laid siege to it for six months. Eighty thousand people in the city succumbed to hunger and diseases. The sculptors and artists who built and fashioned the magnificent structures and artifacts of the city, which even today stand without a blemish, killed one another and ate human flesh. The stench of rotten human flesh emanating from the city ultimately forced the barbarians to abandon the siege and flee. It was not the courage, weapons or technological competence of the inhabitants that drove away the invaders, but the stink of their rotting corpses!

As he sat in the portico of the abandoned haveli, now converted into a restaurant, Kundan wondered whether he, a petty official of the Sarkar, was actually conducting a farcical imitation of the tense drama enacted under a solitary tree four hundred years ago by a hunted raja and his hunter, a sultan.

Kundan walked several times around the hill on which Rambhagarh fort stood, in search of the site of that strange rendezvous which remained a secret even in those days. He was looking for the spot selected by the hunter and hunted for a fiercely fought game of chess and a glass of wine in a daily interlude in the terrible life-and-death battle they waged against each other. The tree must have withered, turned into firewood and returned to the earth, converting someone's wheat flour into bread in the process. But the rocks which shielded the drama from the subjects of the raja and the sultan must still be standing somewhere around, though it would be difficult to locate them now. They remained ordinary rocks which nobody had sought to identify.

It was, however, not difficult for Kundan to find the jauhar kund of the queens inside the administrative block of the Project. It was a circular well with rows of chambers constituting the king's harem in three storeys around it, one chamber for each queen. Each chamber had a window without grills which opened out to the jauhar kund. When the fort was attacked, the king's standard was hoisted at a spot which was visible from all the chambers. If the king fell in battle or when his defeat was a foregone conclusion, the standard would be lowered and a blazing fire lit in the kund. From each chamber on the three floors, through the ungrilled windows, the queens jumped into the kund.

The king visited each of his queens in their chambers according to a roster prepared by the harem administrator. The women received him in the decorated beds in their chambers. Did their eyes wander to the ungrilled windows at the moment of their orgasm in the arms of the king? When they shed their clothes before him to dissolve in his passion, were they troubled by the thought that when the arms that embraced them became lifeless, they would also have to dissolve in the raging fires in the jauhar kund? The predicament of taking pleasure and pain at the same time, of consuming and being consumed at the same moment may be the consequence of man's helplessness, or a sign of his arrogance, or, perhaps, his ignorance. There is nothing anybody can do about it. Nor is anybody called upon to.

Chapter Twelve

It was Daniel again.

But he was not brought there by the police with his hands tied with ropes, as Kundan had feared. Circumstances more compelling than ropes had brought him to the recruiting centre. Daniel had come on his own, wearing the same blue pants. The shirt was, perhaps, different.

Since everything had already been talked about and discussed, Daniel had nothing to say. Kundan too did not repeat the refrain that he was helpless to do anything for him.

There was not much of a rush at the recruiting centre. After dealing with the few candidates in the line, Kundan sat back in his chair, scratching his chin with the pen in his hand. Everybody—Yogeshwar the jailer, Jagtap the security officer, and even Gulshan, his orderly—kept repeating that he had authority. Yogeshwar and Jagtap had also suggested that he should use that authority for the benefit of the Sarkar. What would be beneficial to the Sarkar in this case? The Project needed more workers and Kundan should provide them. Desertions from the work force should be prevented.

Those who had deserted should be apprehended and brought back. The re-captured ones should be awarded exemplary punishment so that they would not run away again. Those prisoners who reported sick, instead of being boarded out, should be cured and fed to make them fit to work again. Only one thing remained to be said: the dead should be brought back to life!

Kundan called in Daniel, jotted down his particulars and passed them on to the clerk. Daniel moved on as the tenth man in the line of recruits to fill in the form for medical examination and to receive kits and uniforms. After running and jumping before the doctor to demonstrate his physical capabilities, back to the clerk, and again from the clerk to the stores. . . Kundan watched the new recruit progressing step by step, stage by stage.

Normally, every man and every event move on in this world like beads in a string, following a cause placed ahead and leaving an effect behind. Some mavericks stray out of the line or are thrown out of it. But they too invariably come back and insert themselves into the line again. Even the dead return to drink from the fountain of life, while others, alive and progressing along the line, might have actually died long ago.

Not everything, however, happened in such an orderly and disciplined manner. Even if there is a God who determines a time and place for each object and event, he is no more than a booking clerk or a conductor in a railway coach. The conductor of a coach struggles with the list in his hand and the clamour of the poromboke passengers, losing his temper, or softening down by turns, and occasionally pocketing a few rupees gracefully. But beyond the conductor's jurisdiction, somewhere outside the time-space coordinates, out in the cold air, there are hundreds of passengers without tickets, affidavits or identity cards, hanging on to the train. The train with the conductors and the passengers—the ones inside and the ones hanging outside—moves on . . .

It was Jaswant who woke up Kundan from his reverie. 'What have you done sir?' he asked Kundan in an excited tone.

'Well, what have I done?' Kundan tried to smile.

'Sir, Daniel is a dead man.'

'No, Daniel is alive. You can see it. I touched him on the sly, you know.'

Jaswant was not amused. He stood his ground. 'He is dead according to the records. Suppose this fellow is someone else.'

'Forget the records, Jaswant,' Kundan said. 'The Daniel of the records is dead. We are taking a new recruit called Daniel. As you have pointed out, this is another man.'

But Jaswant had no intention of leaving it at that. He pulled a chair towards the desk, sat on it and pondered for a moment. 'I had another angle to the problem in mind. Suppose this fellow was dismissed from the Project for some reason—a serious reason?'

'But the Project did not dismiss him. He went on leave and did not return. Later he was reported dead.'

'It is not uncommon, sir. The Sarkar may have used it as a short cut to get rid of a dangerous or undesirable recruit. You see, sir, there is no mention in the records of any document or proof in support of his death. It only says he died. As for this man, he has been knocking at our door again and again, on his own accord.'

'Jaswant, a little while ago you were wondering whether this man was Daniel or somebody else.'

'But, sir, we have to consider all possibilities.'

Kundan's smile disappeared. He was visibly irritated now.

'Why is the Sarkar doing all these things, in your opinion?'

'I don't know, sir. I was just thinking loud. Suppose this man is a spy . . .'

Kundan plunged into the depths of irritability from the

heights of fear that Jaswant had been building up. He got up abruptly.

'You are unnecessarily blowing up the whole thing, Jaswant,' Kundan's voice was raised. 'What is this grand security about which we all shout from the top of the roof? What is it but the starched uniforms of some pretentious men? Even the machines and equipment which are being installed here come from some other country, don't they?'

Jaswant did not say anything more. Neither did Kundan. It was time for them to leave the recruiting centre. They picked up their things and got into the jeep.

73

Chapter Thirteen

There was a dargah in the street in which Kundan's house lay. The road drew a semi-circle around it. The pedestrians, therefore, unwittingly did a semi-circumambulation of the dargah each time they passed it. There were a few shops wedged in among the houses on either side of the street. One of them, the one nearest to the dargah, sold flowers, incense sticks and other materials of offering.

Some said the dargah was of a Sufi saint whose year of death was unknown. There were others who held that it was not a dargah at all, but a place where some king used to have criminals executed and that a tomb was later erected for one of the victims. Perhaps the Sufi saint himself was one of those unfortunate men who earned the badshah's wrath. Nobody seemed to know anything about the life of the saint. But they were all quite sure he used to perform miracles, which his dargah continued to do after his death. The visitors came to the dargah with prayers for a miracle or two which could change the course of their lives. Nobody prayed for getting his salary on the first of every month, or for a child to grow older by one year by the next birthday.

Supernatural powers were invoked for seeking something which was beyond one's expectation, or which defied reason, or which one could not rightfully claim as one's own.

The shop which catered to the visitors at the dargah was the only one of its kind in the street. The rest of them attended to the various needs of the residents in their daily lives: a grocer's store, a flour mill, a book binder's shop and a butcher's. People went to these shops to satisfy their needs which could be measured in kilograms, metres or numbers. Since the business consisted of the exchange of a certain unit of money for a certain unit of a commodity, with the casualness that goes with it, there was no need for anyone, the buyer or the seller, to show reverence or generosity towards the other while going through the job. The faces of the shopkeeper and their customers displayed a kind of mechanical expression, or a bland smile that conveyed nothing.

Strangely, to Kundan, the faces of the visitors at the dargah did not look any different from those of the people at the shops who bought grains, sugar or pulses. The visitors at the dargah were mostly the residents of the same street or of the streets nearby. An occasional pilgrim arrived once in a while. Then there were fakirs and vagrants who did not offer flowers or burn incense. They just sat on the veranda or the parapet for hours, or even for days. They sang songs and slept there and then left as unobtrusively as they had come. Rather than the fakirs or vagrants it was the regular visitors with their vacant faces who attracted Kundan. They came out of the dargah with the same lack of expression with which they went in. The customers who go to a shop may return with a kilogram of wheat flour or a can of oil in their hands. The weight they carry is reflected in some way on their faces. Those who go to a place of worship may, instead, unload their burdens there. Why was it that the expression of relief, which was to be expected, was absent from the faces of those devotees?

Take the case of the old woman who came to pray at the dargah every day. She came in the evening when the slanting rays of the sun and the lengthening shadows added a touch of mournfulness to the atmosphere. She came sailing gently like a boat through the mournful atmosphere. Her greying, tattered burqa left only her face open. The dargah was an open shrine with no watchmen, keepers or priests. There was no one to stop or advise the devotees. She stood at the gates, prayed and returned quietly without looking around or stopping to talk to anyone. Evidently, she was coming to seek a favour from the dead saint. Perhaps her husband had divorced her or turned her out of the house with the children. Perhaps she longed to return to the good old days, or she was tormented by the thought of a son who had left her, never to return, and in whom she had reposed all her hopes, or of an unmarried daughter whose hair had already started greying.

The sorrows and yearnings of these people remained unknown. They were a silent lot. They rubbed their grievances against their own worn-out minds. They knocked at the doors of dargahs or temples, groped in the darkness of their chambers for some sign or omen, and returned without receiving any. Lizards squeaked from the walls of their houses and cats crossed their paths. Black and white cats. Dark and grey days. Idle evenings. Routines and rituals visited them with the precision of clocks. Wearisome chores with the musty smell of soiled clothes kept returning like repulsive flying curls of hair. Cancer or ailments of the heart arrived with a touch of compassion, quietly and without fanfare, in the form of a stomach ache or a giddiness.

There was nothing which made their lives different from one another, it seemed. They all walked about on two legs, exhibiting the same eyes, nose, mouth or ears. They moved from one place to another like migratory birds. Got wiped out in wars and upheavals. Perished or survived or just dragged on with their lives through droughts, floods, famines or epidemics.

And yet, on each idle evening, somewhere, someone from this very lot braves a firing squad or a hangman's noose. At the barbed-wire fence of some concentration camp, someone waits for his dream to come true. Year after year, a barricade comes up somewhere, a rebellion flares up, or a revolution is ushered in.

Chapter Fourteen

A riot had broken out in a neighbouring village. The area
within a certain radius around the fort had been declared
the security zone of the Project and anything taking place
within that zone had to be inquired into. The Station
Commander, an inspector from the security wing, and
Kundan were entrusted with the inquiry into the incident.

Kundan was delighted when he heard about the incident.
Anything even remotely resembling a rebellion was
welcome. Especially when it came from a world lying
perennially under the tyranny of dust, with no hope of an
outlet from the routine of drudgery. Only when he reached
the village did Kundan realize painfully that it was not a
rebellion, but an affliction the villagers had brought on
themselves. The people involved were of the same class,
undergoing the same suffering. It all started with some
remarks being made by somebody about somebody else,
who promptly returned the compliment. The epithets used,
it turned out, were equally applicable to all those who were
involved. In fact, their indignation was against their
common fate and the sufferings they shared. But their fate

and sufferings were not things on which they could rain their blows.

All the cattle and most of the sheep in the village had perished in the drought. Only the goats had survived. The riot claimed a good number of them on each side—and a larger number of humans. Convinced that the violence had nothing to do with the business of the Project, and that the Project's security was in no way affected, the members of the inquiry team returned cheerfully to Rambhagarh.

The head of the team was Brigadier Chandan Roy, the Station Commander, who was Kundan's superior officer. He was categorical that no more time was to be wasted on the inquiry.

'Don't take one step more than what is required,' Chandan Roy said with the air of worldly wisdom. 'Don't look one moment more than necessary at any face. Now these people think they can solve their problems by fighting among themselves. We should get out of here before the equation changes.'

The security inspector threw back his head and laughed. At the end of the prolonged laughter, he too had a piece of wisdom to offer: 'They are nice people. We are nice people. And the world is a wonderful place to live in.'

There was a good deal of truth in the Station Commander's assessment, especially in the fear he harboured about the people of the poromboke. His matured mind could foresee the encounter that was to take place somewhere at some critical moment between the people of the poromboke and the Sarkar which functioned from the fort. Whether it could be called a confrontation or a rebellion or a siege was immaterial. The stars and constellations were coming together, going off target and again regrouping. But Jaswant's remark about the Project getting increasingly involved in the poromboke's lives and problems seemed to point to the opposite—that the critical moment for the encounter had already passed.

The waves created by the Project's recruitment must have already spread beyond its security circle. It was drawing into its vortex all the working men from the surrounding villages. But for the villagers, it was time for growing fodder. The fodder now raised would last till December. After that the migrations would begin, the cattle first, followed by the sheep, and if conditions worsened still, the goats. Men too moved along with the animals, and sometimes perished with them. For the women and children who stayed back in the villages, life was a long, dreary ordeal lasting for three months. With nothing to bank on—the men took the wool, which was their main product, to sell in the bazaars— it was a mystery how they survived during these months. Every year there were some who did not live to see their dear ones return. With the advent of summer, the hungry eyes of the women and children scanning the horizon would be rewarded by the sight of the men returning with their animals. But the joy of reunion was tempered by the mourning over those who had departed for ever—both among the migrants and among the women and children who had stayed behind.

During the previous years many of the men had found themselves at the gates of the recruiting office, instead of on the long, dusty road that led them on their migrating journey. When the fodder was exhausted, the cattle took to migration on their own without waiting for their masters. It was an irreparable loss to the villagers who in their despair quarrelled among themselves over trivialities—the droppings of goats or the foul language someone allegedly used. It took little time for the quarrels to develop into violent attacks and riots which claimed several lives.

What Jaswant said was proving true. There had been a perceptible growth in recruitment during the last few days. In the previous week not less than fifteen men had lined up for recruitment on a single day. This, at a time when the villages were bustling with activity. It was a strange páradox; on the one hand there were not enough men for work in the villages, and the Pioneers were deserting the lines; on the other, even the few remaining men in the villages were making a beeline for the recruiting centre. It was no longer possible to say that their problems were confined to the little circles of their villages and that the Project had nothing to do with them, that the village and the Sarkar had nothing to do with each other.

On reaching the town, Kundan took leave of the others and went to the restaurant, took a seat in a corner and ordered a beer. A lean and short bearer, who looked as young as a boy, brought a bottle of beer and a glass. He blushed like a girl when Kundan thanked him.

As it grew dark, the minstrels clad in their colourful dresses and huge turbans arrived. There were not many people in the restaurant. And those left were also rising to go. It was as if the musicians had arrived to sing solely for Kundan. Or they were just trying to express themselves, not singing for anybody in particular. They took a few moments to time their instruments. Then, suddenly, they burst into song. It was an extraordinarily poignant song:

Oh, you who go away
Go away, if you must.
But never come back,
Never—even if you can.
Don't cast a glance at us
Even if you come back.
And if you must see us
Don't weep for us—
Even if you have tears.
Die and fade away
If it is in your hands to die.
Just spare a thought:
What was this life of yours worth?

As the song reached its crescendo, it appeared that the

minstrels were dissolving themselves into their song and disappearing.

It was an old song. The worn-out words that had been passed from generation to generation rose up into the sky, swinging and swaying. When the migrants returned, they say, the women often did not dare to come to the doors to welcome them, fearing that some of their dear ones may not be among them. A woman standing behind a closed door with bated breath, hugging her children together, at a loss as to how she could account for a son who was no more . . . The approaching footsteps and a knock at the door . . . Or, there may not be a knock at all.

The night advanced. A gentle wind, winding its way through the narrow streets, entered the restaurant, wheeled around and went out through the gates. The curtains ruffled for a moment and were still again. The restaurant was deserted now. Not even the bearers were around. Only the empty glasses and plates remained on the tables. The minstrels were still singing, lost in the silent voyages within themselves. They had withdrawn into their colourful dresses and the huge turbans on their heads. The clothes and the turbans seemed to carry on the song by themselves.

Chapter Fifteen

By 'space' we usually mean the area occupied by something. We can also define it differently, depending upon our approach. For instance, we may measure it as the distance between two different objects, or as a system which relates one object to another. Space dominates objects in the former while individual objects become the reference points to define space in the latter. Consider the two kinds of animal movements, grazing and migration. In grazing, the animals fill the space, moving in a diffused manner without any particular direction. Migration is a movement across space. Here space is only a scale by which the movement is measured.

When a man comes to a desert leaving behind a green valley, the immediate sensation is of a strange kind of freedom. He stands before an immense expanse of land with no fences or boundaries. A rocky outcrop or a khejri tree shows its head, then a shrub here or a hamlet there. Animals graze around at will. The vast spaces are nobody's private property. The visitor, a person of sedentary habits, is used to seeing his space as an island of his rights, surrounded by similar islands of others' rights. The rights he knows are subject to limits and the system he understands is one which recognizes his neighbours as individuals who have their own rights. In short, space is a variant which he uses to establish relationships with others. But this life too secretly nurtures a resistance in him, a resistance against the limitations and restraints which rule his world. Then the desert opens up before his eyes and he suddenly discovers his passion for moving around unrestrained. It is this passion to rush in all directions, this greed to grab and possess things that is the strange freedom of the desert which he experiences for the first time.

But what seems freedom to this man is something else for the desert-dweller. The latter can only see scarcity and destitution around him. In the desert it is not only fences that are conspicuous by their absence, but also resources. There are no fences precisely because there are no resources. One can walk and walk in the desert without trespassing on anybody's property. If one does not think of moving on, it is because there is nothing to lose or acquire there. Scarcity stands in the way of abilities, growth, even aspirations. It looms like a dark shadow before the promise of freedom. Scarcity is a kind of tyranny that weighs down on life, the destiny that blocks all exits.

Yes, freedom in the midst of such emptiness is no freedom, concedes the outsider. The mere absence of controls does not lead to freedom; there must be something to achieve too. But then, how did these majestic forts rise from the barren wastes? How could they be filled with such luxury and pomp which is unfamiliar even to those who have come from the rich, green lands?

It showed that even in the midst of this barrenness somebody had exercised his freedom. Scarcity was no obstacle to him. On the contrary, scarcity and the absence of controls incited him to violence and plunder. He took the whole desert as his possession, just as an outsider would consider his house or field his own, and marched beyond it to the green lands he coveted. The wealth he amassed became the measure of the distance his horses could travel.

The standard of the plunderer's prowess is not the quantity of the booty, but the intensity of the desire or passion to loot burning within him. This desire or passion stems from the thirst for vengeance against the barrenness of the landscape or the natural revolt that even dwellers of green lands feel against controls and limits. The animals grazing listlessly in the desert gather together and form a group. Suddenly their movements acquire a direction. They get ready for migration, leaving one pasture in quest of another, converting the space that used to weigh down upon them into a measure of their movements.

Thus, one day, on the promontories of the green land appear, like a black line, the horsemen unleashed from the depths of the hungry desert. They begin to cast their shadows over it like a swarm of locusts, and thunder in like a dark cloud of dust. The tolls and taxes and rules of the road that civilization imposed on the land cannot stop them. In a moment, the green land is reduced to a wasteland, the wasteland on which the laws of scarcity shall rule hereafter.

As time passes, one witnesses a fort rising up in the midst of the subjugated land to protect the wealth sucked from it and from its people. The laws of rights and privacy having been already done away with, they can only stand and watch helplessly the growth of this new monster. It distances itself from them deliberately. It has no ears for the groans and sighs emanating from the dilapidated and broken houses lying around it. But it certainly watches, through the narrow slits in its high walls, every movement of every object in its domain. The inhabitants of the ravaged land have not seen—or if they have seen, they have already forgotten—the faces of the occupants of the forbidden palace. Like the unfortunate desert people, they too look with their vacant eyes at the object standing far away, a dark, sombre shape silhouetted against the sky in the cold light of the stars, and start calling it by a vague epithet: the Sarkar.

Chapter Sixteen

A wordy duel was in progress between the assistant labour officer, Jaswant, and the record clerk, who sat in his cubicle in the record room, separated from Kundan's by a partition.

A security policeman had come to get information about the relatives of a Pioneer who had died, and Kundan had directed him to the record clerk. After glancing through the dossier of the deceased, the clerk remarked: 'This man too has no relatives!'

Jaswant wrote this piece of information on the paper brought by the policeman and signed it. The policeman took the paper from him and went out. Jaswant had not uttered a word during the whole exercise. As soon as the policeman was out of sight, his expression changed.

'Where did you get the idea that the Sarkar pays you to remark, "this man too has no relatives"? They wanted only the name and address of the dead man's relatives, not your profound analysis of the situation. You seem to forget that you are just a clerk.'

The dead man was the third Pioneer to die of pneumonia in the camp. Like him, the first two deceased had no known relatives. The clerk was referring to this coincidence.

'But, sir, it is a strange coincidence,' the clerk tried to explain his point.

But that only provoked Jaswant again.

'Couldn't you see that this note was brought by a security policeman? Don't you know that it is usually the administrative staff who come on such errands?'

'Yes, that is strange too!' the clerk could not help exclaiming.

'I did not ask you to prepare a list of strange phenomena. I am trying to drive into your head the seriousness of the matter. Didn't you notice that it was the security policemen who came in the other two cases too? You should be more careful when you blurt out your impressions.'

'You are right, sir,' the clerk admitted meekly.

Jaswant cooled down at that.

'They sent this note after having sent the body to the crematorium,' he continued in a kindlier voice, as if he was initiating the clerk into the intricacies of the Project's administration. 'They did the same thing in the other two cases as well. According to the rules they can't do that without inquiring whether the dead person has any relatives. That means they knew the facts even before they got our certificates. I am not narrating yet another case for you to enter into your book of mysteries. This is a security classified project. You may see many things here which may appear strange or unusual to you. That doesn't mean that you should go about proclaiming it to the whole world. What you should do is talk less and do the work given to you more carefully.'

The clerk did not say anything further. Accepting Jaswant's advice, he bowed his head and went back to his work.

Kundan rose from his chair. He took out his green identity card from his shirt pocket and fixed it on the chain around his neck. He picked up the cane with the Project's insignia on it and walked out of the office.

The records office was inside the fort though the Pioneer camps were outside it. It was the usual practice to keep the records of the employees well out of their reach in a protected area. Kundan could not, however, understand why the hospital had to be inside the fort as well. Except the prisoners, all the others, including the security policeman, lived outside the fort. It was difficult to believe that this was done for the prisoners' sake. Prisoners were freely admitted in the government hospitals of the mofussil towns, where anyone could go in and out, and where even stray dogs ventured freely in and occasionally carried away a newborn baby.

The hospital stood just a few steps away from the gates of the fort on the left. The offices of the Project were located in the old palace built by the raja of Rambhagarh. After the fort was taken over for the Project, new buildings were constructed for the jail and the hospital. The hospital was a three-storeyed matchbox-like structure built of stone ashlar masonry. The policeman at the hospital's main gate glanced at the green card on Kundan's chest and saluted him. Kundan walked along the corridors and entered the wards making enquiries about the patients. It was something he ought to have been doing all along, but had not done so far. He felt happy and guilty at the same time. Not that the inquiry would bring about any change in the quality of the treatment, or in the behaviour of the staff towards the patients. But when a man comes to ask about their health, the faces of the patients, who are never visited by anyone, light up. Kundan had been leaving everything to the administrators. It had eluded him that there are certain things which an ordinary administrator cannot do even if he wants to.

He met the doctor on duty and asked him about the cases of pneumonia. The doctor admitted that there were a few such cases. 'There are all types of cases here. There are quite a few diseases people can contract, you know,' the doctor remarked evasively, which meant that Kundan had better mind his own business.

'But pneumonia? And that too in this weather?' Kundan would not let it go as the doctor would have liked him to.

'What do you mean?' The doctor was visibly annoyed. 'Diseases can attack anyone, at any time. Why should the government run hospitals otherwise?'

Neither the doctor nor anyone else in the hospital seemed to be concerned about the unusual manner in which the disease was spreading. No one appeared to have even noticed it except the poor clerk in the records office, a simpleton who saw mysteries as mysteries. But then he was silenced with the same callousness.

It was not the anxiety caused by the disease, but the solace of having hospitals around that mattered to the people. Nobody complained about soldiers getting killed in wars. The pleas were for taking care of their widows and children.

Convinced that it was futile to pursue the problem in the hospital, Kundan went to the mortuary. The guard at the mortuary told him that the body of the prisoner who had died the previous night had already been removed to the crematorium. Jaswant was right. The security men and the doctors knew that the deceased had no relatives. They asked for the certificate from the records office merely to complete the formalities. There were two aspects of the pneumonia cases which made Kundan uneasy. It seemed that pneumonia attacked and killed only those who had no relatives, and whose bodies could, therefore, be cremated in the Project crematorium. Secondly, Jaswant appeared to have an inside knowledge of everything that was happening in the Project.

There were other irritants too. The persistent objections Jaswant raised when Kundan took Daniel back on the rolls, and the security officer's remarks about Bhola's daughter. Jaswant knew that the girl brought milk for Kundan, for it was he who had arranged it. Besides Jaswant, there were a few others who seemed to be regularly acquiring such inside knowledge: the warder of the Project Jail, the warder of the City Jail and, of course, Yogeshwar. Kundan was realizing that a group of people who always had their eyes and ears open were operating around him. They could throw a cordon around him any time. But he was determined not to let himself be browbeaten by them. He was not a naive novice who could be intimidated. He was the labour officer of the Project. And a labour officer had certain duties which he had been neglecting. It dawned upon Kundan with a start that he had not been keeping his eyes and ears open, as he should have.

Kundan came out of the mortuary and walked towards the old palace which housed the Project offices.

The palace was a four-storeyed building. The Security Section was on the ground floor. The Administrative Wing under the control of the Station Commander, which supervised the Pioneer Force, the Prisoner Force and the Labour Office, was on the first floor. The Project Commandant, who was the supreme authority of the Project, sat on the top floor. Except there—only red card holders were admitted to the top floor—Kundan, who held a green card, was free to go about anywhere in the Project, even at the work site. To his own surprise, Kundan had seldom visited these places. He had never visited the Construction Wing. Only once had he stepped into the work site. His visits to the Administrative Wing to which his section belonged had also been rare. He went there only to collect the papers when he had to take in or hand over a batch of prisoners and to receive instructions at the time of VIP visits. The last time he went there was when the riot broke out in the neighbouring village. The Station Commander had then held a brief meeting there.

Kundan climbed the stairs at the end of the corridor to the Administrative Wing. He walked along the meandering corridors which branched out as in a labyrinth. The doors were so low that an assailant would have to put his head in first before entering and the guards could chop off his head before he attacked! The rooms which were occupied by various departments and sections could have been harems, treasuries, armouries or the chambers of petty officials of the raja. The names of the Project officials who now occupied the rooms were written on the doors. Kundan went into the toilet and washed his face. He then climbed the stairs to the third floor which housed the Construction Wing with its engineers and scientists. Kundan read the boards on the doors: Laboratory, Instrumentation, Design Office, Planning, Coordination, Computer Room . . . names which were common to all projects. None of them told him what the Rambhagarh Project was actually accomplishing. Like the rooms on the other floors, these too faced the jauhar kund. Iron grills had been fixed on the windows of the rooms which once opened onto it. The floor of the well had been levelled and paved with stones. Any old man walking aimlessly in the narrow streets of the town, or a guide in a shabby jacket with unshaven face, yellow eyes and blackened teeth who had lost his livelihood with the coming of the Project, and was now reduced to the role of a pimp patronized by stray tourists, would give you the exact number of the raja's queens who had jumped to their death in the well.

But the numbers meant nothing, for those women had to die; if not at the kund then somewhere else; if not as the queens of the raja of Rambhagarh, then as the queens of some other raja; if not by a husband's torture, by starvation or disease. And this principle applies to people who live in the present day too. And since everyone has to die in the end, why should anyone get worked up over such matters? If a clerk strains his eyes with wonder to ask if the dead man is the third to have died of pneumonia, let him spoil his eyes. Whether a man dies of pneumonia or by drinking

for the whole of his waking hours like Pasupati Singh . . .
such discussions were best left to silly, sentimental clerks.
The Security Division which subscribed to this philosophy
had decided to pave the jauhar kund with neatly cut stones.

Kundan descended the stairs and walked towards the
work site. Once the prisoners were handed over to the jail,
they were placed under the charge of their Commander. So
Kundan did not normally visit the work site. The work site
had two security rings, the restricted and the most restricted.
Kundan crossed the first security ring and went around the
places where the Pioneers were constructing walls,
underground shelters and tunnels. The workers did not
seem to recognize the labour officer who had recruited them.
Kundan's eyes scanned the faces of the prisoners. But the
face he sought was not among them. He crossed the second
security line and entered the inner circle. Nothing of any
significance seemed to be happening there. The same sights
and sounds—a concrete mixer, iron girders and the
humming of the air compressor—greeted him. The khaki-
clad engineers and technicians with helmets on their heads
recognized Kundan and nodded to him. But Kundan was
watching the prisoners in shorts and vests. Their slow and
mechanical movements reminded him of a scene in a film
he had seen years ago: the slaves of ancient Egypt building
pyramids. The scourgers with the whips were absent here,
but the movements and expressions on the faces of the
prisoners were the same. The name the Egyptians gave to
their slaves, 'the living dead', appeared to be apt for these
prisoners too. The Mesopotamian word for slaves, which
meant 'those who do not raise their eyes', also suited them.
But Kundan did not like to call these people slaves. They
were prisoners, and prisoners were different from slaves.
He spent some time arguing with himself as to who was at
the lower rung of the scale of human degradation—slaves
or prisoners.

Suddenly Kundan saw Sulaiman. He was returning in a

group with other prisoners after completing some jobs.

'Sulaiman!' Kundan called out.

Kundan had not seen him since the day he instructed the jailer to take him on the roll. Months had passed after that. The last time he had been terribly angry with Sulaiman. What had happened to change his attitude to Sulaiman? Why had he come here to meet him today? Kundan could see no clear reason for his wish to see Sulaiman.

Sulaiman, looking thin and exhausted, flinching under the burning heat of the sun, stooped, pretending to wipe the sweat from his forehead, rubbed his eyes and smiled at Kundan, a smile that did not get washed away in sweat or tears. Then suddenly he stiffened, as if reminded of something, turned and walked away. Prisoners were not allowed to stand alone anywhere at the work site for long. It was now Kundan's turn to wipe the sweat on his forehead.

If an officer and a prisoner were to meet and exchange smiles in such a manner, would their relationship remain that which normally prevailed between an officer and a prisoner?

But this was not what Kundan was thinking of then. Why hadn't he come here earlier? Why hadn't it occurred to him to meet Sulaiman before?

Chapter Seventeen

When the cultural officer arrived, the officers' club welcomed him with a cocktail party. He was to stay with his troupe at the Project for a month. It showed the importance the Sarkar attached to the Project, the Commandant said while introducing the cultural officer. He then talked about the growing discontent and indiscipline among the employees of the Project. These were not to be seen as mere aberrations, but the results of serious causes. This was where personnel management came in. But personnel management was not everything. It was the function of culture to direct man's mind to duty and discipline. In short, to boost his morale. He would call it cultural management.

Concluding his brief, cryptic speech, the Commandant, General Jagannathan, took the cultural officer around among his subordinates. Both had the form and air befitting their office. Tall, slim, clean-shaven and wearing metal-rimmed glasses, the General was a true Commandant, every inch of him. He had a voice that refused to be raised, a thin-lipped mouth that did not open beyond a gentle smile, and a manner of keeping aloof even while striking up quite intimate relationships. After letting loose the cultural officer among his subordinates, he drank a small whisky for formality, excused himself and went out. The cultural officer with his well-trimmed beard and twinkling eyes mingled with the men with a glass in hand.

Once inside the club, it was the convention that the officers should keep away from their wives. Similarly, they were to change their companions frequently without conversing too much with anyone in particular. Everyone observed these conventions. So when Kundan saw, instead of Amala, a woman he had not seen before with Yogeshwar, he didn't pay any attention to it. But Yogeshwar was not just having a chat with a colleague's wife. With arms around each other's waists, with their faces almost coming together in a kiss, they moved around as if they had been glued to each other. Yogeshwar's companion was a woman who could capture anyone's attention with her looks, dress, make-up and loud laughter. Everyone went up to the couple and greeted them.

On seeing Kundan at a distance, Yogeshwar dashed across to him with the woman in tow. He introduced her to Kundan as his wife. Their marriage was only a two-week old baby, he told him with a loud laugh.

When he saw Yogeshwar at the club, Kundan had expected to meet Amala. He wanted to speak to her. He had not been able to do so the last time. Now it was out of the question. Amala was gone—the woman whom Yogeshwar had described as his greatest fortune.

Still holding his new wife close to him, Yogeshwar began to talk about Sulaiman. Perhaps that was the purpose of his dashing to Kundan like a dart the moment he saw him.

'Keep an eye on that man. Fellows like him may prove troublesome.

'But Sulaiman is now wholly under your charge,' Kundan said innocently.

'In this man's case, your responsibility is no less than mine.' Yogeshwar's eyes narrowed to the size of pinheads.

Kundan, however, did not want to discuss the topic with Yogeshwar then. He looked away.

Yogeshwar left him and moved towards the crowd, holding close to him his new, beautiful 'fortune'. Kundan found a sofa in a corner to retire to.

He felt terribly lonely. Seeing his condition, and as if to help him get out of it, a fat man with a thick moustache, his eyes twinkling with mischief, accosted him.

'Hello, I am Brigadier Jogi Handa,' he introduced himself.

He looked a true brigadier to Kundan. It seemed to him that everyone there was true to his designation, the Commandant, the cultural officer and the Brigadier. Kundan introduced himself.

'Where is your glass?' the Brigadier enquired.

'I have already had a drink. And that is enough for me.'

'Ah, yes. Each man to his taste. But have a small one for my sake all the same.' He took a small whisky from the bearer's tray and handed it to Kundan.

'This culture stuff, you know, is something men like me can't understand,' the Brigadier said with an arch smile. 'We are a class of people trained to rule by imposing discipline. Hard things should be learned the hard way . . .'

'The Commandant has no difference of opinion with you on that point.'

'What is the use of his opinion? Though it is a defence installation, this project has a civilian set-up. Look at the way the government has sent a party of dancers to teach this bunch of unruly workers discipline!'

He laughed aloud, moving his hands in imitation of a dancer's pose.

'By the way, aren't you the labour officer here?' the Brigadier closed his eyes for a moment, as if to refresh his memory.

'You have guessed right.'

'Labour—labouring! This labouring is a complicated business, you know.' Setting his legs apart, he made an obscene gesture with his hands, laughing aloud and spilling some of his whisky. Then restraining himself, he moved closer to Kundan and lowering his voice, remarked in mock seriousness: 'For dogs, even intercourse is painful. But man has transformed even childbirth into a pleasure.'

'You can be a little more decent, Brigadier,' Kundan said curtly.

'Oh, I am sorry, you should excuse me,' the Brigadier shook his head. 'What I meant was this: pain is the price we pay for our pleasures. We cannot get anything without paying a price for it. That is the golden rule, and a government that is serious about governing must make its people understand this. In a book I have read, there is a reference to a country where the price of all commodities is paid in the form of punishment. Ten lashes for a kilo of wheat, five for a kilo of potatoes, and so on.'

Kundan's eyes fell on the cultural officer standing alone in a corner. He walked up to him and introduced himself.

'Oh, yes, my whole business is with you. I wonder why they didn't introduce you to me.' The cultural officer grinned, showing his teeth through the neatly trimmed beard and moustache.

'I was talking with a Brigadier just now,' Kundan looked up at the cultural officer. 'He thinks the only way to curb indiscipline is to use the stick. He wonders how you can make men obey you by dancing before them.

The cultural officer bowed and, as if he was revealing a secret, whispered in Kundan's ear: 'These soldiers know only about ordinary, plain sticks, not the ones with poison smeared at the end. But the Sarkar knows everything. It is not for nothing that it gives so much importance to culture. There are carnivals and casinos everywhere. They have even opened a department for culture. Plenty of funds too. We have brought a good troupe here.'

'A department for culture? I think the Sarkar itself is a department of culture!'

'Oh, no, no! You shouldn't say things like that. You are a labour officer,' the cultural officer pulled a long face, allowing his spectacles to slip down his nose. Stroking his beard and carrying his glass, he retraced his steps and vanished.

Kundan went to the bar counter, sat on a stool and asked for another drink. The barman placed before him a plate of fried peanuts along with a glass of whisky.

'No cheese, sir,' the barman who knew Kundan's preferences said apologetically. 'Nothing made from milk.'

Even milk was not available. Bhola's wife had stopped bringing milk to Kundan. Bhola was still working in the Pioneer camp. Kundan couldn't manage to get him out and his wife had stopped asking him for it. The mischievous smile on her daughter's face would have dried up now. With no grass or water, their buffaloes would have died. Or they might have abandoned their animals when they found they could not feed them any more . . .

The bearer handed Kundan a note sent by Jaswant. Daniel, who had deserted, had been caught by the police at the railway station. He was lying unconscious on the platform.

Kundan was brooding over it when Hassan tapped him on the shoulder from behind.

'Something seems to be worrying you, Kundan.'

'Grief, I think, will be a better word,' Kundan muttered.

'They say that grief, unlike happiness, is lightened when you share it. Can't you tell me what is bothering you?'

'This one is different, Hassan. I have to keep it all to myself.'

Chapter Eighteen

The day broke with the news of Daniel's death. He had died in custody the previous night.

There could have been only one reason for his desertion—fear. As a previous deserter who had returned willingly, there could be no other reason for his running away again except fear for his life. He had pneumonia and collapsed as soon as he reached the station. After being arrested, he was taken either to the police station or to the hospital. He could have died of illness or torture. It was no use trying to find out how.

The news of the death reached the Pioneer camp in the morning when the companies lined up for the parade. The Company Commanders, as they usually did on such occasions, informed the men of the death of a Pioneer named Daniel, and asked them to observe two minutes' silence to mourn the deceased.

One of the men who had reported sick and was standing alone outside the formations had signs of fever. During the two minutes' silence he fainted. The Company Commander asked two others to remove him to the medical inspection room. Suddenly a murmur arose from among the Pioneers who stood in three lines: 'Pneumonia', 'pneumonia'. In an instant the whole company gave up the formations, dispersed and followed the patient to the medical inspection room. Surrounding the building, they began to shout that proper medical treatment should be given to the patient.

As the news spread, the other companies too followed suit. Before long, the whole Pioneer Force under Hassan's command gathered before the medical inspection room. All the Company Commanders and officers were rendered irrelevant and superfluous at one stroke.

When Kundan arrived at the site after receiving a message from Hassan, he could not believe what he saw. Though he was a civilian himself, he wondered whether such a thing was possible. But it was happening before his eyes. A couple of stones hit the windows of the inspection room. It seemed that the Pioneers were going to attack the building and the doctor. The mutiny caught the officers unawares, and they merely watched the scene, dumbfounded.

The doctors were trying to take the patient to the hospital inside the fort. But the jostling crowd blocked their way. It was necessary to bring the irate men under control, at least to provide proper treatment to the patient. The Project Security Police was expected to arrive any moment. The problem had to be solved before their arrival. A crackdown would worsen the situation. Kundan and Hassan ventured to intervene and tried to plead with the Pioneers to calm down. At first, it seemed their pleas had some effect.

But it did not last long. If the patient was taken to the hospital, the doctors would kill him, the Pioneers shouted. Could Kundan and Hassan guarantee that the patient's life would be saved, they asked.

It was an issue on which Kundan could not give any guarantee, especially because he had his own doubts about the nature and circumstances of the cases. The workers were expressing the same doubts. All he could say was that pneumonia was no more a terminal disease and that it could be cured if proper treatment was given in time.

But the Pioneers would not be pacified. Then how did so many of them die, they shouted at Kundan and Hassan. Not a single patient had returned from the hospital alive. The doctors were experimenting on the patients like guinea pigs. Could he deny it, they asked Kundan in one voice.

At least one thing was becoming clear to Kundan. The nuances, which he had believed only a trained intellect like his could distinguish, the mysteries unravelled by the records clerk after analysing the records and circumstances of the deaths due to pneumonia, the doubts the doctors thought they could suppress by posing rhetorical questions about the government's motive in building hospitals, and the questions which Jaswant thought would be stifled by the theory that security was beyond all questions—all these were fresh and fully alive in the minds of these illiterate villagers who lived in the company of sand and rock. Thorny or poisonous, these buds and shoots of rebellion showed that everything had not dried up in their souls. They had stopped their comrade from being taken to the hospital, reacting not emotionally or arbitrarily, but with logic and reason.

Yet, Kundan could not speak for them. The allegation that patients were being experimented on, or killed in the hospital, still lacked evidence. Besides, it was possible that the patient would die if he was not removed to the hospital quickly. He took a step forward and entreated the rebellious Pioneers in a dry voice: 'If you don't give way, please try to understand, we will have to use force, at least to take the patient to the hospital.'

At this point, the security police arrived, a whole platoon of them with lathis. They spread out and took up their positions. At their head was Jagtap, the security officer. The handsome Jagtap with his chubby nose and dark eyelashes stood glaring at the Pioneers, his arms akimbo and his legs apart. Kundan took a step towards him.

'Jagtap, for God's sake, don't do anything to worsen the situation. They have some apprehensions about the matter. If a doctor explains things to them they will understand. It was only yesterday that the Commandant spoke about personnel management at the club, you know.'

'When we arrived, I heard you giving them the last warning, that force would be used if they did not give way,' Jagtap replied, 'you may please allow us to do it.'

Like the dismissed workers of a factory, or students turned out of their classroom, Kundan and Hassan were ignored by the security police. They were pushed back rudely as if they had ceased to exist. They had to hop and jump to avoid stepping over the stones that were strewn about.

What followed lasted only a few seconds. Uttering a deafening cry, the policemen charged the Pioneers with lathis. The Pioneers scattered instantly. Some fell bleeding to the ground. The rest ran helter-skelter, and without anyone's command, fell in three lines and stood to attention. The police van drove to the hospital with the patient.

*

The papers in the records office had acquired a musty smell though they were only two or three years old. Surprisingly, it was like the smell of dried horse dung. Paper, like horse dung, is an organic substance. When a living thing dies, it changes into some organic compounds first and then the organic compounds too, in the long run, break down to become inorganic substances. However, in the midst of these processes, they leave behind some smells which roam around, perennially, like spirits or ghosts trying fervently to communicate something to the living.

Jaswant, whose head was buried in the documents, raised it to ask Kundan what had happened.

'What should not happen has happened,' Kundan replied.

'The Security Wing had sent their man to get the address of Daniel's relatives. But without waiting for the certificate, they removed the body for burial.'

Kundan said nothing.

Daniel's relatives had already been eaten by fish during their long journey through the flood waters, digested and thrown out by them, broken down into organic matter and then into the basic elements. Daniel, who escaped this process by clinging to the branch of a tree, also had his long and lonely ride along the narrow and risky borderlines of freedom and bondage. Now exhausted, he had surrendered to the germs of pneumonia and then to the bacteria that had managed to survive five feet below the surface of the dry desert soil.

'What is going to happen now?' Jaswant asked.

'I don't know. The mutiny is crushed, at least for today. Force has won. The cultural officer's troupe will not be performing today.'

Kundan was wrong. While he was munching his two slices of bread and sipping his glass of coffee during the lunch break, a security jeep suddenly pulled up before the stable. The inspector who got down from the jeep spoke to him.

'The instruction is to go down. The situation is bad again. The Pioneers have left the camp and gone out.'

As the jeep drove downhill from the fort, negotiating the hairpin curves one after another, the uproar from the town was audible.

The workers who left the camp went to the town where the people of the town joined hands with them to become a sizeable crowd. Intoxicated by the frenzy of a new-found liberty, the crowd shouted and screamed. The shops downed their shutters. Excited men took up positions at windows and doors or on the balconies of houses. The mob had no sense of direction or purpose. It marched along one street for some time and then turned into another. Apart from the security police, the civil police too had to be involved now. In fact the civil police had already swung into action and cordoned off the streets. Meanwhile the security police had closed the entrance to the labour camps. The crowd was bottled up. Before Kundan could make a survey of the situation he heard the sound of gunfire and the screams of the people. The helpless crowd tried to rush into the shops and houses in the street. The commotion continued for some time. Then the firing stopped. Everything became quiet and the police started removing the bodies.

It was already dusk when the bodies of the dead and the injured were brought to the fort. The next task was to identify them. The women and children were separated first. They were clearly outsiders. Now the problem was to identify the remaining men who had to be divided into civilians and Pioneers. This task was entrusted to Kundan and Hassan.

Kundan decided not to count the bodies. The idea of counting human beings always revolted him. The only way to get over this revulsion was to see them as individuals with faces and feelings. This privilege he had enjoyed while handing over the prisoners at the railway station and recording the biodata of the new recruits at the recruiting centre. But it had also led him to perilous encounters with cases such as those of Sulaiman, Daniel and Bhola.

And here it was happening again.

One of the faces he recognized among the injured was Bhola's. Yes, the same Bhola. Bathed in blood, his head smashed, his eyes still fiercely defiant. Kundan wanted to pretend he had not recognized him or to take his eyes off him. But he could not help staring at the face as if his eyes were riveted to it. Bhola too appeared to be staring at him. The security police removed him the next moment.

The greater part of the night was spent in identifying the dead and the injured. The civil police took away their share of men, and the security police theirs. Dawn was not far away when the last body was accounted for.

Gulshan opened the door as Kundan got down from the jeep. He had been waiting for Kundan.

'I was worried about you, Gulshan.'

'Saheb, can anyone fight and win against the Sarkar?' Gulshan offered his old doctrine again. 'I did not go anywhere. I just shut myself up here.'

'Leaving aside questions of fighting or yielding for the moment, why do you always think of the Sarkar as something to be feared?'

Gulshan did not give an immediate reply. He waited until Kundan sat on the bed and began to take off his shoes.

Gulshan sat on the floor and picked up the shoes. Then he spoke in a half-soliloquy: 'I don't know how it is in your part of the country, saheb. My mother tells me that there are three things you come across in a desert: sand dunes, sandstorms and mirages. If one loses one's way among sand dunes or is caught in a sandstorm, there is little hope. As for mirages, they deceive the travellers and lead them to a thirsty death. Nobody asks why they are there. We should fear what is to be feared.'

Gulshan was a youngster at the threshold of adulthood. A lonely young man full of wanderlust. Had he finally married the girl he had rescued from the clutches of the soldiers?

Kundan drank the glass of water Gulshan brought him, went to the window and looked out. Here was a town that had broken into a revolt during the day, but was sleeping quietly now. The steep lines of the corners of walls that separated light and shadows, the windows that were lost in themselves, the doors that had been silenced, the plinth lines which faithfully followed the ups and downs of the stonepaved paths . . .

Kundan suddenly realized that the grey night was very cold. It was November, the middle of autumn. The earth cooled quickly, and along with it the air too. A full day had passed after Daniel's death. Though Daniel died like the others before him, there was something vitally different in his death. Before the day had passed, Daniel had taken many others with him. Many more were thrown into the cold prison cells. One should fear what is to be feared, Gulshan had said.

Chapter Nineteen

'What are you going to do with these men?'

Instead of replying Jagtap looked at Kundan without any expression. A kind of truculence seemed to have come over his effeminate face. Perhaps he owed it to the glasses he wore—bare, rimless glasses with a brown tinge which concealed his dark eyelashes. Jagtap had not been wearing glasses till the day before. Why did he choose to wear them today, of all days? That he was not fully at home with them was evident from the way he kept adjusting them frequently.

Kundan repeated the question.

'The civilian casualties have been handed over to the civil police.'

'I know that. I am talking about the Pioneers.'

'They will be dealt with according to the laws.'

'I am the labour officer,' Kundan decided to assert himself. 'It is my duty to show them what the law is.'

'My dear labour officer,' Jagtap crumpled a piece of paper he was holding in his hand and threw it away. He then spread out his hands, 'You have done your duty as a labour officer. Now please let the rest of us do ours.'

Kundan knew he was arguing in vain with this man. There was a chief security officer above him, but he was not any different. He had better see the Station Commander. Kundan's impression of Brigadier Chandan Roy was that of a soft-spoken, mellowed man. Besides, who else but his superior officer should he approach for help in discharging his duties?

Kundan hastily climbed the stairs to the first floor of the Administrative Block. Without waiting for ceremonies, he went directly to the office of the Station Commander. The Station Commander raised his eyes from the file before him.

'Yes, Kundan, what can I do for you?'

'Sir, it is very urgent. I learned that the Pioneers who revolted yesterday are being taken to some unknown place. I don't know if it is true. If it is, as the labour officer, I . . .'

'Of course they are being taken away, and they should be.'

'But how can they do it? They are under my charge. There are some rules to be followed in these matters.'

'You are right, they are now under your charge. You can prepare a list of them and hand it over to the Security Wing. You may strike off their names from your rolls.'

'But sir, on what authority am I to strike off their names? Or hand them over to the Security Wing, for that matter? Does it mean that their services are being terminated?'

'Well, not exactly. Be seated, Kundan.' The Brigadier gestured forcefully, as if he was pushing Kundan down into a chair. 'They are being proceeded against according to the rules.'

'But sir, we cannot do anything that is not according to the due process of the law.'

'According to the procedure established by the law,' the Brigadier corrected Kundan, shaking his head gently. 'I suppose you know the difference between the two.'

'But that does not entitle the Security Wing to take away these men. I haven't even seen them. Since yesterday they have been in the custody of the security officer. Even the patient who fainted yesterday was not brought to me although that's what it says on paper. The doctors have not informed me about his condition either.'

'The patient is being treated by the doctor. You know that, don't you?'

'The patient is in the custody of the doctor, and the workers in the custody of the security police. I can't understand this.'

'My dear, dutiful labour officer,' the muscles on the Station Commander's face became taut, the corners of his lips curled and his voice hardened, 'don't you agree that it is the doctors who should treat the patients and that it is the Security Wing who should deal with the mutineers?'

Descending to the first floor of the building, going in through the open panels of the stable, Kundan reached the cubicle at the end which was the records office and sat in the chair that lay vacant for him. Hearing the scraping of Kundan's chair on the floor, Jaswant came out of the adjoining cubicle. They looked at each other for some time in silence.

'Jaswant,' Kundan spoke at length, 'have you ever thought of this: how did our species survive on this planet?'

'Why do you ask such a question, sir?'

'It is no less than a miracle that a creature like man, so handicapped and helpless physically, has survived.' Kundan's eyes met Jaswant's. Noticing the vacant expression on Jaswant's face, he continued: 'I am talking about our ancestors. Surrounded by a variety of fierce, carnivorous animals, without any effective weapons to fight them, without the physical strength to drive them off, or even to outrun them . . . I wonder if they ever had a sound day's sleep.'

'Yes, yes. You are right, sir. Now I understand,' Jaswant's face lit up.

Sometime that day, the vehicles carrying the arrested

workers were to leave the fort. They were prisoners now, not workers. Their destination was unknown. Perhaps they would never return. No one knew what awaited them, for they had challenged the security of the Sarkar. There was no place in a country for people who were not faithful to it. That was why Kundan had to strike off their names from the records. But he could not just prepare a list of their names and hand it over to the Security Wing, as suggested by the Station Commander, for the simple reason that he did not know where they were. The prisoners as well as the list of their names were in the custody of the Security Wing. Perhaps he could get the list from them tomorrow, the list of the names to be struck off the rolls. Whether the men in the list were dead or injured, or arrested for starting a mutiny, he need not inquire. Was this the nature of the sandstorms that Gulshan had spoken about, the sandstorms about which no questions were asked as to how or why they originated? The sandstorms which constantly shifted sand dunes and dug graves for every grain of sand?

Kundan had nothing to do till the next day. He collected his things and left the office.

The doors and windows of the house were open. As Kundan climbed the steps he heard the fan turning in the bedroom. He pushed open the door and his eyes fell on Ruth lying on the bed, reading a book.

'Surprise!' Ruth grinned at him.

Leaning against the door with one arm and holding his folded coat with the other, Kundan stood on the doorstep, tired and exhausted, unable to respond to Ruth's greeting.

'Surprise and solace are two different things. But today I find them the same,' Kundan said when he regained his composure. 'I don't know how I should thank you, Ruth. While sitting in my office today, I wished fervently that you were here. I wanted somebody to talk to, urgently.'

'What happened?' Ruth asked innocently.

'A journalist asking me what happened! The whole town . . .'

'I heard everything, Kundan, everything,' Ruth got up from the bed and walked up to him. 'What did *you* do?' She was looking intently into his eyes.

'Nothing,' Kundan shook his head.

'Didn't you feel like doing anything?'

'Don't be so cruel to me, Ruth.'

They sat down.

'I am not trying to be cruel,' she said. 'We—our team—have been going through a very cruel ordeal during the last few days. On reaching here, I remembered you. I must see you, I thought, and learn what you have discovered.'

'Ruth, I am afraid the more I discover and the more I know, the more ignorant I become.'

'As the island of knowledge grows larger, the shoreline of wonder stretches farther.'

They laughed.

After dinner, they went out and wandered through the narrow streets. They gazed at the fort perched on top of the hill in the distance and the silhouettes of the tall havelis that hemmed in the streets, making them look like deep ditches. At night they sat in the chairs at Dewan-e-aam and talked for a long time.

Ruth was describing some traders whom she met in the train on her way from the city to the desert. 'One was a leather merchant, and another a dealer in bones. The merchants who used to live in these havelis dealt in pearls, gems and silk. The traders I met dealt in bones and hides. So much for the change from feudalism to whatever you want to call what we have now!'

Animals had died in thousands in the drought and the famine that followed it. The villagers removed the hides of the dead animals and collected the bones left by the vultures to sell in the town market. The mutiny in

112

the Project was not unexpected or inexplicable, Ruth said. The conditions in the villages were horrifying. The Pioneers wanted to go back to their families, at least to die with them. Instead, they were now being taken to a destination they knew nothing about.

Chapter Twenty

Ruth had to rejoin her team in a village nearby. It happened
to be the one where Kundan had gone to arrest Bhola. When
he heard this, Kundan said he would go with her. He
wanted to meet Bhola's family. They belonged to the village
and he reckoned that they might have gone back there after
their milk business in the town had failed. He did not know
what to say to them. But it seemed to him that he owed
them something.

The last time he visited the village was four months
ago, before the monsoon clouds arrived. Since then, for the
last four months, the clouds had moved across the sky, but
without ever precipitating into a shower. Sometimes they
appeared in a bunch, but soon dispersed and melted away,
leaving the sky clear again.

'It is not for want of clouds that there are no rains here,'
Kundan explained to Ruth on the way. 'The clouds here
carry as much vapour as clouds do elsewhere. But they
never consolidate vertically to form rain.'

'There must be a reason for it. Somebody has to find it
out.'

'If you ask Gulshan, he will tell you it is not necessary.'

'Have you noticed something, Kundan? There is no dearth of wildlife in the desert. Peacocks, camels, deer, hares, sand-snakes, lizards, beetles, not to speak of the countless shrubs and the few trees. Man digs wells and lays pipes to bring water. But how do these plants and animals find the moisture they need?'

'I am glad we are still able to ask such questions,' Kundan smiled. 'While sitting in the office the other day, I put a similar question to my assistant. He did not understand it. Later when I came here, Gulshan told me not to ask such questions. Perhaps he was right. If he had asked such questions, he would, perhaps, be rotting under the earth now, or lying in a packed, dark dungeon.'

Kundan realized that the appearance of the village had changed a lot during these four months, though there was not much to change in a place like that. The dry, twisted trunks of khejri trees reminded him of the stunted limbs of lepers. Even the roots of fog-shrubs had been dug up, as the heaps of sand around them indicated. Except for a few rocks here and there, the sand dominated and ruled over the whole landscape. From body to soul, it was sand all the way.

The few men who were left in the village were all old and incapacitated. The walls of the old houses and the sides of the dried-up tanks seemed to be holding long-lost memories which the whole village seemed to be making futile attempts to draw out. Stray cattle, reduced to skin and bones, were sniffing at the sand. No smoke rose from the chimneys anywhere in the village.

The villagers had dug a deep well in the middle of the dried-up tank. The whole village collected its drinking water from it. Nobody even thought of washing their clothes or taking a bath.

The arrival of Ruth's team had created a stir in the village. Men, women and children gathered around them.

Some dialogue seemed to be in progress between the two groups. Kundan stood apart and watched the scene. He did not want to interfere. He had nothing to ask, nothing to learn. He was a mere onlooker.

Suddenly, Kundan spotted Bhola's daughter in the crowd. At first he thought she had not noticed him. But he was mistaken. She glanced at him intermittently, but showed no signs of recognition. The restless girl with bright eyes who used to burst out laughing at the slightest provocation had suddenly become impassive—like a wall without doors or windows. Numbed by the sight, Kundan averted his eyes.

The villagers began to disperse. Ruth came up to him and explained that they were going to do something which they did only in extreme situations. Unable to feed and look after their cattle, they were going to set them free. They could have sold them in some distant market or fair, but the expenses involved in taking them to the market were more than the prices they expected to get. What tradition dictated in such situations was to release them into the desert. Since the animals would instinctively try to return to the families that kept them, they had to be taken to a considerable distance before being set free. It was a ritual performed strictly in the traditional mode.

The whole village assembled at the head of a small path that led into the desert. Some leaves and hay, especially kept for the occasion, were fetched. Lamps were lit and the animals to be set free were herded before the crowd. A puja followed with the women waving lamps in the air before the animals. To complete the ritual, the animals were given some water to drink. The journey of the animals began.

The animals were at the head of the procession, followed by the villagers with Ruth's team behind them and Kundan at the tail end. Kundan noticed Bhola's wife and daughter among the villagers in the procession.

When Bhola's wife had approached Kundan earlier, her

fear was that her husband would not return. But events had overtaken her with breathtaking speed. Drought and famine had dried up the little moisture that was left in the lives of these two women. They walked in silence with the group of villagers accompanying the animals. Now they had nothing to ask from Kundan. Like the cattle, they too were left to their fate. Ruth's team which came from the capital with their questions too was irrelevant to them, if not a nuisance.

Neither the villagers nor the journalists spoke a word. The hoofs of the cattle made a clanging noise when they struck against a projecting piece of rock or gravel in the sand. Suddenly someone began to sing. Though subdued, the sharp notes of the song ran through the empty sky like a slender, weightless thread.

Finally the procession reached its destination. As if they had a premonition of what was going to happen, the animals stopped. Small bundles of hay were hung around their necks, followed by a last hug and a pat on the back. Then the ropes were untied and the animals were set free. A gentle push, and the cattle began their long journey into the desert to die a thirsty death. The lamps were put out and the people turned back.

Kundan stared at Bhola's wife and daughter as they walked back with bowed heads. They did not know that Bhola had been abandoned in another desert like the cattle to die a thirsty death. At the moment they were thinking only of the abandoned cattle—some of them may have been theirs.

Chapter Twenty-One

A week after the mutiny, the town and the labour camps had returned to normal. There was a nip in the air. Winter had a way of arriving unawares. A sudden storm or rain lashes the town, the temperature dips and the people exclaim: ah, winter is here! But other things were hotting up, particularly security and enforcement of discipline at the Project. The cultural officer and his troupe had melted away into thin air. Nobody remembered his beard or his mischievous eyes. Instead, Jagtap, who had by then reconciled himself to the light brown glasses that concealed his eyelashes, dominated the scene with his stiffness and gravity undiminished. Without resting for a moment, without allowing even a wrinkle to form on his uniform, he strode like a colossus in the Project.

The Project administration pounced upon everyone with a vengeance and tried to restrain every man's movement. Petty offences which were formerly ignored now resulted in severe punishments. From the supervisor at the site to the Station Commander, every officer seemed to be intoxicated with the spirit of authority and sadism.

In an unusual move, Kundan visited the Pioneer camp

to watch the morning parade. An army officer who had recently taken charge as the Company Commander took the salute of the A Company. The untrained rustics saluted awkwardly and in different ways. But they were all dressed in the same uniform with the colour of the grey sky. They had learned to stand to attention, though in a clumsy way, and, of course, to receive punishments without a murmur. The A Company had a distinction: the mutiny had begun in its ranks.

The mornings were cold. But as the sun rose the sand and the air heated up, which was why the workers had not yet begun to wear their winter uniforms.

Kundan watched the long shadows of the men standing to attention stretching obediently behind them, passing over the gravel on the ground, rising vertically up over the bodies of the men in the rear line, but never clashing with shadows of the men on the sides. As the sun rose higher, the shadows diminished in length. An expression that could be recognized as despair or resignation spread like a thin veil over the faces of the workers.

The Company Commander withdrew after taking the salute, and the Havildar Major appeared. He divided the workers into three groups: the sick, those on fatigue duties and those going to the work site. The sick were quite a few in number. This was surprising, for, if certified fit by the duty doctor, they would have to face the penalty of a pack-drill or a crawl on the belly from one end of the parade ground to the other. They must be genuinely ill, Kundan surmised. Not too many would take the risk of faking illness. He went up to them and found them to be of four different categories: those who had been ill for some time, those who had fallen ill recently, those who had been called for check-ups and those who had venereal diseases. Every one of them stood in the lines with their faces downcast. On the parade ground it was embarrassing to report sick.

'All these fellows are liars, sir, damned liars,' remarked

the Havildar Major. He lifted the faces of a couple of the men with his cane. 'Don't want to work, bloody liars.'

'The ones called for check-up too?' Kundan enquired pleasantly.

'Yes, sir. Now there are such doctors too. One can only guess what commission they extract for reporting them sick.'

'Really?'

'Obviously. Nobody wants to work. But they want to get paid all the same. All these fellows would have been scorched to death, had it not been for the Project. They should be grateful to the Sarkar. But what do they do the moment your eyes are turned? Go on a rioting spree! If this had happened in the army, they wouldn't be alive now to tell the tale, not a single one of them.'

Though the Pioneers heard every word that was said about them, none of them protested. Their expressionless faces seemed to be as dark as their shadows on the ground. Suddenly one of them collapsed in a heap on the ground.

The Havildar Major walked up to him and kicked him with his boot. Still no one protested. Kundan bent down and felt the forehead of the man lying sprawled on the ground with the back of his hand. He was running a high temperature. Nobody would call it pneumonia now, for pneumonia was no longer reserved for the ones with no known relatives.

Kundan had the man removed to his jeep and driven to the hospital.

*

'It is now two weeks since it happened,' Jaswant complained loudly, 'they haven't sent us the figures about the dead and the injured. The security chaps have their excuses ready when I ask them about it.'

'Ask them again,' Kundan suggested idly.

'Oh! We are not going to get anything from them, sir. I

can see only one way out. Go to the companies and make a list of the men who are still at work and record the rest as dead.'

'Do it then.'

Not long ago, he had racked his brains over Daniel's record-folder, Kundan recalled. He had even kicked up a row with Jaswant who had advanced a variety of interpretations over the report of his death in the records. He had even made a speech ridiculing the Project security. He was prepared to make another speech on it now. It was not the death of a single Pioneer, Daniel, that stared Kundan and Jaswant in the face now; death was crawling over the Pioneers like a python swallowing its victims one after the other. Unlike in the case of Daniel, the question Kundan and Jaswant asked now, as they grappled with the records, was not 'who?', but 'how many?'. And they had to devise a method to get the answer from the Security Wing.

The Havildar at the parade ground did not see faces. Trained to stand vertically and look horizontally, he could only spot vacant spaces, if any existed, in the three rows of men who stood to attention before him. He took count of the men by multiplying the number in one line by three and subtracting the vacant spaces from the sum. After that, using the toes of his left foot and the heel of his right as a fulcrum, he turned round clockwise and spat the number to his superior officer who watched the parade. To swallow and to spit—that was the function of every link in the chain of command.

'Where do they cremate the pneumonia-corpses they cart away even before they get our certificate saying they have no relatives?' Kundan asked Jaswant.

'Somewhere at the foot of the Chhatri Hill.'

'Have you ever been there?'

'No.'

Kundan thought for a moment. 'Oh, today is Saturday. A half-day, isn't it? Well, I won't be coming in the afternoon.'

Chapter Twenty-Two

The sun had begun to set when Kundan got down from the horse carriage. He sent back the carriage and walked towards the Chhatri Hill. The Chhatri Hill stood beside the road leading to the desert from Rambhagarh. In fact there were two hills in the area. The one dotted with chhatris was the Chhatri Hill. The other bore the ruins of a fort and a temple. Perhaps it was on this hill that Raja Mansingh's ancestors wanted to build a fort. They began constructing it, but were unable to finish it. The incomplete structure they raised had perished as there was no one left to look after it. The Chhatri Hill was different. The bodies of all the dead rajas, whether they died at the palace or in the battlefield, were laid to rest on the hill. A whole dynasty of kings, wherever they had lived or fought or died, came together in their final abodes on Chhatri Hill.

A shepherd boy who was grazing his sheep became Kundan's companion as he climbed up from the foot of the hill. The boy seemed to know everything about the place. He showed Kundan several pits on the ground on which the shadow of the hill descended as evening approached.

Not all of them were pits, however. Some were black patches indicating spots where bodies had been cremated.

'They used to cremate the bodies,' the boy said. 'Then firewood became scarce. Now they only bury them.'

Kundan was not interested in the pits. He followed the boy, listening to what he said.

During the three years since the Project was set up, there had been a number of deaths among the work force. Some were due to accidents. At least two of them had committed suicide, Kundan had learned from Jaswant. But there were no murders.

'This is where they buried the people killed in the mutiny.' The boy stopped before a large mound of earth. It was a mass grave. The heaped earth was still loose. It would take quite some time to flatten and harden and for grass to grow over it. Rain was scarce, after all.

'Nothing to see here, saheb. You should climb up the hill if you want to see the chhatris before it gets dark.'

They climbed up the slope, holding on to rocks and shrubs. Surprisingly, there was a lot of greenery on the summit. Trees, grass and even flowering plants were in bloom. There was a fairly large water tank too. The caretakers had grown a garden around the cluster of chhatris.

There were a number of chhatris, big and small, at different levels and facing all directions. They were too numerous to be counted, all crowded together, making it difficult to walk among them. Built of heavy stones, with a surfeit of carvings, a mandap in front and a gopura behind, a pennant fluttering on the gopura, the chhatris resembled temples. There were no idols inside, only the models of a throne under an umbrella. On them were inscribed the names of the rajas who were buried there. An interesting feature of the chhatris was that their height increased in chronological order of the succeeding rulers. The highest chhatri was that of the ruler last buried on the hill. Raja

Mansingh, who was the last ruler of his dynasty, had no chhatri, for he had no successor to build one for him. His body was flung into the desert sands by the sultan's soldiers. A whole dynasty perished in the desert, and its last member, his wives, courtiers and army were left to rot on the open sands. Raja Mansingh sacrificed everything for the honour of his dynasty—even a tomb and a funeral! The vultures had a good meal of his body. That is perhaps how all dynasties end—without a grave or a burial.

The magnificent mansions of human civilization, its works of art, its intellectual heights and philosophical depths and the diverse life forms on earth themselves may, perhaps, be waiting for such an unceremonial end, just as all rivers are waiting to finally end in graves of sand, and all greenery, fighting to the bitter end, to walk ultimately into the open mouth of the desert . . .

Kundan went round taking a look at the picture gallery of valorous princes and chieftains built at the end of the row of chhatris. All the heroes of a dynasty, in their full armour, their moustaches twirled up, looked down from the walls at him. The pictures of their exploits and the methods of punishment enforced by them on their subjects, so graphically described on the walls, seemed to admonish him. They hunted wild animals with their spears. They hacked their enemies with swords longer than themselves. They punished their subjects who disobeyed their orders by piercing a spear through their rectums to their heads or quartering them by tying horses to their limbs and driving them in four different directions.

In the solitude of the picture gallery, where only the princes, the chieftains and their victims gave him company, Kundan was startled by the shuffling of feet behind him. He turned round and was startled to find Amala standing before him. She wore a soiled sari and a blouse torn above the shoulder. She had become visibly frail since the last time Kundan saw her. Her face was darker and her eyes restless.

'I have been watching you going through the chhatris for some time. Kundan, I must speak to you.'

She placed her hand on his shoulder.

'Amala . . . I . . . I can't . . .' Kundan spluttered, bewildered.

'There is a temple here. I am staying there for the time being. Don't bother about what happened to me. It doesn't matter. But don't let Sulaiman die. If anyone can prevent it, it is you, you alone.'

'I don't understand.'

'Just as I suspected,' Amala shook her head in despair. 'Pasupati had a death sentence on him. Now Sulaiman is going to be . . . '

'Oh God!'

Kundan felt his legs buckling under him. He leaned wearily against Amala's shoulders.

Footsteps were heard outside the picture gallery. Amala hurriedly detached herself from Kundan and started walking away. Before she disappeared, she turned and said in a hushed voice: 'You must meet me. Not here. Ask for Dayaji at the sultana's haveli. If you don't find me there, try Vrindavan's shop. I want to speak to you.'

Amala went out in a hurry through a side-door of the gallery. Looking at the picture of a young prince with a spear poised in his hand, Kundan stood rooted to the ground.

Chapter Twenty-Three

Was it excusable to remain ignorant of what one ought to know, especially when it was part of one's duty and when even those who were in no way connected with it already knew all about it? Kundan turned the question over in his mind. Six months earlier on the platform of the railway station, when he signed the papers for taking charge of a short, frail man with all his fingers intact, in place of a tall, stout man with a part of one of his fingers missing, he had felt proud of himself for having done a good deed. But the Kundan who did that good deed was now no more. The Kundan who stood leaning against a newly constructed concrete column had, like the prisoner, lost a part of himself, a part he could not even identify. He had become one of Pasupati's henchmen. The only plea he could make in defence of his transformation was that he was unaware of it.

And yet, he was congratulating himself for having the good fortune to come in contact with a variety of men, something which nobody else could boast of. When Sulaiman, Bhola and Daniel entered his life one after the other with their problems which were enough to destroy his peace of mind, he felt gratified. He was proud of the fact that he could identify and understand each man by his name and marks of identification, that he was moulding into individuals that molten mass of humanity lying at the bottom of the Project. Today they had risen from their moulds to confront him. They were not asking him whether he looked at them as human beings, or whether he entertained their personal problems with sympathy and understanding. Instead, they wanted to know why he had failed in his efforts to perceive certain things which lay beyond them, things that were much more relevant to them. Each one of them had grown from an individual into something larger. The face of Bhola, who had risen in revolt against injustice, was red with indignation. The lips of Daniel, who was hounded and killed when he tried to run away from a system which made guinea pigs of men, were now curled in scorn. What would be the expression on Sulaiman's face when he learned that the Sarkar not only hangs the innocent for saving the guilty, but also extracts the last measure of energy from their muscles before the hangman's noose tightens around their necks? None of them were going to forgive him and let him go scot-free merely because he patted them on their backs or stretched the corners of his mouth in a sympathetic smile.

As the island of knowledge grows larger, the shoreline of wonder stretches farther. Did Ruth know of a situation when that shoreline of wonder became a path of isolation, a long fence of barbed wire inflicting pain and suffering?

If he had known everything right at the beginning, what would he have done? A procession of men who knew everything appeared before him. The City Jail warder, who kept repeating that everyone would be in trouble. The frail, bespectacled man with a stoop, resembling a railway clerk, who fell ill the next day and disappeared into the intensive care unit (was he still alive?). The Project Jail warder, who nodded indifferently when Sulaiman confessed in tears that he was undergoing imprisonment in place of Pasupati Singh in return for a monthly allowance to his family, that he was doing it for his wife and children, that he had done no wrong except being poor. (He was now quietly marking Sulaiman's attendance in the register every morning and striking off one more of his numbered days every evening. He then went home untroubled by a guilty conscience to enjoy a good supper and to sleep with his wife). The same Yogeshwar who argued that Sulaiman got his name merely because his mother called him so, and that the Sarkar did not need such men who produced more children and more botheration for the country, but needed Pasupati instead who rendered some worthy, though unknown, service to it. Yogeshwar, who sailed smoothly along the rails of duty laid by the Sarkar, balancing his newly-wed wife on one arm and a glass of whisky in the other hand.

Why did these people behave so strangely? For the security of the ubiquitous Sarkar? How did they look upon the Sarkar, with respect or with fear?

At the construction site only the sounds of a concrete mixer operating in the foundation pit and of a crane idly raising and lowering girders in a corner could be heard. There were a few prisoners and some technicians and engineers around. They went on with their work in silence, as if each one of them knew exactly what he was supposed to do. A number of columns had come up and were now being connected by girders. The site was being walled up from one side. Only the engineers and scientists knew what feat was going to be performed by the installations in the end.

Kundan's eyes searched for Sulaiman. He asked the workers who came up in a single file from the pit about Sulaiman. Some shook their heads and passed on. Others did not even look at Kundan. Perhaps they did not know each other, or they merely desisted from speaking to each other at the site.

Kundan went down into the pit, scrutinizing every prisoner's face. The engineers watched him curiously. One of them asked him something, but he did not reply. Another placed his hand on Kundan's shoulders. Kundan freed himself and walked on. He did not care who watched him or what they thought of him. He was looking desperately for the one man he wanted to meet.

At last he caught sight of Sulaiman. He was pulling a girder with some other prisoners to hook it on a crane. Kundan rushed towards him, jumping over the obstacles in the pit. He stumbled and pitched headlong into a pile of wet concrete. Trying to extricate himself from the mound, he narrowly escaped being hit by the dangling hook of a crane.

'Sulaiman!' Kundan shouted over the din of the concrete mixer. Sulaiman turned. His face lit up like the rising sun. The smile that broke on his lips pierced Kundan like the stab of a knife.

'How long is your sentence, Sulaiman?'

'Eight years, they said.'

'Eight years!'

'Doesn't matter, saheb. Time flies. By the time I come out, my son will be old enough to do some work.'

'Oh God!'

It was for the second time in two days that Kundan was invoking God. But, instead of God, it was the hook of the crane that came sweeping towards him again as the crane operator suddenly swung its boom. Kundan ducked. The prisoners fell flat on the ground. Kundan heard one of the engineers swearing loudly.

If that hook had struck Sulaiman on the head, if the terrible ignorance in his skull had scattered like a plate of Chinese noodles, if crows and vultures had pecked at it . . . If the eggs of the fattened crows and vultures hatched, if Sulaiman's son grew old enough to work, to question, to revolt, to fight the crows and vultures that peck at human intelligence . . .

Kundan extricated himself from the cacophony of engineers, crane operators and concrete mixers and started walking away quickly. He had really broken into a run, under the scorching sun, kicking up a cloud of dust behind him. Kundan was no longer conscious of his body. He ran with a haste, with an urgency that had taken possession of him—an urgency he had never felt before.

Chapter Twenty-Four

Kundan walked briskly along the veranda of the Project Jail. There was a high wall with ventilators on top on one side. On the other side was a row of cells with heavy iron bars. The cells were empty as the prisoners were out working. However the doors of the cells were locked, the fat locks looking like potbellied Chinese figurines with swollen cheeks.

Somewhere in the frightening silence of the jail, Kundan could hear a subdued sound—like bubbles coming up from water. He realized that it came from one of the cells. Holding the bars with one hand and shading his eyes with the other, Kundan tried to peer into the cell. He saw a man suspended upside down from a rope that hung from the ceiling. There was nobody else around. In the darkness of the cell the man hung from the rope without struggling, bereft of the company of even his torturers. His arms hung down from his shoulders, motionless. Foam and froth were oozing from his nose down to his hair.

Suddenly a scream arose, followed by a series of painful groans. Kundan did not know where they came from. The rest of the cells seemed to be empty.

Pioneers convicted on various charges were given upto twenty-one days' imprisonment according to the provisions of the Army Law which was made applicable to them. Such convicts were sent to the quarter guards maintained by the Company Commanders under Hassan. The workers of the Prisoner Force were already housed in the Project Jail. Where would the offenders among them be sent to? Was there a jail within the jail? Or perhaps these were the methods of punishing them—flogging, suspending upside down on a rope . . .

Kundan went to the jailer's cabin at the end of the building. Though it was about Sulaiman that he wanted to talk to Yogeshwar, when he began speaking it was about the sight he had just seen. Yogeshwar could have sent him back by retorting that the matter fell under his jurisdiction and that Kundan need not rack his brains over it. But Yogeshwar was not in a mood to be provoked just then. It was true that he was overbearing and rude on occasion, but generally he was soft-spoken and amiable.

'Yes, Kundan, I understand. But that fellow is in the custody of the Intelligence chaps. We have no say in these matters, you know.'

'I didn't see anybody from Intelligence there. The prisoner is hung up alone—in one of your cells.'

Once again Yogeshwar tolerated the intrusion into the domain of his authority. 'They are not here at the moment,' he tried to explain.

'Ah, I was forgetting. You must be right. I heard the evidence of their presence from elsewhere. But why should they do this? Before they torture a man of yours like this, they should at least inform you about it.'

'Yes, they do inform us beforehand. In fact, they are very cooperative. It is only natural, because they need our cooperation too.' Yogeshwar chuckled meaningfully. 'This fellow had been convicted in a sensational case of espionage. He landed up here from the jail. While in jail, he had sent a letter to one of his friends which was intercepted by Intelligence.'

'Is it forbidden to write letters from jail?'

'What do you mean?' Yogeshwar threw back his head and laughed as if he had just heard a very funny joke.

'I was wondering why they should torture him for that.'

'A spy should be kept under constant observation, Kundan. The Intelligence chaps are trying to find out what he actually conveyed in the letter.'

'Was there anything suspicious about the letter?'

'Nothing of the sort. In fact, he just enquired how his friend's wife and children were doing and wished to convey his regards to them. He also enquired about his own family, his mother and sister. His sister was bedridden at the time. Moreover, he asked everybody to face all adversities with fortitude and constancy.'

'You mean to say he is being tortured for writing that?'

'You never know,' Yogeshwar shook his head. 'When a spy writes such a simple letter, that in itself will arouse suspicion. They are trying to find out whether there was any coded message hidden in it. They want to squeeze the last bit of information out of him before the hangman's noose snuffs it out.'

A shudder went down Kundan's spine. Yogeshwar's voice was cold and detached, lacking even the minimum of liveliness which people display when discussing the price of vegetables in the market. A poor prisoner hung upside down from a rope was rotting like a crushed tomato. Everything had to be extracted out of him before it became too late. The Intelligence men needed what was in his mind. The Project needed what was in his muscles.

'So . . . this man . . . you mean to say he has been sentenced to death?'

'I thought you would have known it. All the prisoners sent to work here are on death row. Pioneers can't be put in the high security sections of the work, you know.'

It was all his fault, Kundan thought. Simple and straight-forward logic did not enter his head. That he did not know it was what surprised everyone.

'I can understand your fears, doubts and good intentions, Kundan. You are an outsider. You used to work in factories.' Yogeshwar extended his hand and placed it on Kundan's. 'Tell me, what did your factories do? Didn't they make use of human beings? Here, we are dealing with criminals. Jails, though they are closed areas of darkness, play an important role, like factories, in the life of a country. The Sarkar is not only a protector, but a dispenser of authority too. It expresses its authority through punishments given to its people. Of course, there are no kings who go hunting in the forests these days. Today the human body is not looked upon as the target of the spear, but as a usable commodity. In this respect, jails merely follow your factories. The Sarkar uses everyone, Kundan. Everyone, including you and me.'

Kundan let Yogeshwar withdraw his hand from his and rose from his seat. A tremor ran through his body.

'Time is running out, Yogeshwar. There, in one of your cells, a man has been hanging upside down. As we were discussing the causes of his incarceration and torture, his intestines, stomach and spleen might have pressed a little more onto his lungs. More spittle and froth might have flowed out of his mouth. There is another prisoner of yours, innocent of any crime, who does not even know that the hangman's noose is tightening around his neck every moment. Who uses whom does not interest me at this moment. It is not a part of your duty or mine to snuff out a man's life before its time or to execute a prisoner who is not sentenced to death. You have certain responsibilities, just as I have mine. We can't excuse ourselves from that. I have come here in a hurry to make this statement. Time, Yogeshwar, time is running out.'

Kundan turned and walked out.

Chapter Twenty-Five

One of the boys pretended he was running away. His friends seized him and pulled him back. A mock fight ensued. When it ended, one of them cracked a joke, and they all laughed. A song came next. One of them started it and the others joined him in a chorus, tapping rhythmically on their thighs. It was a way of overcoming the monotony and boredom of the afternoon for the boys.

Kundan watched with interest the shadows of the boys on the road which had started lengthening as the sun began sinking into the horizon. They crossed the streams of sunlight flowing along the road like a bridge. But all the shadows were not alike. Some shrunk like dwarfs and some lengthened depending upon the slope of the ground. Where the stones paved on the road were uneven, their edges broke and became serrated. The shadows also changed their length and shape as the boys moved about. Sometimes a shadow suddenly disappeared behind the others and they all joined together to become one black mass. Then the black mass exploded like a bomb and scattered into pieces. How different were the shadows from the objects that cast them!

They only followed the movements of the objects, that too ineptly, and did not reflect the boredom they suffered. Without being faithful to the objects, they let the ground they fell on manipulate them. And as the evening darkened, they broke away from the objects altogether to start their long journey through the night. Contrary to what has been presumed, shadows have no commitment to the objects that cast them. Shadows are not shadows at all!

A grocer in his store in the street, surrounded by his colourful provisions, suddenly burst into song. It was a bhajan:

O Lord, I have set out on my voyage from this shore
You are my boat and my boatman now.

The mattress on which the grocer sat was long enough to allow him to stretch himself for a siesta. But he preferred to sit on it and sing his bhajan, tapping rhythmically on his thighs and rocking his head. When Kundan looked at him, he beamed him a smile that spread widely beneath his grey moustache and bowed. Was piety another way of escaping from boredom, Kundan asked himself.

A cart with a horse stood on the side of the road, clinging to its own shadow, unmindful of the bhajans about journeys to unknown shores. The wheels made contact with the ground only at a single point each. Yet the horse was inseparably bound to the cart, to the yoke, to the ropes, straps, bridles and reins. Anything that touched it had stuck firmly to its body. Puffing its nostrils, putting out its tongue and shaking its body to drive away flies from the festering sores on its back, it endured its wait. The cart-driver was not seen around.

Kundan was on his way to the sultana's haveli. The name instantly brought two images to Kundan's mind. One was that of the sultana's and the other of Amala's. The sultana had refused to end her life in the jauhar kund. But she could not escape the ordeals that awaited her after that. She had to share the bed of the very sultan who had exterminated her clan. Pelted with stones for violating the traditions of her clan, she turned into a prostitute and accepted as her customers the very people who stoned her! To sustain her will to survive was like walking through fire! How did she look back on her life in her mellowed years? As a bridge-burning rebellion against tradition? Or as a series of compromises with each changing situation? How thin was the line that divided rebellion from compromise! Even yielding to tradition is often acclaimed as braving the temptations of desire! The society that worshipped satis as brave women condemned the sultana for being a coward. At the fag end of her life, as she sat on the lavishly decorated balcony of the biggest haveli in town and surveyed the vast expanse of the desert around her, what kind of thoughts must have crossed her mind? Did she expect another sultan to manifest himself from the depths of the desert at the head of his fierce horses with war cries that sent chills through the spines of the people? Or was she overwhelmed by a regret she secretly preserved in her mind about her failure to heed the glorious call of the fire in the jauhar kund? How would Amala, who was getting crushed between the hanging rubble of the dilapidated havelis and the massive walls of the prison rising all around her, be judged by the coming generations?

There was a shadow in every man, extending inwards into himself. It might be lengthening, or shortening or exploding into fragments; or be in the process of fusing into a vast darkness. Or it might, if it wishes, embark on a long journey to unknown shores in a boat without a boatman. The first pre-condition for a rebellion is the loss of faith in the master and the first flames of revolt are ignited when the shadows in men declare independence.

A group of schoolboys emerged through a hole in a wall beside the road, after climbing over a garbage heap behind it. Thrilled at discovering a new route, they uttered whooping cries as they came out of it one by one. Dressed in uniforms, with their hands raised, running in all directions, they looked like a swarm of butterflies emerging from their holes in the earth. Kundan almost collided with the rushing children. For a moment, it appeared that the rush of freedom had swept away all the shadows. But the spectacle vanished like a passing cloud.

As the spectacle of the schoolboys vanished, Kundan saw an urchin of about nine years, wearing only a pair of torn shorts running towards him. As he jumped over the mud and garbage, he scared away the pigs rummaging for food among the filth. A fat man was chasing him with a stick in his hand. The boy collided with Kundan and fell down. But he quickly scrambled to his feet and took shelter behind him. 'You rogue! I will suck your blood,' the boy muttered, shaking his fist at the man with the stick. The man retraced his steps hastily with the blood the boy wanted to suck still safe in his veins. Kundan peered at the boy whom he had unwittingly protected. The muscles of his face were taut with fear and anger. But soon they gave way to grief, and the boy began to cry. Kundan did not ask him what his problem was. In any case, he had no solution to offer him.

Kundan suddenly discovered that he was standing in front of the sultana's haveli. Perhaps the boy lived in it. He followed the boy into the haveli.

It was not difficult to locate Dayaji. The first man he stopped to ask pointed to one of the numerous 'holes' in the haveli. An old man in an old coat with a muffler wrapped around his head emerged from it.

Dayaji listened to Kundan with a faraway look in his eyes. At last he spoke. 'It is not a good place, that Chhatri Hill.'

Why did Amala go there? In fact Dayaji had no idea that she had been there. She had lived in the haveli for some time. Then one day she vanished and was not seen again. Dayaji knew nothing more.

Kundan gathered from Dayaji that he knew little about Amala. However, he had great affection for her. Typical of a polyps colony, each member in the haveli related to the others only through the coral reefs they built together.

Amala could not complete what she had wanted to tell him at the Chhatri Hill. She was urging Kundan to save Sulaiman. But wasn't she herself getting trapped in a dragnet? Kundan could not even make a dent in the mystery that surrounded her.

To him Amala was not different from the others with whom he had recently become involved. He did not know much about any one of them. Why was he carrying all these people like crosses on his shoulders? But he had no strength of will to get rid of even one of them.

Kundan walked back along the same road he had come. A few moments ago, a small boy running away from a fat man had taken shelter behind Kundan. A group of schoolboys had exploded like colourful fireworks and crossed his path, unmindful of him. A carthorse had stood on the road, probing deep into its own wounds. None of them were seen now. All the shadows that had caught Kundan's attention had vanished with the objects that cast them. Only the grocer sat on the mattress on which his colourful wares had etched their designs. The brisk business at his store seemed to indicate that his boat had returned from unknown shores. As his eyes met Kundan's, he again extracted a smile from under his grey moustache—like one of the items he pulled out from the shelves to hand to his customers.

Chapter Twenty-Six

'I have got some coal. Shall I make a fire?' Gulshan enquired.

'All right,' Kundan leaned back in his chair wearily.

Gulshan took some time to get the fire going.

'Saheb, may I bring a drink for you?'

'Isn't it cold? Bring one for yourself too.' Kundan spread a sheet of cloth on the floor near the fire and sat on it.

Gulshan was going to marry the girl from the village. He was to leave for the village in a day or two.

'Saheb, is everyone at home all right?' Gulshan asked hesitantly.

Kundan nodded.

'When will memsaheb be coming?'

Kundan did not reply to that. Gulshan waited expectantly for a moment.

'Saheb, you do not appear to be all right for the last few days. Is anything the matter?'

'Gulshan, have you heard of a place called Pataliputra?'

Gulshan shook his head.

'Let me tell you a story. Once upon a time there was a king in Pataliputra. He was fabulously rich. To keep all his wealth safely, he decided to have a secret treasury built. But he had a problem. The workers who build the treasury would learn about all the secret paths and tunnels connecting its chambers. How could the treasury remain a secret then?'

There was a glitter in Gulshan's eyes as he sat huddled before Kundan. But he did not seem to have an answer to the question.

'Do you know how the king solved the problem?' Kundan went on. 'He summoned his faithful builder. The builder, the master builder of the city, stood expectantly before the king. The king turned to him and said: "There are some prisoners in my jails awaiting death. You can put them to work building the treasury. I shall hold back their execution till the work is over."

'The master builder began his work. Busy and restless days followed for him and the prisoners who worked under him. At last the secret treasury was ready. The king saw it and was pleased. The master builder was rewarded with a fat purse, a gold chain and a silk shawl. The prisoners were taken back to the jails. The king was happy with the prisoners too. He sent gifts to their families.

'Deep into the night, when his courtiers and subjects were fast asleep, the king's men began to fill the treasury with gold and diamonds. The prisoners had a feast that day. They were to be beheaded the next day at dawn. But the master builder got no peace of mind that night. Carrying his gifts, the purse, gold chain and the silk shawl, he walked aimlessly through the streets of Pataliputra.

'The master builder stopped at a tavern. A tax collector sat at the door and invited the passers-by in. One-tenth of the tavern's collection went to the king's treasury. The tax collector's commission was one-tenth of the tax collected. The waiters at the tavern soaked the master builder in liquor. Soon his purse was in their hands and he staggered into the street with the rest of his possessions, the gold chain and the shawl.

'His next stop was a brothel. Before he knew what was happening, the tax collector at the door had sucked the master builder into it. One-fifth of the earnings of the brothel went to the king's treasury and one-fifth of the tax to the tax collector. The prostitutes vied with one another to hook the builder with the gold chain. They lavished their bodies on him.

'Relieved of his purse and the gold chain, the master builder dragged himself through the streets with the last of the king's gifts, the silk shawl on his shoulders. It was a dark, moonless night. The master builder had no destination . . .'

Kundan paused. Gulshan was not listening to the story. He had fallen asleep. He lay curled up on the sheet of cloth before the fire. The silence of the night covered him like a blanket.

. . . But the master builder did not stop. He walked on. Having sacrificed for the state the gifts it gave to him, and yet with no peace of mind, he trudged through the streets, across the night, across centuries . . . One, two, three . . . more than twenty of them passed. Treasuries, military camps, taverns and brothels . . . He passed them over and over again. Palaces and mansions were inhabited, vacated and inhabited again. Invasions, battles, plunders, massacres and arson recurred. But people kept multiplying and filling the places left vacant by the dead. The master builder walked on and on and reached the gates of a burial ground. The watchman did not stop him. He lay sprawled on one of the wooden steps, stone drunk.

The builder wandered among the countless graves in the burial ground. They were no longer in shapes that could be identified as graves. Rainwater had run over them, and over the flattened mounds plants had germinated, grown, fructified, fallen and decayed in succession. But, as the builder's feet touched them, they started pulsating, heaving and splitting open. Men and women emerged from them, like seeds sprouting from the earth. They followed him like somnambulists.

The master builder walked to the end of the burial ground, turned, gripped the barbed-wire fencing and gazed at the resurrected human forms: loyal subjects who fought faithfully for their kings and got hacked and shot down by their enemies; men who were slaughtered as they held aloft the standards of their countries; women who flung their bodies into the fire to save the honour of their clans and dynasties; men who slaved, coughed and spat their lives out, building forts, palaces, factories and tombs; men who were conferred medals and trophies for their skills in enhancing their countries' pomp and splendour . . . The medals and trophies had vanished. The armour and costumes and vermilion marks which adorned their bodies had all withered away like dry leaves. The honours, ideals and ideologies they had invented in order to create a halo around their heads had all dissolved into thin air. They were mere naked bodies with no names or history attached to them. Exhausted, with their faces cold and expressionless, rocking their heads, rubbing their sides against each other, grunting and bleating like animals they waited, for the master builder of Pataliputra to leave them and move on . . .

Chapter Twenty-Seven

There was a grocer's store in the lane that led to the Kali mandir. As it was the only grocer's store in the lane, business was always brisk.

At the head of the lane on the left was the long compound wall of a primary school. Children had used stone, charcoal, cowdung or anything that could make a mark to imprint their ideas on it: a white man wearing a hat and smoking a cigarette, an incomplete monkey, a crude, obscene figure. At the end of the wall was a small restaurant which sold tea and refreshments, on top of which was the familiar picture of a girl hawking a popular brand of soft drink, drawn by a local artist in imitation. The artist had given the girl's eyes a slight squint. The grocer's store shared a wall with the restaurant. The board which hung in front of it read: 'Sukumari Grocery Shop. Proprietor: Vrindavan Lal Shukla'. Vrindavan was the second reference Amala had given Kundan.

Vrindavan Lal had become quite an intimate friend of Kundan's. As his was the nearest store, Kundan used to buy his provisions there. In the process they became good friends and Kundan took on the role of an adopted uncle to Vrindavan's invalid daughter, Sukumari. It was mystifying how Vrindavan became Amala's confidant. But then, there were other equally mystifying questions: how did Amala land up in the sultana's haveli? Why did she take shelter at the Chhatri Hill?

There were a few customers at the shop. An assistant was handing out the items while Vrindavan made the bills and collected the money. Kundan quietly took a seat on a stool in front of the traditional mattress on which Vrindavan sat. Yellow and brown pulses, deep red chilli powder, black oil cakes, golden wheat, flour, rice . . . Customers often miss the dazzling display of colours in a grocery store, dismissing them as mere commodities with a single quality—price.

If a customer needed more than a few items, Vrindavan totted up the figures by jotting them on a paper on the table. Otherwise he just added them up in his mind. The thick moustache that drooped over his lips was probably a nuisance when he ate. His eyes were dull and dry, which was natural, considering what he had gone through. Kundan could not think of this unfortunate man possessing the kind of information he was seeking. To think of him as a mere grocer was difficult, but the role he had now taken on—the possessor of potentially dangerous information—was also too frightening for Kundan to feel comfortable in his presence.

When the customers left and Vrindavan was free, Kundan came directly to the point.

'Vrindavan, I have come to learn more about Amala.'

The smile on Vrindavan's lips faded. As the muscles on his face contracted, the wrinkles and furrows showed up again.

Vrindavan got up from his seat, picked up a woollen shawl and wrapped it around him. Leaving the shop to his assistant, he came out. 'Let us go upstairs.'

145

Vrindavan lived with his family above the store. Instead of taking Kundan into his house, Vrindavan led him to the terrace. It was cold out there. A chilly wind made the open terrace colder.

'Where is Amala?' Vrindavan asked Kundan as soon as they climbed up to the terrace.

'I saw her on the Chhatri Hill a few days ago. She asked me to look her up here.'

'Oh, the Chhatri Hill!' Vrindavan turned it over in his mind for a moment. 'She could have stayed with me. After all, I am like a father to her. Her father was a good friend of mine.'

Kundan was relieved to find that there was somebody in the world who knew Amala intimately. But that was not good enough. His problem was to find out where she was and what she was doing.

After leaving Yogeshwar's house with nothing more than the clothes she wore, Amala had taken refuge in Vrindavan's house for a few days. Then she had suddenly disappeared. She came back after a few days, only to disappear again.

'I am frightened, Kundan.' Vrindavan did not say why he was frightened. But there was fear in his trembling voice and his lustreless eyes.

'Has anything happened?'

'Somebody murdered Pasupati. Amala was afraid the police would suspect her. So she went into hiding immediately. But she can't do such a thing. It is impossible. I know her well. And I don't think the police suspect her.'

Something flashed like lightning through Kundan's mind. Suppose Amala had really done it? Didn't she have a right to do it?

They were silent for some time. The cold wind flowed between them like a river. As they argued over whether Amala could really have done it, she floated down the river of uncertainties that flowed between them and disappeared from view.

Was it about Pasupati's death that Amala was trying to tell him at the gallery when the approaching footsteps cut her short? That was perhaps the only way she had found to save Sulaiman. The man who had been sentenced to death was now dead. His murder was now on the records. How could they hang another man as Pasupati?

'Don't you want to see Suku?' Vrindavan looked up at Kundan.

'Oh, yes.' Kundan rose.

There was no question of Kundan leaving without meeting Suku, Vrindavan's only child—a girl who lived in a sad, unreal world. If she was not to get lost in her absurd world for ever, the occasional presence of people like Kundan was necessary.

It happened a few years ago. Suku and her younger brother were playing hide and seek. Suku's brother was a timid boy scared of being alone. He was always with his sister. To remove his fear, Suku forced him to hide so that she could seek him out. It was a lonely deserted place full of shrubs and rocks. Crying and protesting loudly, he finally yielded. But Suku could not seek him out from his hiding place. Ten years after the incident, he still remained untraced. Nobody knew what happened to him. Since then, Suku had been living in a make-believe world of her own. To assuage the sense of guilt that haunted her, she would imagine and tell everybody that her brother was hiding behind every object that her eyes fell upon. She would call out to him, tease him and ask him to come out.

As Kundan went in, Suku came running to him. When she started speaking to him, he was distracted. But soon he too laughed and cracked jokes. Suku's mother brought some sweets for them. As they ate the sweets, a song floated from the radio and the bells in the Kali mandir tolled.

Vrindavan held the bars of the window and looked out into the street—like a prisoner or a traveller whose progress was arrested. Clusters of buildings stood frozen in the cold

147

air—old havelis and houses built in modern style.

'We have reconciled ourselves to it, Kundan. But she can't. It is just a brief respite now. After some time, when you are gone, she will begin to hunt for her little brother again.'

Suku came to the door to see off Kundan. Suddenly an expression of grief came to her face. 'God help you, Kaka,' she said. Then she smiled again.

What Suku said was unusual. And her laughter too. On his way home, it kept echoing in his mind.

Chapter Twenty-Eight

There is a popular theory that the happenings in our lives are the residual effects of greater events taking place at the social level. In order to see the real action, that is where we have to look. Society acts and the individual is acted upon—there is perhaps some truth in this argument, and many of the events in history induce us to accept it. However, when we see the marks left on individuals by these great events, we begin to suspect the 'greatness' attributed to them. After all, a great event need not always be pleasant or progressive. It could be destructive or painful, like a bloody war or a tyrant's reign.

Sociologists tell us about the sacred covenant between the society and the individual. It is a kind of marriage, they say. When it comes to the stage of decisive action, they go a step further and tell us that we should yield our private interests for the sake of public good. A relationship with such ramifications parallels a feudal matrimony, where marriage establishes a hierarchical relationship and pulls down a purdah between the two partners who enter into it, rendering all intimacy fake or mechanical. For Kundan, the unquestionable public good was manifesting itself in the form of the Sarkar to which he was supposed to be 'married'. He was thus called upon to yield to its lust. He was yet to see it face to face, for everything had been happening from behind the purdah. Yielding meant submitting to rape. What Yogeshwar said to him had the stink of a rapist's sweat. Yogeshwar had kept going back to the same argument—those prisoners were going to die anyway, so why not make use of their bodies while they were alive? The compulsions of justice and fair play were applicable only to those who might live and come back to challenge you. Bother only about those who were free. In other words, freedom was for the free!

Carrying the argument a little further, what is the stage at which one can say that a man's fate is sealed or that his days are numbered? The prisoners on the death row, yes. But what about the aged who cannot be expected to live long? What about the sick? In a sense, all those who were weak and helpless could be brought within the ambit of 'utilizable stuff'. What is any man's life worth before the eternal Sarkar? Instead of the individual lives becoming the residual effects of great events, we see here an entirely different paradigm: a big tower called the Sarkar is erected with the bricks of individuals who are either dead or broken. Its shadow erases all the great events and ideas of public good.

Kundan discovered that in this stream of thought, somewhere, at some time, he had begun to use the term Sarkar for society. Was it the root cause of all the aberrations? When did the Sarkar take over society's functions? Was this monster, which was recognizable in the darkness only by its foul smell, an usurper of society, or just its outgrowth?

When Kundan lifted the receiver and dialled Hassan's number, he did not mean to ask these questions. He had only Sulaiman's problem in mind though he knew it did not concern Hassan.

'You can't solve the problem that way, Kundan,' Hassan told him.

'I admit I don't know which way I can solve the problem. That is why I woke you up at this hour. But what did you mean by "that way"?'

'You created a scene in quite a few places, it appears. At Yogeshwar's office, at the construction site, at the hospital, at the Security Section. In fact everywhere you went. What did you achieve by all the fuss, except making enemies?'

Kundan felt a lump in his throat. Even Hassan could not understand him. After a moment's pause, he spoke into the mouthpiece again. 'Hassan, could you please tell me what I should do?'

It was Hassan's turn now to be silent. Kundan waited. At last Hassan's voice came through the wires.

'Kundan, I can understand your feelings. The world is full of evil and sorrow. How much of it can you fight? And for how long? Amala's brother was a nice boy. But you can't bring him back to life now.'

Kundan said nothing.

'Perhaps Amala too.'

Again Kundan said nothing.

'Sulaiman . . .'

'He is not dead yet.'

'H'm.'

'Hassan, I followed events farther than you expected. I allowed everything to happen—more than I should have. Now they have overtaken me. Running after them is useless, ridiculous.'

'Kundan, I feel I should meet you to talk things over.'

'Time is running out, Hassan.'

'I will come down to meet you tomorrow.'

Kundan put back the receiver mechanically. Hassan's wife would have already put their son to sleep.

Gulshan had gone to marry the girl he loved.

Chapter Twenty-Nine

'The seventh batch of prisoners(.) Keep in readiness to move(.) Likely date of move—20 Dec.,' the Warning Order read.

The office of origin of the telegram was not clear. The clerk at the Rambhagarh telegraph office had cut out the message that come through the wires, affixed it on a sheet of pink paper and despatched it. A copy of the same message must have already reached a jail somewhere in the country, far from the desert, across fertile fields, rivers and woods. Like Kundan's office, the prison office too—which was like an unknown planet to Kundan—would be kept busy for quite a few days by the message.

Kundan had received a similar message when the sixth batch was to be sent back. He had worked the whole of a holiday to complete the formalities. He remembered vividly the prisoners changing hands from one set of policemen to another, one of them losing control of himself and creating a scene and getting beaten up by the policemen for his histrionics.

It was not with the innocence of that day that Kundan

looked at the message which announced the moving of the seventh batch. The white strips of the letters pasted on the pink paper appeared to grow thicker and thicker. Kundan got the feeling that they would reach out and punch him on the nose.

All the openings of the stable were towards the open yard where the horses for the cavalry used to be assembled for the soldiers to mount. Kundan came out of his cabin and walked along the hospital to the wall of the fort from where the space between the turrets gave a view of the surroundings. No part of the town was visible from there, only the desolate desert stretching out to the horizon could be seen. It was somewhere there that Raja Mansingh and Sultan Alam Khan had had their rendezvous in those fateful evenings. Kundan stood gazing through the space between the turrets for a while, drawing in his mind the picture of those two unusual personalities who communicated through the rattling of swords during the day and across a chessboard at night.

Kundan was waiting for Hassan who had promised to come and see him there. Of course, he would not be coming with a gift package of solutions to all his problems. No new window was to open out from Kundan's stable. He wouldn't have anything to say other than that the horses had their freedom to run at the beck and call of the cavalry men on their back. Nevertheless, he had decided not to take the next step without hearing what Hassan had to say.

At noon, he ate the packed lunch he had brought. In the evening he collected his things and got into the jeep. He drove home down the hill and through the narrow lanes of the town. He waited the whole evening. The night descended on him. Still there was no sign of Hassan.

He opened the cupboard and took out a bottle of whisky. He emptied the remaining liquor into his mouth, got into bed and stretched himself.

Hassan may have run into some problem of his own. At any rate, Kundan had a tomorrow. The time from tomorrow to the twentieth of December, to be precise. But he was alone—just a single individual against the Sarkar.

154

Chapter Thirty

Yogeshwar's face hardened. There was no sign of friendliness or cordiality on it. Nor did his hands move awkwardly as they used to. The grave countenance on his face made him a moving statue.

'Well, what is your problem now, Kundan?' Yogeshwar's question seemed to indicate that he had solved all the previous problems.

Yogeshwar had not offered Kundan a seat, nor did Kundan take one. Kundan placed the Warning Order on the table.

Yogeshwar glanced at it without picking it up and nodded his head as if he already knew about it.

'The term of a batch is six to eight months. They have to go back after that. Isn't that the routine?'

'Yes. They will be hanged after that—as a reward for their services.'

Yogeshwar knitted his brows and narrowed his eyes. The expression on his face and the tone of his voice suddenly changed.

'Come on, Kundan. They are convicts on death row. They

would have met their end long ago but for the Project. The last six months have been a bonus to them. They should only be happy for getting it.'

'Please, Yogeshwar, please don't reduce human beings to their bodies, and their life to the count of months and years.'

'What are you driving at? Do you want all these criminals to be let off? It is no use discussing philosophy. I have no time for it.'

'At least one of them is not a criminal. Do you want him to be hanged too?'

'Don't ask me such questions,' Yogeshwar raised his voice.

'I won't allow him to be sent back to jail,' Kundan's voice was unwavering.

'How do you propose to do that?'

'In a very simple way. Let out the truth about his identity. Since Pasupati Singh is dead, it is not going to be a problem. We can do it. Both of us know the truth. It is not necessary to pretend that we don't.'

'Have you thought of the consequences? It will be a scandal for the Sarkar. Many people will be involved, including you and me. I will never do it. I know you too won't.'

For Kundan, there was now no time to think of the consequences. He had nobody's mantle to inherit and needed nobody's orders for doing things as he thought fit. He was a one-eyed cyclops who saw only the lengths and breadths.

Like a cyclops, which had emerged from its cave, Kundan wandered into the security officer's cabin on the ground floor. He knew that Jagtap would not do anything on such an issue. But Kundan was out to bell the cat, and so could not keep Jagtap out of his one-eyed rebellion. There is bound to be a certain amount of recklessness in every rebellion which proliferates as the rebellion spreads, but the one who dares to start it always remains terribly alone. Even when he works with others, he remains isolated. Kundan had been on his own—right from the beginning.

Jagtap did not raise his eyes. He sat in his chair, looking straight ahead like a sepoy on the parade ground.

'Jagtap, listen,' Kundan pressed his hands on the table. 'There is a prisoner called Sulaiman in the Prisoner Force. His name here is Pasupati Singh. When Pasupati Singh, convicted for murder, was sentenced to death, he hired Sulaiman and sent him here in his place. Now Pasupati Singh himself is dead. So no one can send Sulaiman to the gallows. So he will now go back—home.'

This speech, as Kundan expected, brought Jagtap back from the parade ground. He raised his eyes and looked at Kundan.

'Pasupati Singh, or Sulaiman, if you like, is not going home,' Jagtap declared in the manner of a judge pronouncing a verdict.

'Why?'

'Pasupati Singh, or Sulaiman, if you like, has been working inside the security section of the Project for months. He knows all about it.'

'So?'

'So it is dangerous even to let him live, not to speak of letting him out.'

'What is your secret? A bunch of concrete columns and girders?'

'You have not heard what I wanted to say,' the judge continued to read out the verdict. 'It was you who smuggled this Pasupati Singh, or Sulaiman if you like, into this project, into a section which is vital for the security of the country, where only those who are condemned to death are allowed to work. You smuggled in a civilian with an assumed name, one whom a court could set free. You have the freedom to decide whether to put your head into the noose, or Sulaiman's.'

After pronouncing the verdict, the judge rose and walked to the door. Holding open the door, he said kindly, 'Now you may go.'

Chapter Thirty-One

'Do you think a sensible man would say such things? I don't.'

Kundan was speaking to the chief security officer who reclined in his chair and listened to him patiently. But his face was blank. It seemed that his elliptical face had no eyes, nose, or mouth on it. But Kundan had not lost hope yet.

'Security is certainly important. I won't say it is not. But it should not be stretched too far—as far as to send an innocent man to the gallows—especially when everyone from top to bottom knows he is innocent.'

'Have you come here to complain against my officers?' At last the chief security officer opened his mouth.

'No, that is not my purpose. The matter, in fact, concerns me. I have not gone against any rule which governs the Project. I have obeyed every order, every directive given to me. But this . . .'

'This you will not obey?'

'This is . . .'

Kundan had not finished when the security officer

sprang from his chair to his feet with lightning speed, and before he could realize what was happening, Kundan felt the officer's right hand on his cheek. The punch was so strong that he fell down and rolled a few paces.

Kundan took a few seconds to adjust himself to reality. He pressed his hand on the floor and lifted himself up into a sitting position. Blood was oozing from his mouth and one of his teeth, torn from its roots, was dangling. He pulled out a handkerchief from his pocket and pressed it against his cheek.

The chief security officer had gone back to his chair. He sat there as if nothing had happened, with the same blank, oblong face.

When Kundan, bleeding, shocked and humiliated, got up and stood before him dazed, the officer spat out a few more words: 'Go to the bathroom and wash your face and get lost. Don't leave any of your dirty teeth on my floor.'

Kundan did not leave his tooth on the floor. He went to the bathroom and spat it into the washbasin. He doused his face with water and went out quietly.

Kundan climbed the stairs at the end of the corridor to the next floor. Kundan's boss was the Station Commander, not the chief security officer.

On his way up, Kundan sat on one of the steps, tore a sheet of paper from his diary and wrote a petition, addressed to the Station Commander. It looked silly, a labour officer complaining to his boss like a schoolboy that the chief security officer had slapped him! For a moment Kundan thought of tearing the letter to pieces, but changed his mind immediately. When the first letter was finished, he wrote another. This was certainly not silly. It was a petition which revealed the identity of Sulaiman, with a request to free the innocent man as early as possible. Kundan felt contented when he affixed his signature to it.

The Station Commander glanced at Kundan's bleeding mouth, his bloodstained clothes and his dishevelled hair.

Kundan placed the petitions on the table before him.

After reading them Brigadier Chandan Roy picked them up and extended them towards Kundan.

'Here, you can take them back.'

Kundan held his hands close to his sides without moving them an inch. The Brigadier tore up the letters and threw the pieces into the wastepaper basket under the table.

'What is this? Aren't there any rules in this office? I am the labour officer. Don't think I know nothing,' Kundan protested vigorously.

'I am sorry, but my labour officer does not even know where he is working. This is not a court to check the identities of prisoners and to pass verdicts on their innocence. Do you think we arrested this man?'

'Sir, precious time will be wasted if . . .'

'You have already wasted my time beyond reckoning. The door is before you, it would be very helpful if you go out through it yourself.'

Doors. They were all too eager to push him out through doors, while he could not even make a dent on the walls surrounding an innocent man.

Chapter Thirty-Two

Kundan had a long sleep. On getting up he could not recollect when he had reached home the previous night. It was a dark, cold night. He remembered walking through the streets dragging his feet. Opening the door, he had gone straight to bed and pulled the quilt over his head. He had fallen asleep instantly after that.

The sleep had done some good to him, and he felt a little relaxed. Suddenly he thought of his tooth. With that, everything that the sleep had laid to rest rushed back to his mind, like a crowd of men who made a ruckus and wandered wherever they liked. He got up and went to the mirror. His left cheek was so swollen that his left eye looked like a tiny aperture. The swelling had also made his lips twist grotesquely. The absurdity of the situation was difficult for him to accept. How did such a disaster descend upon him?

He felt glad that he had stood by the truth, that he had told it to everyone he faced up to, that he had put it in black and white with his signature, and, above all, that he was prepared to accept the consequences. But what had he achieved? Nothing had moved an inch. Everything remained exactly where it had been before—except one of his teeth. The face of truth which he had tried to hold high now looked like the face of a clown who only knew how to jump up and down at the same spot.

He opened his mouth and felt the gap left behind by the missing tooth. It was an incisor. The bleeding had stopped. He passed his fingers over the swollen cheek and felt some relief.

A postman was coming up the walk. Kundan got up and opened the door before the man knocked. He recognized the handwriting on the envelope. It was Ruth's.

Ruth was coming down again. Her group had completed the study they had undertaken. They were taking a break now.

An unprecedented excitement passed through Kundan which almost upset the balance of his mind. Had he yearned for her so much? Or was it the appetite of his solitude which had burned everything inside him? If only she had written when she was coming! He opened all doors and windows . . . Voices of the pedestrians on the street, the cold, the wind, dust and sunlight were all welcome to him then.

Gulshan had left him for good. The supply of milk had stopped long ago. Kundan cooked a frugal meal, and after taking a shower, ate it hungrily. He pulled out an armchair, sat in it and looked out through the window.

Rickshaws, horse-carriages and handcarts passed along the road. Villagers in soiled clothes and crumpled turbans, who seemed to be in no hurry, looked like ticketless travellers playing hide and seek, or pawns let loose on the chessboard—pawns which had not yet found the squares where they would be trapped, cut and vanquished.

Kundan dozed off in the armchair.

When he woke up he found his head in Ruth's hands. She was gently stroking his swollen cheeks. He could not get up. His hands and legs had gone numb. It was late in the afternoon. The room was only faintly lit now. It seemed to him that his eyes too had become numb. But he could see her face which was dark and tired. He extended his benumbed arm towards Ruth and buried his face in her chest. She pulled him to her.

They woke up in the middle of the night hearing a fakir's song. The fakir had taken shelter from the cold in the veranda of the dargah. The faint light of the lamps in the street came in through the window and draped them like a sheet of silken cloth. They lay idle for a while listening to the song.

> Sukhia sab sansar hai
> Khave aur sove
> Dukhiya Das Kabir hai
> Jage aur rove

The whole world is happy,
Eating their fill and going to sleep
Kabir Das alone is sad,
For he wakes up only to cry.

Ruth and Kundan had not spoken a word to each other since Kundan woke up in her hands. Once they began to talk, it was like opening the gates of hell.

Chapter Thirty-Three

For two days, Ruth and Kundan had only each other for company. They talked and walked a lot, ate little and slept even less.

Kundan unfolded the story of a long drama of savagery mixed with buffoonery, enacted by villains, clowns and fools. How a group of workers rose in revolt en masse in a few minutes and then, in the same way, pulled down the curtains on it and stood to attention in three lines without anyone even having to blow a whistle. How gallows came up at the gates of the work site along with the columns erected inside, how innocent lives ran dry over the sands like desert streams. Faces reduced to zeroes with the eyes and noses effaced from them. And finally, the story of his comic experiments with truth culminating in a swollen face with a lost tooth. But Kundan was not aware of the sandstorms that raged in Ruth.

'Do you remember the play we staged once at the University about a tribe in Africa?' Ruth suddenly asked Kundan. 'It was their custom to kill the chieftain after a fixed period of rule or when his hair turned grey or his teeth started falling off. The playwright had, perhaps, packed subtle meanings into it. But we foolishly presented it as a comedy.'

'It was not comic, at least for me,' Kundan grinned. 'I was the chieftain's attendant. The rule was that anyone talking or coughing while the chief ate his food would be instantly beheaded. And that happened to me!'

'Kundan, some time after that, I had an opportunity to study the customs of certain obscure communities when I tried my hand at anthropology,' Ruth suddenly became serious. 'I came across an extremely interesting custom. In a certain country, when the king died, the jails were thrown open and the criminals were set free. The law enforcing agencies like the courts and the police were withdrawn. Might became Right. Theft, murder and robbery became the order of the day. Everyone, whether he was a chief or a commoner, was forced to protect himself. Anyone who succeeded in controlling the anarchy and bringing back order would be the new king.'

'The logic behind the system was, perhaps, that society should overhaul itself periodically and start from scratch again,' Kundan observed. 'It may be one way to cope with the changing situations. Of course, if there are changes!'

'Exactly. I thought the same. A tribal society is an unchanging one. Why then did they go for this practice? Unlike tribal societies, our societies do change. We, therefore, have revolutions which seek to follow the same sequence of anarchy to order. But ours are also continuous societies and they break down under such convulsions. They cannot afford to start from scratch at any time.'

Kundan told Ruth of what Hassan had once told him about the cyclopean characters in a society—individuals who followed their own laws and lived in their own dens. Though Kundan did not hold them up as ideals, he still felt that every society, to defy its own rusted laws, needed some individuals who enter into it laterally, who have nobody's mantle to inherit.

They were returning to the town after a long walk into the desert. The warm sand flew into the air at the slightest provocation of a breeze. As they approached the town sand dunes retreated and gravel and stones appeared. The stones in turn gave way to projecting outcrops which gradually merged with the buildings of the town. Finally the whole process came to an end at the large rock at the centre of the town and the fort erected on top of it.

The giant sandstone fort had acquired a golden glow in the sunlight. Rounded watch towers jutted out from its corners like blended ends of its jagged history. A mysterious silence emanated from the dumb giant, like the heat that exuded from rocks exposed to the sun. People in the slums and decaying buildings around seemed to greet its silence with a variety of subdued noises and sluggish movements.

'Ruth, the chasm between this fort and the people living around it sometimes amazes me. Though both the settlement and the building of the fort started together the moat between them grows deeper and wider every day.

'Isn't it the nature of every system? At each stage of its advance, the Authority sheds a section of the people, and reduces the size of the circle which it recognizes and protects. As the centre of authority shrinks and becomes more compact, the poromboke around it grows larger. That is how regimes get isolated from the people they rule.'

As they entered the town, night closed in on them. Their footsteps echoed in the cobbled streets as they crossed the beams of light and the curious gazes that came from the open doors and windows.

'I was a mad man to set out on such a journey,' Kundan said as if to himself. 'Mounting a horse that knows only to prance; wearing as armour the motley of a clown; making spears out of candlesticks, without a clue about the destination or the route of my journey . . . Did anybody call me for help? What tree am I watering, squeezing water out of the rocks and sand of the desert?'

Ruth took his hand in hers.

'Doesn't it make a difference to know that you are not the only one on such a road?'

Kundan drew her to him. Sheer madness too makes sense when there is someone to share it. But they were not merely sharing, they were dissolving into one another, not only in their resolutions and illusions, but also in the warmth of their bodies.

They woke up before the night ended.

'Let us go out,' Ruth suggested.

They wriggled out of the quilt and put on their clothes. Thrusting their hands into the pockets of their overcoats, they went out into the street. The moon was about to set, but dawn was still far away. They sat on the white sand and waited for the darkness between moonset and dawn to abate.

Ruth pressed her chin on Kundan's knee playfully. 'Let us get out of this place, Kundan. Why do you want to work here?'

Kundan shrugged his shoulders and smiled.

'A place where people know each other, trust each other . . .' Her voice grew sad. 'A place where the sincerity and totality in the love between a man and a woman is reflected in every human relationship . . .'

'Why, Ruth, these two cannot be compared. You know that.'

'But faith is expressed in the highest form in the relationship between a man and a woman. In fact there is an element of faith underlying every kind of human activity. Everything is tolerable—even the most terrible act of cruelty—except duplicity or deceit.'

'Perhaps you are right, but . . .'

Ruth was looking curiously at Kundan.

'Kundan, till now, you have been concerned only with the plight of Sulaiman, Bhola and Daniel. You have never had any suspicions about what is actually taking place in this Project.'

'What do you mean?'

'The project you work for is a sham, a hoax. I know it would be difficult for you to take this. But the fact is that your project is nothing more than a few columns and beams, and like the dome they are going to place over them, it would cover up one of the largest scams in recent times involving misappropriation of a colossal amount of money.'

'How can it be? All these engineers, technicians, army men, the big design office . . . '

'Some of them know it. Some, like you, don't. But you are all responsible for it.'

Kundan stared into the distance without a word. The moon had set and darkness had obliterated the white glow of the desert sand.

'I am sorry, Kundan. I know the emptiness that is filling you up. Forgive me.'

'All that security and secrecy, punishing the helpless prisoners and Pioneers to protect it . . .'

'Security was necessary. Not for preventing sabotage, but for covering it up. To make people believe that something really hot was going on there. It is like defending an imaginary attack by a non-existent enemy. It was not just a few prisoners who were led to the gallows, but a whole people.'

'Why are you so helpless?'

'Why are *you* so helpless that you cannot save the life of a prisoner whose innocence is known to everyone, from the jailer to the judge?'

They returned through the moonless night trying to cheer each other up.

When the first shock was over, Kundan, to his surprise, felt a great relief. It was as if he had suddenly received the answers to a number of baffling questions—simple and straightforward answers which made him feel he had known them all along. But Ruth had not realized that it added one more item to the long list of impossible things before them—the non-existent enemy, imaginary attack, meaningless columns, sleepless gallows, sleeping men—a vain quest. After shedding the cloaks of absurdities, clownishness and madness, one after the other, they now had a new mantle to put on—the mantle of nakedness. Helplessness was nothing but nakedness.

At the tall, arching gates of the town, they saw a group of people leaving the town for the desert: whole families, the young, the old and the children wrapped in woollen clothes, trudging the desert road with downcast eyes. The dim light from the dust-covered street lamps crawled over them as they walked. They had come to the town leaving their hearths and homes to escape drought and famine. Now they were going back defeated. Silently, they walked. Their sandals and shoes struck against the stone-paved path and made rhythmic beats which sounded loud in the dead of the night. They had started their journey before dawn so that they could reach their villages before the sun became too hot.

Kundan and Ruth stood on the kerb, watching the column of human beings—a defeated column abandoning the siege they had laid on the town. Whether they had knocked on the gates of the town for domestic work or robbery or prostitution was immaterial. Whatever they had done, it had been an invasion; an invasion of the town by the poromboke. It had failed. They were now returning with downcast eyes, covering their heads with shawls and holding their children close to them.

Chapter Thirty-Four

Defeat need not necessarily be a condition of men who have fallen prostrate on the ground after a battle fought with swords and spears. Nor that of men returning to the wilderness after abandoning the siege of a town. It may be a general feature of life acquired through generations by a people.

After each robbery involving much personal risk and the loss of several lives, Valmiki entrusted the booty of gold and money to his wife and children. He also asked them a question which one of the plundered travellers had asked him to put to them before he died. 'No, no!' they replied horrified, 'we will accept the gold and money you plunder, but not any part of your sin. The sin is yours—yours alone.' In a flash, Valmiki saw the life he had left behind and the life that lay before him. He was a man of the poromboke. Born a Brahmin, he developed a contempt for Brahminism early in life and strayed into the ghettos of the Sudras. He lived with a Sudra woman and fathered her children. He joined a band of dacoits, plundering and killing wayfarers. Depressed by the reply he received from his wife and children, he withdrew into the inner recesses of the poromboke, the forest, where he sat in meditation. He meditated till an anthill grew around him and enveloped him. Though he was later acclaimed a sage, he essentially remained a man of the poromboke. He saw inveterate moralists dumping their sins surreptitiously in the thickets. A certain *maryada purushottam* even dumped his wife there to protect his honour. Valmiki took upon himself the sins that others refused to own up and the burdens they relieved themselves of.

To some people defeat is a condition, not an event.

All civilizations have moved along the same path, following the same doctrine. The path of slavery and the doctrine of the robbing of the labour of the many by the few who ruled over them. If mankind had stuck to the primitive tribal communism, there would have been no Egypt, no Sumeria, China or Harappa; none of those cities, edifices or works of art we dig up from the earth and admire in our museums. All civilizations germinated in deserts. They grew by drinking the water carried to their areas by rivers which had their catchments elsewhere. Wasn't this history, wasn't this the custom, one may ask. Yes, it has been. But then you are only talking about receiving the benefits of civilization and forgetting its sins. Like what Valmiki's wife and children had said: The wealth is ours, the sin yours! Where are the Valmikis to own up to the sins of our civilization?

As Ruth and Kundan leaned against the walls of the sleeping houses in the freezing cold of the dawn and watched the column of the defeated men that passed them silently, the questions which were lying curled up within them evading their understanding all along sprang up once again. The rhythmic sound of the sandals and shoes of those people as they struck the cobbled road knocked at the doors of their mind, shouting, wake up! Wake up!

History was passing them like a river, cutting arrogantly

into one bank and liberally building up the other. Kundan and Ruth could not sit on its bank and drink from it like Valmiki's wife and children. Taking up the burden of sin was the only way to defy sin. Defiance ran through them like a flame. And through the defiance they saw their nakedness and helplessness melting away. The numbness of their hands vanished and they became themselves again.

Chapter Thirty-Five

Ruth left in the morning for some unknown destination.
Life was becoming more and more dangerous for her, she
said. However, there was nothing she could do about it.

The house was in a mess. Ruth had tried to clean it up
but before she could complete the job, more pressing
assignments had taken her away. Looking around in the
kitchen, Kundan saw that nearly everything had been used
up. There was some tea still left in the kettle. He heated it
and poured it into a glass. Sipping it, he sat on a chair by
the window.

He felt too lazy to get up from the chair. When he
thought of the long chain of routine before him, he was
depressed. Gulshan was not likely to come back. Neither
was Ruth. He asked himself how long he himself would be
there. Suddenly Kundan felt that he had intruded into
somebody else's house. Everything in it, including the glass
in his hand became strange to him.

Two men standing on the other side of the street caught
his attention. One of them had a dark beard and the other
wore a woollen cap. He was sure that they did not live in

the street. Besides, he remembered seeing them quite frequently during the last few days. Perhaps they were security men set to watch his movements. Was Ruth too being tailed? Again, there was nothing he or Ruth could do about it.

Kundan picked up the phone and asked the Mechanical Transport Section to send his jeep. Someone on duty replied that it was under repair. Kundan locked the door and went out.

The distance was not much. It was a pleasant walk to the foot of the hill. Beyond that, it was a steep climb. He removed his coat and climbed the hill, halting intermittently to steady his breath. While going up the winding path, he got a bird's-eye view of the slums and labour camps below. With men out on work, they wore a strange, disturbing look. Something told him to avert his eyes from them.

There was an enormous stone jar placed at the impressive Gothic arch gates of the fort. As he usually entered the fort in a jeep, Kundan used to get only a brief glimpse of them. Now he walked up to the jar which stood almost as tall as him. Polished to the sheen of glass, exquisitely carved, decorated with engravings, it was a masterpiece of art. It used to be filled to the brim with opium whenever the king organized a raid from the fort to the fertile plains lying beyond the desert. Every mounted soldier took a cup of opium as he rode out of the fort. There were stepping stones built near the jar for them to climb up and scoop out the opium from inside. Kundan placed his hands on the jar and peered into it as if to see if any opium was still left in it. No, the soldiers had finished every grain of it as they went out on their raids.

When he entered the records office, Kundan saw Jaswant looking at him out of the corner of his eyes. Jaswant and the clerks were silently and dutifully hard at work. There was a surprising silence in the office.

Kundan occupied his chair and stretched his legs. After

a while Jaswant rose from his seat and went across to Kundan's table. Kundan did not turn to look at him. Jaswant walked on for a few paces and returned to Kundan's table again.

'Sir, a query came in your absence,' he said haltingly. 'They wanted to know whether you were absent from duty.'

'What did you say?'

Jaswant did not reply.

'I was, wasn't I?'

Puzzled, Jaswant stared at him for a few moments before going back to his table. Kundan had often wondered whether Jaswant was spying on him. Now he did not mind, for everybody knew, to the last detail, what he was doing.

There were only two days left to send back the prisoners. The date of arrival of the new batch had also been announced. Kundan rose to go out.

In the open space between the hospital and the jail, he met Yogeshwar. Yogeshwar was actually walking towards him. As he came closer, his face lit up with joy.

'There is news for you, Kundan,' Yogeshwar took Kundan's hand.

Kundan stared at him.

'You were getting worked up over things quite unnecessarily,' Yogeshwar lowered his voice. 'In fact, so was I. One has to maintain a sense of proportion. It doesn't do if you lose your composure during times of crises. God will find a way out of it, you know. We are yet to learn quite a few home truths.'

'Have you anything useful to tell me?' Kundan did not hide his irritation.

'You don't understand me, Kundan!'

'Perhaps, Yogeshwar, only I understand you.'

'No, you don't. He is dead.'

'Dead? Who? . . . Oh, Sulaiman!'

Yogeshwar nodded.

'Oh God, you could go to this extent!'

'No Kundan, he was not killed. Believe me. I can prove it.' Yogeshwar was pleading in a manner not characteristic of him. 'It was an accident. A girder collapsed and one of the prisoners was trapped under it. Sulaiman, who saw the girder fall, rushed to extricate the trapped man. But as he pulled at the girder he too was trapped under it. The girder slipped and his head was crushed. It was no murder, Kundan. You have to believe me.'

'I don't know . . .'

'It was a tragedy. This Sulaiman was a poor man. But looking at the incident from another angle, I feel he was lucky. As far as you are concerned, the problem that has been worrying you has just disappeared.'

'My problems have only begun,' Kundan muttered and without waiting for Yogeshwar's response, he turned back and walked away. He heard only his footsteps and saw only the earth beneath his feet. Why did everything have to end like this? Everything he touched? Everyone he came into contact with: Bhola, Daniel, Sulaiman, Amala, or even Ruth. They had all left him alone in the end. He could not go back to where he had begun, convincing himself that all his problems were over, adding everything up and bringing the balance to zero. All those who had left him had also left some burden for him to carry, though none of them would admit it. Nothing had been brought down to zero. Or, perhaps, they had crossed zero and gone beyond it to the other side of the axis, to minus, to the other side of the looking glass where they could enter blissfully like Alice and from where they could only hear the anguished cries of human beings.

Kundan walked into the office and called Jaswant.

'Jaswant, what action has been taken on Sulaiman's death?'

'Sir, he was a prisoner. So it is not necessary to wait for the relatives. They took his body straight away for cremation. We were just informed about it.'

'You mean a prisoner's body need not be handed over to his relatives?'

'The bodies of prisoners condemned to death are not returned to the relatives. They belong to the Sarkar.'

'Yes, you are right, they belong to the Sarkar . . . wait a minute, what did you say . . . it was cremated?'

'On the records he was Pasupati Singh, sir.'

'That means Sulaiman's family was not informed.'

'The letter has gone to Pasupati Singh's family.'

Sulaiman's family had to be informed. They had at least a right to know. Kundan must do it. There was no other way.

Chapter Thirty-Six

The bus had been running through the desert for the whole of three hours, jolting, protesting and halting. Twice it broke down and started again. The villagers who sat by his side told Kundan that it would be a few more hours before it got over the 'hump'. By 'hump', they meant the slender range of hills which separated the land into desert on one side and fertile tracts on the other. The southern end of the ranges which were said to be about two thousand metres high gradually sloped down and merged with the plains in the north. The desert was the western rain shadow region of the ranges.

Sulaiman's home town was on the other side of the 'hump' which, the conductor of the bus told Kundan, they would reach by the evening. This now appeared to be improbable. Most of the passengers were to get down at the villages nearby. The men wore colourful frilled shirts and huge turbans while the women wore heaps of clothes from which clumsily tattooed hands, wearing a number of bracelets, protruded. The women rarely showed their faces and spoke little. Only brief, intermittent sounds, like the chirping of birds, came from the layers of clothes. A boy of about seven, sitting near Kundan gradually shifted to his lap, and leaning back on his chest, dozed off. Kundan put his arms around him so that he did not slide down to the floor.

The bus broke down again, this time for good. After making some attempts to repair it, the driver announced that it would not be going any further. The passengers got down quietly with a foolish smile on their faces.

The sun was setting and light was vanishing behind a screen of dust. Most of the passengers decided to walk to their destinations. But Kundan had a long way to go. So he waited on the side of the road, hoping to hitch a ride.

He must have spent quite some time squatting on the kerb of the tarred road and springing up and waving his arms whenever a truck came along. The sun was sinking into the ·horizon. It was almost dark when a lorry, responding to Kundan's frantic waving slowed down and pulled up. Kundan got into the front seat beside the cleaner. The driver and conductor of the broken-down bus waved to him as the lorry started moving.

The lorry driver was in high spirits, shouting boisterously to the cleaner and cracking an occasional joke. They moved deeper and deeper into the dark night. It was a moonless night and everything around them was invisible, except the black ribbon of the tarred road illuminated by the headlights and rushing backwards under the wheels.

The driver dipped the headlights for a vehicle coming from the opposite direction to pass. For some reason, he continued to drive in the dimmed light even after the vehicle had passed.

A tiny speck of light, like a glow-worm, came into view in the distance. As they drew near, they could discern a human figure, wrapped in a blanket squatting on the road with a hurricane lamp on the side.

It was a woman—a solitary creature waiting on the road

with a lantern. Perhaps she had dozed off in that posture. When the lorry appeared she started and scrambled to her feet. The driver applied the brake, put his head out and spoke to her. Though Kundan could not hear the conversation clearly, he got the drift of it. The driver turned to Kundan. 'Poor, helpless people, saheb. Nothing to eat, no work. Drought and famine have made them take to the road. Would you like to help her, saheb?' He winked at Kundan.

Kundan said nothing. The driver drew the vehicle to the side of the kerb and parked it.

'We will be leaving only in the morning, saheb. These people have a camp a short way from here. I think I'll share their supper and spend the night with them.'

He lifted the lantern and followed the woman.

Kundan stood staring into the darkness for some time. The lorry driver had chosen an unusual way of taking leave of him. But what could he do about it? There was nobody to complain to. After all, the driver too needed some rest and cheering up. And the woman her daily bread. That was all there was to it.

There were some lights glowing in the distance in the direction the lorry driver and the woman had gone. Some faint sounds too came from the direction, which made the silence of the desert deeper and lonelier.

Kundan walked towards the lights. After some time he came upon the ramshackle camp of a group of tribals who had been displaced from their homes by drought and famine, and were now moving in search of greener pastures.

As their destination proved illusory, their movement too had lost direction and they were left to fend for themselves with their camps and their meagre possessions—a cluster of torn and patched up tents, a few camel carts and heaps of rags and pots scattered everywhere. The men danced to keep themselves warm, while the women waited on the road with lanterns for prospective lorry drivers.

Some women were sitting huddled together a few paces away from the camp. Spotting Kundan, one of them got up and walked towards him, pulling her ghoonghat aside.

'Could you give me a roti, if you have one to spare?' Kundan asked her as she stopped before him.

Kundan felt a lump in his throat as he spoke these words. The picture of another woman came to his mind, a picture which had remained etched in the brain of a man before it rotted and mingled with the soil along with his brain after it had been crushed to pulp by a girder. It was for the love he had for her and the children she bore him that he had taken upon himself the death sentence handed out to a murderer.

Kundan took some money from his purse and extended it to her. She almost snatched it away from his hand and walked away. Kundan squatted on the ground and wrapped the blanket he had brought with him around his shoulders.

Surprisingly, no one from the group of men who were dancing, or merely idling, paid any attention to him. It appeared that the job was reserved for women. Every kind of suffering, drudgery, pain and humiliation always seemed to be passed on to them—even in this community which had been driven into a nomadic existence by circumstances. The woman came back with two rotis made of bajra and a raw onion. The ghoonghat had been pulled back completely to reveal her sharp, impassive features. Kundan took one roti and returned the other to her. She took it back without any hesitation.

Gradually the noise from the camps subsided and the desert withdrew into its eerie silence. Kundan leaned against a rock and stretched his legs.

In the plains, the dust rising up into the atmosphere during the day settles down at night. Not so in the desert. Fine particles of dust remain suspended in the desert air at night absorbing even the faint starlight and making the sky a grey canopy. The grey, starless sky makes you feel forlorn, lost and trapped.

Around Kundan, under the canopy of a dusty light in which even the stars had been melted down, lay asleep a community betrayed, deprived and forgotten by civilization. As the the women embraced the bodies of strangers, the men, emasculated and resigned to their fate, were lost in themselves.

Two camels squatted near Kundan, the huge bulks of their bodies resting on their folded, slender legs, their heads rising up into the sky like minarets.

A dust storm was brewing in the distance. Kundan withdrew his head into the blanket and waited for sleep and the break of dawn.

Chapter Thirty-Seven

The lorry driver woke up Kundan early in the morning. 'Come on, saheb. We have a long way to go.'

They got into the lorry and resumed their journey through the dry, barren landscape. Soon the hills appeared. As they came closer Kundan saw that they were just huge rocky mounds. Once they were covered with vegetation, even lush woods, the driver said. He had seen it with his own eyes when he first came into the area, driving his lorry.

As the woods disappeared, the top soil was easily washed away, baring the rocks. The wind and the sand worked on the soft rocks, giving them a variety of queer shapes with curves, cavities and holes. People compared the shapes to animals calling them Frog Hill, Bull Hill and so on.

As the road cut through the hills and entered the plains, the landscape changed. But desolation was evident there too. It seemed that nature's fort was crumbling and the invading soldiers were entering the harems and laying them waste.

The driver stopped at a watering point. The man in charge had started rationing the supplies. His well had started drying up. 'You may not find water here on your way back,' the driver warned Kundan. 'Everything has lost its roots,' he said philosophically. 'The foundations are shaking. The people are selling their last drop of fluids, water or blood, allowing themselves to dry up like uprooted trees.'

It was noon when Kundan reached Sulaiman's home town. The town wore a deserted look. Kundan suddenly realized that he had not given much thought as to how to go about his task. It was not easy to go to a household and announce the death of the head of the family. But Kundan had to do it. This was the retribution for all that he had done, or rather, for all that he ought to have done, but did not. Now he had to look straight into the eyes of a woman and tell her that he had been about to send her husband to the gallows in place of another man. That he had been using Sulaiman for a fake and fraudulent enterprise, that Sulaiman had sacrificed his life for it, that he was helpless to obtain any compensation for the family from the Sarkar . . . In short, that he was solely responsible for everything that had happened.

The first thing he saw on the way to the bazaar was the horrible sight of two monkeys kept for sale. The hind legs of both the animals had been chopped off and the wounds were still fresh. The pathetic but fierce look in their eyes seemed to be directed at Kundan. There were quite a few curious onlookers around. Unable to control himself, Kundan pushed aside the onlookers and pounced upon the hawker. Uttering a kind of war cry, which sounded strange even to him, he caught hold of the man by his shirt and rained blows on his face.

The onlookers did not take him for a mad man. Perhaps they too had felt the indignation which had taken possession of Kundan, though they had not reacted like him. They separated Kundan from the hawker and led him gently away, trying to pacify him. 'Bhaisaheb, will you attack the whole market? Today is market day. There will be buyers and sellers coming from all surrounding areas. You will see many such sights today.'

They took him to a small restaurant, made him sit on a bench and asked the shopkeepers to give him a cup of tea.

'Nobody knows where they come from and what they do with all these things,' the shopkeeper said, as if he was talking to himself. 'All sorts of things are sold here. There are buyers for everything. They buy living animals as well as their hides and bones. Perhaps human beings are sold too. People are ready to sell anything, yes, anything, including themselves.'

It was true. There were no products of human labour left to sell. People were starving and were incapable of producing anything. Nothing grew in the arid soil. All trees and plants had been cut down and used up. They had turned to catching animals now. To prevent them from running away, they maimed them. Kundan had already seen them selling their women. Perhaps they sold their children too. These people had to live. No, they were not people, they were just individuals. Each one for himself and against everyone else. Drought and famine had rewritten the laws of society.

Kundan had just brought the cup of tea to his lips when he heard a piercing shriek from one of the monkeys. He threw up everything in his stomach convulsively.

The shopkeeper gave him some of his precious water to wash his face and sprinkle on his head. Kundan did not have the nerve to inquire what was happening to the monkeys. He became bolder when he began to walk. He was more successful now in reconciling himself to the sights he saw. Besides monkeys, there were a variety of birds, including peacocks, and reptiles too, for sale. A man sat with a few iguanas and a frying pan. Starvation had brought the creatures to the verge of death, but the man had seen to it that they did not die. Their feeble movements were perceptible only to a careful observer. When a buyer came, the hawker would put one of the iguanas into the pan, fry it and extract its oil. The fat of iguanas was popularly believed to have miraculous curing powers.

Hides of cattle, bones which had been picked clean by vultures, and every animal alive which had some use, was up for sale. Merchants from various parts of the country gathered at the bazaar to make the best use of the harvest of starvation and death.

After the animals, it was a human body that met Kundan's eyes. It was the corpse of a girl of about ten years, uncovered, borne by two children, a boy and a girl, on their shoulders. Two other children followed them.

Death, especially of children, had ceased to touch the minds of the people, it appeared. The children carrying the body and accompanying it too showed no emotions.

Following the directions given by a passer-by, Kundan reached Sulaiman's house. It was not a house, but the ruins of an old mosque or tomb. The winter sun shed its weak rays on it. As Kundan lifted the clothes hung on a line in front of it, two boys of about ten and eight years came out. They were Sulaiman's sons. They told Kundan that a girl in the neighbourhood called Nabeesa had died and that her parents had gone away leaving the dead body behind. Their sister had to take care of the burial. Their mother too was away, having left the previous day. They did not know where she had gone or when she would be back.

Everything seemed strange. There were not many grown-ups in the village. They had all gone out on various jobs or had just disappeared. Children were managing the households everywhere. Sulaiman's daughter was now the head of her family.

Sulaiman's daughter, whom Kundan had seen carrying the dead body, returned soon. She asked Kundan whether he had brought anything from her father. Hearing this, her little brothers too gathered around Kundan with expectation. What could these starving children be expecting other than something to eat? But Kundan had not brought anything. He felt guilty. He drew out his purse and took out as much money as he could spare.

'Your father has sent some money.'

She took it from him.

'Where is Abba? He did not say anything to us when he left. He does not write to us these days. His last letter came two months ago. He had given us quite of bit of advice in it. Tell us, kaka, is he all right? Did you come here to tell us . . .'

'Where has your mother gone, child?'

'I don't know. Sometimes she comes back after several days.'

'Give me some water to drink, child.'

Kundan sat on the broken parapet wall.

When he had drunk the water, she asked him again about her father. She had sensed that something had gone wrong.

'Saira, I am sorry. Your father is no more.'

Saira did not cry. There was no expression of shock on her face. She just stared at Kundan. Kundan saw two teardrops roll down her eyes. Perhaps she had been expecting it. The teardrops that rolled down her cheeks were performing the last rites for her drawn-out agony.

She called her younger brothers who were playing and walked away with her arms on their shoulders.

What was the purpose of his coming here and breaking the news to these kids? The monthly allowance paid by Pasupati must have stopped after his death. With no letter from him for two months, they were already in the process of losing him. Sulaiman would have disappeared quietly from their memories, like the innumerable men and women who disappear every day. It is easier to accept the biggest of afflictions when they set in gradually. But this bold feat of Kundan's, which he had boasted he was committing as duty, had only short-circuited that process.

Kundan walked back along the path he had come. Dust rose from under his feet with every step. The sun was rapidly going down and dusk was settling. Kundan kept kicking the rocks that protruded on the road in a show of impotent rage.

He waited for the bus at the point where the lorry driver had dropped him. Now there were no shrieking monkeys or frying iguanas anywhere around. In fact, the market was deserted. Picking up their things the hawkers had all withdrawn into their holes.

Kundan managed to catch a bus going to Rambhagarh. He sat in a corner seat like a piece of luggage as the bus hurtled through the fading twilight.

Chapter Thirty-Eight

Julius Caesar overran eight hundred cities and annexed three hundred nations. His armies waged war against three million people, one million of whom were killed and another million captured and enslaved. What a valiant emperor, what a formidable commander, the reader of the chronicles of Caesar's exploits exclaims. But before he can read further, a historian, or a philosopher, or the two rolled into one, steps out of the shadows to confront him. Look, my friend, he says, all the cities Caesar overran, the nations he annexed, the people he fought and subdued, without exception, survived him. Poor Caesar! He could not even survive his senators. He was only fifty-six when they did him in.

What the philosopher-historian means is that nations and people are vast, unfathomable, eternal oceans while emperors are trivial, ephemeral phenomena incapable of creating more than a few ripples as they splash about on the surface before going down to the bottom.

The philosopher-historian's arguments, convincing as they may be, are not quite consoling or reassuring. It is not just tyrannies and despots that people survive; they pull themselves out of floods, earthquakes, epidemics and famines, which are often more devastating. But it is not the survival of nations and races, but the sufferings and agonies that individuals undergo, the little pleasures and contentments that they weave around themselves during their brief lifespans that make human life what it is. Before the two drops of tears that quietly rolled down the sunken cheeks of Sulaiman's daughter, before the silent, parting looks of the three children retreating into defeat, that ultimate victory the philosopher-historian gloats over pales into irrelevance.

Chapter Thirty-Nine

It was late in the evening when Kundan reached home. He was shivering in spite of the woollen blanket he had pulled over his head. At the door, a security officer suddenly materialized and placed a forbidding hand on his shoulder. The officer could not obviously recognize him because of the way he had pulled the blanket over his head.

'Who are you?'

They were no longer shadowing him incognito. The security men wore uniforms and carried guns.

Kundan pulled down the blanket from his face. 'I am the Project's labour officer.' The security officer hastily withdrew his hand from Kundan's shoulder. 'I am sorry sir, I couldn't recognize you.'

As Kundan went in, the security officer called him. 'Excuse me, sir. You must meet the Station Commander first thing in the morning.'

When Kundan looked around, he saw more of them. They had surrounded the house.

'Am I under house arrest?' he asked the security officer, bewildered.

The officer merely repeated what he had just said, adding that Kundan was not allowed to go out.

Kundan got the message. He went in quietly without any more questions. He was hungry. There was nothing to eat in the house but he could not go out to get anything.

A layer of dust had settled over everything in the house. The house itself had acquired an ancient look. Every flat surface was covered with dust and there were cobwebs in every corner. If the skeleton of a dancing girl, walled up by an emperor, had come crashing down, Kundan would not have been surprised.

There was no water in the tap. But he located a bucket full of water in the bathroom. There was a dead cockroach floating in it. He removed it and carried the bucket of water to the kitchen. A long search yielded some rice and dal at the bottom of two tins. He poured some water from the bucket into a vessel and put it to boil on the stove and put the dal and rice in it. When they were cooked, he sprinkled some salt and chilli powder on top and stirred the mixture. He was so hungry that the concoction tasted delicious to him. But there was not enough to appease his hunger.

Trying to ignore his half-empty stomach, Kundan got up and went over to the bed. He passed his hand over the bed and the soft quilt. The only warmth left in the room which had suddenly taken on a sepulchral air was the warmth of Ruth's body lingering on the bed. The last two days he spent in the room were at once the happiest and the saddest days in his life. While on the one hand he felt the roof was coming down on him, on the other he was trying to sense the warmth of Ruth's presence among the debris. It was not just the warmth of physical intimacy that they had discovered there. They had been drifting on two lonely rafts till they met on this island. In those days Ruth became an island to Kundan and Kundan one to Ruth. His hand lingered on the bed. Ruth had left and now he too was leaving that abode which, together, they had made a cosy nest.

The security officers were making their presence felt by banging their batons on the walls. Kundan put out the lights and lay quietly in bed for some time, allowing the security officers to relax.

A few minutes later, he got up, collected all the money left in the house and walked stealthily into the kitchen. Picking up a wooden board he had been using as a shelf, he climbed the stairs to the terrace. On the terrace, he quickly knelt down behind the parapet wall, out of view of the security men. He placed the wooden board like a bridge on the parapet and across to the parapet of the next building. Crossing over quickly and noiselessly, he did the same with the next buildings in the row till he reached the end, where he felt more free to move about. The cold had sent the residents indoors, leaving the terraces and street below deserted. Kundan looked back and silently bid farewell to the house where he had lived and to the security officers who were guarding it. Looking down into the street, Kundan spied a pile of garbage—a piece of good luck, the ideal spot to jump down without making too much noise.

But when he jumped, Kundan could not maintain his balance. He let out a stifled groan as one of his feet struck something hard. As he tried to steady himself, he realized that his other foot was steeped in the slimy slush which a drain was emptying into the garbage heap. The dogs and pigs which were rummaging for food in the garbage were startled by Kundan's sudden landing and scattered all around. But they regrouped in a moment and encircled him snarling and grunting. Extricating himself from the garbage and the mire and breaking the cordon of the belligerent animals, Kundan walked towards the railway station. There was a train early in the morning. The security officers would notice his absence only when he failed to come out of the house in the morning. They would then make a dash for the railway station and the bus stand. But, by then he would have left Rambhagarh far behind him.

His new status as a fugitive from the law both amused and pained Kundan. He had always been extremely punctilious about observing the law. He even derived a certain thrill from conducting himself as a law-abiding, disciplined citizen. Even when his beliefs were not in consonance with it, he obeyed the law to the letter. How or when he started turning his back on it, he could not remember. Now, as a fugitive, he was trying to escape from its clutches. There was something comical about it. But the comedy evaporated when he looked at what lay ahead. Was he going to end up a prisoner, and ultimately a convict on the death row, destined to lift girders and mix concrete in a sensitive project in the midst of the desert with a six months' bonus of life? The Sarkar could not be expected to let grass grow under its feet. It had a way of making those who revolted against it build fortresses to protect the same system.

Dragging his sprained leg and ignoring the slime that had soaked the other, Kundan walked on. He tried to look normal, though it was not normal to walk alone through the street at that time of the night.

Behind the closed shutters of the shops in the street, he imagined he could still see the shopkeepers sitting on their mattresses on which the wares they sold had etched multi-coloured designs. Kundan wondered why his mind was wandering in this strange manner. Perhaps his transformation from a respectable labour officer who used to move freely with the shopkeepers into a deserter, a fugitive from the law, had induced him to think about the world around him as an alien entity. If they had kept their shops open, he would not have been able to walk along the street as he was doing now. His freedom, his life itself was now a gift of those closed shops, or of the deep sleep the residents of the town were enjoying under their quilts.

The picture of the girl with a squint drawn by the local artist as an advertisement for a popular cold drink caught

Kundan's eyes. Then his eyes glided from it to the board hanging over Vrindavan's provisions store. Kundan stopped, as if he was being pulled by a strange force. Exactly at that moment, the door on the side of the shop which opened to the staircase flew open. Kundan stared in disbelief. It was Suku. He recognized her in the light of the street lamps. She had wrapped her face in a brown shawl.

'You may be wondering how I knew you were coming. Take it as my sixth sense, the sixth sense that has kept me alive all these years. I knew you would come out of your hiding place today, at this moment. I stayed awake the whole night for it.'

Kundan, who was standing stunned, was gradually beginning to grasp what she was saying. Tears came to his eyes. Her face was bright, full of joy, as never seen before.

'Why do you cry, my little brother,' Suku was stroking Kundan's hair. 'How timid you were! But how smart you look today! Standing boldly before the whole world after sneaking about for so long. No, don't come in. Go wherever you like. It is enough for me to know you are alive. I always knew it, though everybody called me a foolish girl.'

She held his head close to her heart and kissed it. Suddenly she detached herself from him, waved to him, went into the house and closed the door behind her.

Kundan stared at the closed door. He had no need to hide now, Suku had said. He was a man who had come out into the open at last, not one who was running away. He wiped the tears that had appeared in his eyes and walked on.

The railway station was deserted. There was still plenty of time for the train to arrive. Kundan crossed the tracks and walked towards the stacks of stones the quarry workers had heaped up beyond them.

The quarry workers were sleeping in their camps across the tracks on the other side. He chose a safe spot among the stacks. The pain on his sprained foot returned the moment he stopped. He sat on the ground leaning against a stack and stretched his legs. There were only cold, dead stones around him, stones waiting for the rail wagons to carry them to distant places; big lumps with frowning faces, thin slabs lying in layers, one over the other, flints too small even to make their presence felt.

He came back to the platform wrapped in the woollen blanket. The train, driven by an old steam engine, arrived in time. Halting for a few moments at the platform, it resumed its journey, puffing smoke and discharging steam.

Kundan climbed on to one of the upper berths and stretched himself. Dawn was still about three hours away. He could cover a lot of distance in those precious hours.

Then he suddenly thought of the prisoners. He could not remember the date by which the last batch was to be sent back to the city. Perhaps they had already been taken back to the city. Jaswant might have, in his absence, handled the whole process. They could, like him, be sitting in a train. Or they might have reached their jail already. Or . . . death sentences were usually carried out at dawns like this.

Chapter Forty

It was a stately structure made of pale sandstone, each stone perfectly shaped and each door frame and each window pane neatly painted and polished. At the top of the steeple stood a cross, its arms outstretched into the sky. It overlooked a light green turf and a garden full of flowers in bloom with gravelled paths bordering them. The cathedral in the city was adored by everyone, irrespective of their faiths, and even by non-believers for its sheer beauty. The morning dew had washed and freshened up everything.

The doors on either side of the cathedral opened and a well-trimmed, dignified crowd poured out of them. The crowd filled the empty, gravelled path and moved down it in a gentle stream. There was no jostling and not a single foot trespassed into the lawn.

The cathedral purged the worshippers of their desires and disillusionments during the one hour they filled it and then discharged the human mass through its many doors. The emptiness of their minds seemed to make the crowd light and buoyant and they glided through the morning air like mere coats and skirts. The streams of believers converged at the narrow gates of the cathedral compound and diverged again as they passed out of it into the street. Kundan was attracted by the contented looks on the faces in the crowd. When they come here again, passions would have welled up in them. And, again, after depositing their desires and demands in the safety lockers of the neat interiors of the cathedral, well protected from sun and rain, they would walk out into the open, confining themselves to the gravel path and carefully avoiding the turf.

What was the spirit that blended buoyancy with discipline in these people? The turf they avoided and the narrow gate they respected were certainly not the factors which instilled discipline in them. It must be the timed beats of the prayer put to harmony by the soft notes of the organ that kept these people afloat in the morning air as they came out of the cathedral doors. After instilling the fear of God in their minds for an hour, the cathedral was in fact letting them out into the world where evil and sin bared their fangs.

The two most notable features of this part of the capital were the cathedral and the Government Place. The Government Place had vast sprawling lawns crisscrossed by wide roads, fountains and statues. Like the cathedral, the offices in the Government Place too were made of pale sandstone. Gigantic structures built with huge blocks of stone placed layer upon layer. They stood on both sides of the main road which led to the President's residence, in perfect symmetry, with the same kind of domes, doors and pillars. Every lawn, every lamp post and every fountain had a counterpart on the other side. The architecture followed perfect proportions. The guards stood stiffly like statues and moved like robots, their boots brightly polished, their uniforms well starched and their strides perfectly rhythmic. Music was the soul of the neatness, perfection and discipline exuded by the Government Place. Every year, at the concluding ceremony of the National Festival, the military band performed beating the retreat at the Royal Chowk that lay between the symmetrically placed gigantic offices and the vast lawns of the Government Place. From the President's residence at the end of the road that divided the row of offices into two, the band marched in colourful uniforms to the accompaniment of trumpets, bugles and drums. As the band marched down the road, its tune arrested the whole atmosphere. The drums robbed the spectators of their heartbeats.

Kundan did not know why the neatness, order, rhythm and melody frightened him today. Why did man create such perfections in his life with music? Somewhere in this perfect structure, he should have left a crack or a gap for a wrong or discordant note to come out.

The band marched past Kundan. As it moved away and the music faded, Kundan was left alone with the sombre, petrified offices of a cold Sarkar. They seemed to be mere stones to him, hills of stones. Suddenly it occurred to him that all these offices, the cathedral and every piece of architecture in the capital had assimilated the stoniness of the desert where the sandstones were mined. The desert had arrived in the capital even before Kundan had gone to work as a labour officer in the fort. Before he went to study law. Before he was even born.

It was the anguished cries of the prisoners, the string of lies he heard from the officers, and a contingent of security police that had driven him out of the desert to this city. He could still sense the presence of each one of them behind him. If he had tried to run away from them, then it had been a failure.

What was he now, a crusader or a fugitive? He could not figure out. If he wished, he could throw away everything, buy a new suit and go back to the city that was familiar to him with its cinemas, theatres and restaurants. He had seen what he had to see and suffered what he had to suffer. Now he could forget everything. There were many more forts in the country. He could visit them like a carefree tourist. Scandals come and go in the newspapers. Murder and violence bring out processions in the street for a day or two. Sulaiman's children would wipe their tears and pick up the threads of their life again. A good monsoon could rescue Bhola's family. Prisoners would find their deliverance on the gallows. Kundan's lost tooth would be replaced by a dentist.

Kundan sat warming himself in the January sun on the lawns of the chowk from where the drums beat the retreat. Everyone in the crowd was a stranger to him. It seemed a long time since he had spoken to anyone. He could still feel upon him the stony impassive eyes of the guards who had shadowed him, and the still eyes of the dogs and pigs which surrounded him when he stood with his sprained foot on the garbage heap. He saw the loving eyes of Suku who had come out to meet him in the dead of the night. Perhaps she was the only person who could communicate with him. But she too was strange. She did not recognize him as Kundan. Or was she the only person who recognized Kundan? She did not call him in. Instead she said: go where you like, go boldly . . . and closed the door behind him.

Now, in the ambience of the huge government offices built with massive blocks of sandstone in perfect proportions and the air in which the music of trumpets, bugles and drums lay dissolved, Kundan came face to face with a formidable truth: there was no going back for him. All doors had been closed behind him.

Chapter Forty-One

There was a group of people commonly seen floating about at the crossroads of the city. They wore tattered clothes in strange colours. Emaciated men and women carrying crying babies on their shoulders and holding sickly and naked children by their hands. They had either wandered into the city from their villages, stricken by drought and famine, or had been displaced by development projects. The city was alien to them and making a living was an excruciating task. They could be seen waving newspapers at the vehicles parked at the traffic signal lights or wiping the windshields of vehicles unsolicited, or just begging. As they were usually seen around traffic junctions, they had been given an appropriate name: 'junction people'. But they thrived in other parts of the city too. At night the women would be selling their bodies in the dark corners of the streets and the men would be stealing or waylaying people. Whatever means they chose for a livelihood, these poromboke people were a nuisance to the residents of the city. They were only objects of hatred and distrust to the law-abiding citizens.

A lorry had ploughed through such a family that had

been sleeping on the road the previous night. There had not been enough blankets to go round so the whole family of eight or ten men, women and children were sleeping under a single quilt. The badly mangled bodies now lay waiting for the police to arrive.

The onlookers seemed to derive some kind of relief or satisfaction from the incident. Good riddance to bad rubbish, someone remarked. The whole lot did nothing but whore, steal and kidnap children.

The driver of the bus in which Kundan was travelling had stopped his vehicle for a few moments to enable the passengers to get a good view of the pieces of flesh covered with blood and flies. When he started the bus, the passengers withdrew their heads from the windows and sat upright again.

Kundan too withdrew his head, but his mind was still driving away the flies from the flesh and blood on the road. There were no faces to be seen among the lumps of flesh crushed to pulp. Nevertheless, he thought he knew these people. Were they not the same people who had offered him shelter and bread during a night in the midst of the desert? It was futile to figure out who lands up where in a rootless world. It was even more futile to be surprised at anything. Something like the killer truck had badly mangled the whole human race.

Kundan got down at the stop the passenger sitting next to him showed him. It was a busy street. The houses almost touched each other and pedestrians waded through heaps of garbage and slime, dodging hosts of pigs, dogs and flies feasting on them. It seemed that Kundan's fellow passenger had not heard him right. But then, Kundan's request too was rather extraordinary. He had asked the way to the jail!

The road was going up on a gradient towards a bridge over a rather wide drain. A black frothing liquid slowly flowed through the drain, emitting a pungent stench that made it impossible for him to stand on the bridge for more than a moment. But the people living in the rows of slums that lined the drain seemed to be indifferent to the stench.

As he crossed the bridge, the old pattern of houses, garbage, pigs and flies appeared again. Kundan hesitated a moment before walking further. Suddenly a boy of eight or nine ran up to him and nudged him. Kundan thought he was begging. But the boy came closer and whispered in his ear: 'Babu, only five rupees. Fine stuff.'

Immediately another boy appeared and pushed the former aside. 'Get lost. Who wants your squinting sister?' Turning to Kundan he mimicked a squint and winked. 'That is how this bugger's sister looks. Come with me, babu.'

Kundan looked at their faces one after the other. For a moment he thought of going with them to meet their sisters. But he gave up the idea. He fished out two pieces of chocolate from his coat pocket and handed one each to the boys and walked on.

He had taken only a few steps when a man squatting on the side of the road suddenly put out his foot and tripped him. Kundan pitched headlong on to the road. A few others who were squatting on the road burst into loud laughter, holding their sides and pointing their fingers at Kundan. Kundan got up and caught hold of the man who had tripped him by his shoulders. But the man easily swept Kundan's hand away. Bringing his face close to Kundan's, he hissed: 'Bargaining over the brats' kid sisters, eh? A great one for girlies, aren't you?'

He laughed loudly with the others again.

Kundan said nothing. He walked away, his face downcast. The laughter of the squatting men followed him for some time. Finally he was alone again.

He asked the next man he met the way to the jail.

The man was amused. 'You are on the right track. But you have to walk a bit more. Keep straight.'

'But a man I met in the bus asked me to get down here.' Kundan pointed to the bus stop.

'Oh!' the passer-by smiled. 'People tend to think it is nice to have a feel of this neighbourhood before going to the jail!'

Neither Sulaiman nor Bhola had taken the same route he was taking to reach there, Kundan mused. And he was going there of his own accord. It was a strange fascination that was leading him there. Why didn't he pick a fight with the man who tripped him? Why wasn't he really offended by the laughter of those ruffians?

Chapter Forty-Two

The jail was in the outskirts of the city, beyond the busy crossroads. A long road from the city ended in the jail. What lay beyond that was only an uneven cart-track.

The prison complex was an astonishing sight for anybody who visited it for the first time. If the presence of the guards, the high walls and barbed wire were overlooked, it was difficult to believe that there was a jail inside the complex. The prison appeared to be no different from a small township. Besides the offices and quarters of the staff, there was a small market, a hospital and a school. In fact, these were the structures that came into view as a visitor followed the path that led him inside from the gates. The walls and the barbed-wire fence of the imposing jail built of sandstone lay further up the path.

The identity card Kundan was still carrying in his pocket helped him get through the hurdles effortlessly. But the lanes and passages, like a labyrinth, confused him. Perhaps they were meant to confuse. A prisoner who breaks out, confronted by these endless by-lanes and turnings, may easily choose the wrong ones and find himself at the gates of the jail again.

As the signboard indicated, it was the manager of prisons who was in charge of the jail. He sat in a richly furnished air-conditioned, fully-carpeted chamber. There were all kinds of modern office gadgets lined up in the room, including a personal computer. The manager was an amiable, elderly man with long grey hair which was brushed back, thick glasses, a thick moustache and a generous smile.

He glanced at Kundan's card and immediately rose from his chair and shook hands with him, smiling broadly. He spoke without a trace of formality.

'I have always thought that people like you should visit our establishment more frequently. Sitting in a distant project and sending requisitions is not the way to manage labour. Projects are different. There you have an entirely different kind of work. One cannot miss those details, you know. It is good that you have come here, I must say. You are the first man to do so.'

The manager referred to the batch that the Project had recently sent back. To Kundan's surprise, he remembered everything. Kundan's heart missed a beat when he heard that the prisoners were now in the jail administered by the prison manager.

'Could you permit me to meet them?' he could not help asking.

'What would you like, tea or coffee?' the manager asked in reply.

'I'll have tea.'

While they waited for the tea to arrive, the manager spoke at length about tea and coffee and how differently they affected the human body. Kundan watched the tender tea plants sprouting from the manager's mouth, the shoots growing taller and producing two leaves and a bud. (The officer's brother was, incidentally, the manager of a tea plantation in the hills). The workers nipped them and put them in their baskets, took them to the factories, and after drying and processing them, packed them neatly. From the packets, they fell into the boiling water in pots and kettles. The brewed tea then passed through the alimentary canals of millions of tea-drinkers and corroded their insides. Nevertheless, Kundan and the manager sipped the beverage with relish forgetting the history behind it.

'Look here, Kundan,' the manager, rejuvenated by the tea and the friendship he had struck up with Kundan during the last few minutes, resumed the conversation, 'our duty is to make the maximum use of manpower. Even if the project is a highly sensitive one, we will not clear the people who have returned from it immediately if the experience they gathered can be utilized advantageously elsewhere. Yes, the security rules do insist that the prisoners returned from sensitive projects should be cleared immediately. But every rule has an exception, hasn't it? The Sarkar's needs come first. If it is in the interest of the Sarkar to insert a man's neck into the noose, it will be inserted, however innocent he may be. If it is not, we may pull even a hardened criminal out of the gallows.'

Every time the manager used the word 'clear', Kundan felt a stab in his heart.

'Do you send only prisoners condemned to death to work in projects?' he asked the manager to change the subject.

'If your work is not of a sensitive nature, you can certainly take other prisoners too.' The manager had assumed that Kundan had come to select another batch of prisoners. 'We are even prepared to send undertrials if you are willing to take them. If you ask me, you will find highly efficient workers among them. All types: doctors, engineers, executives, teachers, even lawyers. You can even use them as officers. They have been picked up from all kinds of places: markets, cinema theatres, railway stations, streets or even their own houses. They are like you and me. The only difference is that they are inside and we are outside. Coming to think of it, the next time you go to the market with your wife to buy a sari for her, they might even pick you up, or even me for that matter. Ha ha!'

The mellowed old man seemed to be enjoying his own joke like a child. Kundan did not relish it.

Jokes were shedding their colourful wings and falling to the ground, reverting to caterpillars with big eyes, grotesque feelers and disgustingly fleshy bodies. They were on their slow grinding journeys exposed to predators of all kinds ready to pick them up and fly away.

A brigadier had made some obscene gestures at him, making fun of his job as a labour officer. Then a security officer had knocked out his tooth and complained that it was making the floor of his office dirty. Today, a ruffian on the road had tripped him. Kundan wondered whether the manager of prisons too had something up his sleeve for him.

'Let us come back to the topic,' the manager cut short his jokes and suddenly became serious. 'Of course, there are all kinds of prisoners here in the jail. Hardened criminals, small-time mischief makers, undertrials, suspects and a few who are completely innocent. Depending on the security classification of the work, you can employ these people anywhere. Labour officers who do not know these things keep indenting only the convicts on death row.'

'Arresting innocent people and forcing them to work on top of it—isn't it rather unreasonable?' Kundan used the word 'unreasonable' instead of 'unjust'.

'You see, my dear labour officer, to a labour officer, a worker for whom he places an indent is only a worker. The indent he signs shows only the type of work he has at hand. A jailer does not ask for what crime or how a man is brought here. He is just a keeper. His job is to see that the prisoner does not escape. To escape from jail is a crime even for innocent people. Besides, think of the policemen . . .'

The manager seemed to be enjoying his lecture. After

all, it was his subject. He knew everything about it—and also liked to show off what he knew.

'You see, the policeman's world is the underworld, a closed world where they live in the midst of crime and criminals. When you read in today's papers that the police have failed to arrest anyone for a crime that took place yesterday, you remark in disgust: what useless fellows these policemen are! People expect policemen to work like machines. Under pressure, the helpless fellows often take the son, wife or mother of a criminal into custody to flush him out. Once in a while, they pick up somebody from the streets to extract something out of him. The policemen are poor too, earning not more than what a peon does. There is a price for everyone's freedom. In a sense, you should rejoice that it does not come to you free and that it has a price. Now, if you want someone who is creating trouble for you to be put in his place, what do you do? You grease a policeman's palms and he does the job for you. Suppose you have some information with you that the Sarkar does not want to be revealed to the public. Isn't the Sarkar obliged to protect its interests? It can protect them only by protecting you, perhaps in the safety of a jail. Knowledge is not power in our society. It is a risk. Wherever we start, or however we start, we all get involved in these things as one link passes on to another. That is how we all identify ourselves with the Sarkar ultimately!'

The manager was once again in the mood for joking. The caterpillar had again grown wings. But Kundan could not see those colourful wings. What he saw instead was the huge worm with large eyes disproportionate to its body and long feelers pretending to be flying. After some time the caterpillar suddenly crashed to the ground. Crawling tortuously across the ground, lowering its eyes and freezing its feelers, the helpless creature muttered:

'Look here, Mr Kundan, I know nobody enjoys these things. I was trying to tell you how we, you and I, are helpless in these matters. We move with downcast eyes and folded arms like prisoners of war, along the path of our duty. It is our duty that defeats us. What does a man laugh at, if not at his own defeat and helplessness? But then, even the Sarkar is not spared this defeat and helplessness. What other consolation is there for a tormented man than to realize that God himself is helpless? Let us conjure up some formula like: Help God to get sufficient strength to help you!'

He leaned forward, supported himself with his elbows pressed against the table and continued in a low voice: 'Pardon me if it seems hallucinatory and nonsensical. Some time ago, the Sarkar in a highly risky operation, laid siege to a place where some hostile elements were holed up. The whole lot surrendered in the end. I was then the jailer of a jail inside a fort. A group of people, including old men, women and children, were brought to my jail that night. Obviously not all of them were terrorists. But the Sarkar had no means to screen them and so no charges were brought against any of them. All I got that night was a register with numbers, but no names. I accepted the prisoners and I think anyone in my place should have done the same. Only people like us can understand the helplessness of the Sarkar in such situations. If, after the passing of several years, these people are still held in the prison, I can understand the helplessness of the Sarkar in that too. For, after the lapse of such a long time, there are now certain grounds for not releasing them. If they are let out today, every one of them will be a potential risk to society. They may take their revenge on anybody, people not even remotely connected with their case. If after all these years, these people are brought to me today, I would not hesitate to accept them with just the numbers in the register. They cannot be let out now, and I wouldn't even utter a word if they are to be disposed off in the middle of the night under the pretext of some jailbreak or the like.

Such a course of action is necessary for the security of our society. History can wait. Fair play may hang fire. What is expedient is always the right thing. And let me tell you, that is what every Sarkar does—nothing but that. I will not blame it for that. No, never.'

Sometime in the midst of the harangue, he stood up, pressed his palms on the table and brought his face menacingly near Kundan's. His voice was rising and he was swaying from side to side like a man possessed. Like an epileptic, his face had got contorted. Kundan saw the caterpillar again—its huge eyes, the lengthening feelers, its massive fleshy body. A gigantic caterpillar, helpless and frightened of a predator that might swoop down from the sky any moment to pick it up . . .

Kundan wondered what really frightened him—the caterpillar's massive body, or its avowed helplessness. Weakness could be as frightening as strength, and helplessness as alarming as ferocity.

Chapter Forty-Three

There was no visible order or pattern. Some were hanging upside down, some by their necks. Saliva, mucus, bile and undigested food particles oozed from the mouths and nostrils of those who hung upside down. Those hanging by their necks convulsed violently; there was the all-pervading smell of urine, excreta and semen. Men, women and children, their naked bodies grotesque in the pale twilight, dishevelled hair swinging, fingers wriggling like worms . . .

Workers, artisans, architects, lawyers, scientists, soldiers, artists, prostitutes, pimps . . . all in a crowd with spouses and progeny . . . humble, meek lumps of flesh . . . surrendering and forfeiting everything . . . hiding nothing and spewing out everything they had eaten, produced or processed.

Dazed, Kundan stared at the array of human figures hung up by invisible hooks and ropes. One of the dangling arms could reach out and grab him . . . Kundan shrank back in terror. Then it occurred to him that the hanging bodies were like temple bells, oscillating and striking against one another, but instead of producing resounding rings, they emitted agonized groans and grunts. To which god was the temple dedicated? But Kundan was not looking for a god on a pedestal. He was in search of a heretic, whom the bizarre human bells and their eerie music reminded him of—a professor who had taught him at the University.

Chapter Forty-Four

An unusual tension seemed to have gripped the city. Small crowds collected spontaneously and police vans patrolled the streets. A few small processions passed down the road.

A large mob had assembled before the largest hospital in the city. Hovering over the crowd were a number of vultures which had made the high roof of the building their perch. Though not quite uncommon, the sight was frightening.

Like the hospital taken over by vultures, the sky over the city was occupied by swarms of flies. Kundan tried to shoo them away. But the more he tried, the more they pestered him.

Dead leaves from the trees that lined the road had formed a carpet which lay undisturbed as the traffic had thinned out. An occasional bus carried a bunch of leaves to some distance, and another one going in the opposite direction brought them back to their original position. Kundan did not know why such trifling things, which would have gone unnoticed on any other day, caught his attention and disturbed him.

The plaza was still bustling with shopping crowds and seemed unaffected by the tension in the city. Men and women walked hand in hand in a festive mood carrying large shopping bags with the names of the stores inscribed on them. Their slightly parted red lips, wandering eyes and playful gait, the tunes they hummed as they walked, betrayed satisfaction and assurance at the same time. For a moment Kundan relieved the shoppers of the bags they carried, stripped them of their clothes and hung them upside down. They began to groan and grit their teeth and discharge saliva, mucus and bile from their mouths and nostrils. Kundan hastily untied the ropes, put them back on their feet and clothed them again. He applied lipstick and rouge on their lips and cheeks and sprayed them with perfumes and put the shopping bags back in their hands . . . They started humming tunes again.

A stereo cassette player suddenly started blaring from one of the shops in the plaza. But a band that came along the road killed it.

*

Every city has a music of its own—muffled voices from houses, the cacophony of markets and the cadences of the spoken language evolve a distinct rhythm and melody. They are supplemented by a number of other notes and overtones—the affinity or revulsion of a city towards silence, the pitch and volume of bells and organs ringing in its places of worship, the din made by its crowds, the creaking of footwear as its inhabitants walk, the sounds they make when they cry, laugh, make love or kill, or when hung upside down . . .

Different societies have different kinds of music, and the same society may have different kinds of music at different times—this was how the professor once began his class. He was known in intellectual circles as a liberal and a maverick rolled into one. He had a number of theories to his credit. One of them was about the negative functions of the arts. The systems of music and dances adopted by each society form the core of its identity and together they give an insight into its character. But they are also a measure of its capacity to accommodate and its readiness to compromise. Each form of art has a rhythm. But rhythm is not just a harmonious blending of rising and falling notes. It is also a way to facilitate the co-existence of the ethical with the unethical. Right and wrong, good and evil merge into one in it. Therefore art forms have a way of going beyond aesthetics to promote the assimilation of selfishness, cruelty and exploitation, everything which the conscientious individual finds repugnant, into the social fabric. The roots of Kathak and Bharatnatyam are found in abominable social practices like prostitution. In the harmony of their nimble movements, captivating rhythms and melting notes were drowned the tempests that raged in the souls of innumerable helpless women and the silent agonies they put up with. In fact, the kind of dances and music which exist at a particular point of time in a society are indications of the level of its cultural decadence and its capacity to assimilate evil and injustice.

*

Shopkeepers suddenly began pulling down their shutters. The shopping crowd clutched at the things in their hands and ran for cover or for any vehicle they could get into.

*

'As the island of knowledge grows larger, the shoreline of wonder stretches farther.' The axiom which Ruth loved to quote frequently was the caption of a beautiful landscape hanging on one of the walls of the visitors' room in the professor's house. The room also had a few other curios worth looking at—a Buddha in meditation, a Nataraja in his cosmic dance and the Trinity of creation, preservation and destruction.

In the sprawling and well-guarded enclave of bureaucrats, in the presence of the Buddha, Nataraja and the Trinity, Kundan stood on the thick carpet trying to cope with the situation he found himself in. When he started on his search, he only had the address of the heretic professor with him. He had no idea that it would lead him right into the sanctum sanctorum. The professor had taken over as one of the advisers to the government. Of course, it was too much to expect him to remain a professor perennially and flutter his wings and fly unencumbered in the ethereal firmament of the university.

How could he tell the adviser to the Sarkar the tales he had brought with him? On the other hand, who could be a better person for narrating them to than the adviser to the Sarkar? Only he would understand them. But the real problem lay elsewhere. The professor no more had the time to sit and chat with his students. Perhaps he would be too busy even to give Kundan an appointment.

The professor had gone to the secretariat to attend a meeting of the cabinet which had been summoned on short notice. Nobody knew when he would return. The explanation of his secretary did not satisfy the visitors who had taken their appointments. But that did not seem to disturb the secretary who was more worried about the emergency that had developed in the country.

Kundan gathered courage to ask the man who stood next to him what the emergency was about. 'Anything may happen, my friend, anything,' the man replied, throwing up his arms. 'Even a spell of military rule. Don't you know that a minister was assassinated in the morning? Only a miracle can save the government from falling now. It has to be seen whether the cabinet will resign or decide to act resolutely.'

Suddenly realizing that he had spoken too much to a stranger, the man pursed his lips and peered curiously at Kundan, surveying his dirty clothes and unshaven cheeks. 'Who are you?' he asked Kundan after a pause. 'I was a student of the professor,' Kundan replied with exaggerated humility.

'You mean to say you want to meet him today? Oh my goodness! What a day you have chosen for a professor-student discussion!' 'That is for him to decide. Is it not?' Kundan sat back in the cushioned seat and thought back.

'Like in any other science, in sociology too we have to use the tools of reason and observation. But there is a vital difference'—the professor was launching into his first lecture, introducing the subject he was going to teach.

'The physical sciences study nature which created *us*, while the social sciences study society which *we* created. The laws of nature which the physical sciences seek to unravel can claim a kind of immutability. But in the social sciences, the laws keep changing all the time. Again, in the physical sciences, laws are discovered, while they are discovered as well as invented in the social sciences. What we call theories and ideologies are so mixed up. This makes our science vulnerable to manipulation. Objectivity runs into subjectivity, the "real" gets buried in the "ideal" or "what should be". Believe me, I am leading you into the labyrinths of a treacherous science. Let me warn you, your inquiry is likely to stray away from reality to hyperbole. In physical sciences, they use instruments, machines and chemicals in their experiments. But what do we have in our science? Words! In social sciences, it is the word that assumes tremendous power and becomes a force by itself. Words mean literature, imagination, fantasy. Sociology is, therefore, a subject in which, as in music or dance, a rhythm can be created to absorb and accommodate all kinds of inhuman practices. Revolutionaries fired with the ideals of truth and justice co-exist here with despots who thrive on repression and absolute power. Besides, a revolutionary can easily transform himself into a despot, and a despot can effortlessly don the mantle of a revolutionary . . .'

The professor's voice rose and fell. His arms undulated like the waves of the sea. He made rapid strides to and fro across the classroom. The students in the first year, listening to his lecture, sat stunned . . .

'As the island of knowledge grows larger . . .' the landscape on the wall warned. The Buddha continued to meditate and the Nataraja remained frozen in his cosmic dance.

What had happened to the professor who used to be such an iconoclastic intellectual?

It suddenly occurred to Kundan that the professor would not discuss with him the things he had thought of revealing to him. He may not agree to meet him. He may not even recognize him. Perhaps he would not return home from the cabinet meeting. The night will advance, the waiting visitors will get tired, go to sleep, die, turn to dust. But he will not come back. He was on a journey without return.

A government's fate hung in the balance. A minister's dead body lay in a hospital. People hurried back home.

A swarm of human bodies swung and collided and clanged like temple bells around Kundan. Their rhythmless clanging absorbed or accommodated nothing. They were just naked and hollow bodies, emptied of even their entrails . . .

Kundan rose and walked slowly out of the professor's bungalow.

Chapter Forty-Five

Kundan lay in his bed in the hotel room, too exhausted to go over all that had happened. He was mortified to find himself at a loss as to the next course of action.

The room was on the fourth floor and tall buildings of concrete or stone surrounding the hotel obstructed his view. The slit of sky visible through the narrow vista between the two buildings had turned a dull grey in the lights of the city.

An emptiness was taking over him, making the crowd, the rush and din around him a distant reality. It seemed ages since he had communicated with anyone. Dozing off, he saw the professor stepping in slowly and softly like a friendly spirit, into the vacuum that bridged the desert and the city in his mind.

They were sitting in the lawns of one of the sprawling gardens of the city built around an ancient monument. The silence around them was punctuated only by the chirping of the birds which felt bold enough to express themselves. Kundan was not sure whether it was morning or evening. It was space, not time that mattered. The spacious, undulating lawns, the huge trees which seemed to be brushing against one another high up in the sky, the imposing structures with their painted Gothic arches and vaults co-existing with Islamic round domes . . .

'Do you know why I brought you here?' the professor turned to Kundan. 'Look at these huge monuments, tombs of sultans, noblemen or saints. They were erected in memory of the deceased. But these magnificent monuments, instead of perpetuating their memory, merely attract the visitors with their architectural beauty, and overwhelm them with their sheer size. They forget to ask who lies underneath these tombs. When you erect a tomb, you bury not only the dead man, but also his memory! Later, the fact that it is a tomb too is laid to rest. Look at what we have done here. We have built a beautiful garden around the monument with shady trees, flowering plants, lawns and pathways. Children come to play on the lawns, lovesick couples seek solace in each other under the trees, old men go jogging. Even dogs enjoy their twilight freedom, having been freed from their leashes. We go on burying one thing under another. Man's mind is a playing field of ideas, emotions, fancies and prejudices. All sincere and fervent, but each capable of cancelling out the other. Our ancestors refined this principle of cancellation to such an extent that they ultimately proved that man himself did not exist! They turned everything into maya and buried all realities under it. Then, to demonstrate the unreality of reality, they turned to miracles. They made slaves fight one another for their masters' causes. They made wretched, starving people lynch each other in the name of their gods. They prostituted women by calling them the brides of god.

'Of course, today we don't go to that extent. Politics is different from religion. It is not our aim to lead the whole population to moksha. We only try to solve their immediate, mundane problems, problems which make them restive. For example, I can see that something is bothering you now. That means I should try to solve the problem. But mind you, I am not going to find out its cause. That is none of my business. Suffering has no scientific basis. It is only a way your mind has interpreted a situation. So, if we can get hold of that particular program of your mind which interprets objects and situations and bring it under our control, we can wipe off the tears from your eyes and make you smile again. We can even transform your life without making any change in your material conditions. This is what we call, in our terminology, the Principle of Banishing Suffering by the Comparative Method.

'The first step in the application of this principle is to identify the problems. The multiplicity of problems does not worry us. In fact, the more they are, the better. Our choice increases to that extent, and also our freedom to play with them. The problems divide society into various groups or sections. If there are more problems, there will be more sections. Each section is preoccupied with its own difficulties. It insulates itself from the others and clashes with them under the impression that they are obstacles in its path. So the more the problems, the less the chances of a united struggle against the State for justice. Can you now see the advantage of having a multiplicity of problems? All we have to do is to prevent the anxieties of the people from being posed together. Always keep them in separate watertight compartments. This is the crux of our theory. Now let us go to its application.

'In our science, there are two types of solutions for a problem, the short-term solution and the long-term solution. The short-term solution never solves the problem. Instead, it merely plays with it. When we have cut society into a number of sections and put them into disparate compartments, they have already become our prisoners. The reins are now in our hands. The guiding principle is that the claims of each section come into conflict with those of others. When the rights of tribals come up, push the rights of the industrial workers to the forefront. Similarly, when the rights of women or workers come up, invoke the rights of the minorities. Put each problem in its place carefully and keep yourself out of them, remaining detached like a saint. You will be surprised to see the miseries associated with them evaporating in a moment. They transform themselves into pleasurable exhilarating experiences. Carrying their erstwhile miseries on their heads like trophies, they will merrily beat their drums, set fire to the houses of their neighbours and dance around the flames.

'Sometimes, it becomes necessary to shift the workers from their cells and redistribute them, or to evacuate the cells for women, divide them up and send the groups to the cells earmarked for various religions. This task of redistribution is not as difficult as it appears to be. You may not have to use a whip, or even shout at them, as they used to do in the days of slavery. You have only got to open the cells and announce the problems. You will see them picking up their bags and sheets and pots and moving on their own to the new cells. All you have got to do is to say the right thing at the right time and place. That is the art.

'Now the long-term solution. Here our aim is to reduce all social problems into mere individual ones. As in the short-term solution, here too we have to deal with various sections, but with a difference. In this case, we progress in a linear direction, not laterally. We have to proceed systematically, slowly, step by step and stick to the rules. First, pick up the most serious problem and the section representing it. Push all others to the background. Then split the section into a number of sub-sections and select the most important among them. Push the other sub-sections to the background. As you continue the process, the groups become smaller and smaller. You will ultimately reach the small components of families and individuals. Now we have stripped the problems of all their social garbs and reduced them to the vulgar and shameful level of individual concerns. Then comes the moment to turn around and throw this simple question dramatically in their faces: "What are these personal problems when compared with the interests of the country? You should understand that the country is large and great, while you are small and insignificant. When a giant tree falls, the earth shakes. Do you then worry about the blades of grass that are crushed under it?" With this question you have reversed the process you have so far been following, in one stroke. Tearing them away from their serious problems you showed them their irrelevance and helplessness. Then you pluck them from their lowly moorings and throw them back into the monumental issues. But while doing it, you don't let them perish. You don't leave them to fend for themselves. You are compassionate. Even if they are totally insignificant when compared with the country, you are sympathetic towards them. You come out with a number of welfare schemes which give relief to their individual sufferings. You carry relief to their doorsteps, offer them interest-free loans. The doctor in you with the healing touch will never be missed. The packets of food, water, shelter, blankets, medicines and compassion are always ready for those tormented by drought, famine, floods, war, strikes and riots . . .'

The professor's voice faded away. Kundan saw time returning and space receding to the background. It was getting dark. The chill in the air pricked him like pins. The descending mist was burying not only the dead, their tombs and the ancient monuments, but also the garden where they lay.

Like a ghost disappearing into the netherworld at the crack of dawn, the professor turned and spoke to Kundan again: 'There used to be a girl with you. What was her name? Ah, Ruth. Where is she now?'

'She is in the desert. She is trying to break the rhythm of music and dance which conceals all incompatibles. She is trying to find out how deserts are made.'

'Why have you left the desert?'

'I haven't. I am still in a desert.'

Even after the professor's voice trailed off, even after his face dissolved into thin air, his smile lingered in the air, like that of the Cheshire cat. It floated around in the air and stamped itself on everything it struck; walls, tables, chairs, the tired night, the coming dawn, towns and cities . . .

Kundan sat up on the bed. Loud arguments and voices shouting aloud were heard from the street. Kundan went to the window and looked down.

The noises came from a distance. In the dim light nothing was clear except the outlines of some figures moving in groups in the street. The commotion had brought several people to the doors and windows of their apartments and houses. But nobody dared to venture into the street to investigate.

Then a sudden scream pierced the air. It was so loud that Kundan was startled even though he was too far away to make out where it came from. The few people who had come down into the street quickly retreated inside. Doors were slammed. Then a bomb went off. There were more screams which stifled all other sounds. Kundan hastily put on his coat, closed the door behind him and ran down the stairs. Not bothering to see whether there were others like him going down, Kundan ran in the direction from which he judged he had heard the explosion.

In the street Kundan got a clearer picture of what was happening. A couple of shops were burning. Two men, bathed in blood, lay in the middle of the road. The assailants, about a dozen men in all, armed with sticks and knives, were running away after finishing their work. Kundan could see some of their faces clearly. To his surprise, they seemed familiar to him. They too must have recognized him, for they tried to cover their faces with their hands as they fled.

One of the assailants who was wounded fell to the ground while running. His companions did not stop to pick him up. They ran towards a lorry waiting at the corner. The driver started the engine as soon as they scrambled in. The lorry raced down the road and disappeared from view.

Trying to figure out the situation, Kundan stood between the groaning victims lying in a pool of blood and their assailant who had also fallen to the ground. When he recovered from the shock, he had no doubt that the assailants were convicts, the same convicts whom he had identified and taken charge of and who had been sent back from the Project only a few days ago. They were to be hanged after their return from the Project. Evidently the jailer had not cleared' them yet. Had they broken out of the jail to settle some old scores?

Kundan approached the assailant lying on the ground. The man was unconscious. He had been stabbed in his stomach. Kundan recognized him instantly. He could even remember his name. As he bent to have a better look at the convict, a jeep suddenly pulled up near him. Two men jumped out of it, pushed Kundan aside, lifted the unconscious assailant and put him into the jeep. The jeep then disappeared into the distance.

Chapter Forty-Six

Sitting across the table, Kundan argued his case with the prison manager. He had no doubt, he told the manager, about the identity of the assailants. He had called their names and identified them before inducting them into the Project. They had been in the rolls for six months after that. The manager, however, showed no interest in the topic. The man who had waxed eloquent about the prisoners and their role in society the previous day was strangely silent. His eyes refused to leave the file before him on the table.

'Surely there was a jailbreak last night, if not earlier. I am quite certain, sir. Why don't you check up with the warders?' Exasperated, Kundan raised his voice.

'Don't get excited,' the manager raised his eyes at last. 'A jailbreak is not a joke. If there had been anything like that, it would have appeared in the morning papers.'

'That is very funny! A prison manager learning about a jailbreak from the papers!'

'It is no use quibbling with me, mister. The truth is that there has been no jailbreak. No prisoner has escaped from any of the jails here. You have to believe me. Besides, you should remember that spreading baseless rumours is a crime, especially when the city has been gripped by violence and tension.'

'I am telling you what I saw with my own eyes. I think is my duty to report it here—especially, as you say, when the city has been gripped by violence and tension.'

'All right, you have done your duty. Now, will you please clear out of here?'

Kundan realized that he was banging his head against a stone wall. But why was the manager stoutly denying everything without even bothering to check up with the warders or the other officials who were in charge of the prisons? Kundan had experienced it everywhere he went: flat denials, orders to get out and not show his face anymore, to pick up his dirty tooth . . .

Kundan glanced at the manager's hands on the table. The thick stumpy fingers were twitching involuntarily; certain things had slipped through them, but they had closed ranks quickly before more damage was done. Either the man was afraid of being held responsible for what had happened, or he was clearly an accomplice.

The real shock came to Kundan when he emerged from the building. One of the vehicles parked outside was the jeep that had picked up the wounded assailant after his associates had left him on the road and escaped. Kundan recognized the colour, shape and the crack on the windshield.

He was at a loss now. He could tell the story to the people in the street, or to the editor of a newspaper, but none of them would believe him because he had no evidence to prove it. But what use was evidence? It was not the lack of evidence, but the very idea of it that was being challenged here.

The city welcomed him with a strange spectacle. The entire three hundred and sixty degrees of its horizon was marked with dark columns of smoke. The dull sky which used to lie languorously over the spectres of the tall buildings suddenly sprang to life. Spirals of smoke were rising up everywhere, dwarfing everything that stood high and drawing a completely new skyline.

People were running in all directions. Kundan's attempts to stop them did not succeed. The only thing he could elicit from them was that marauders had attacked several parts of the city the previous night. This, along with the assassination of the minister, had sparked off riots and arson in the city. The violent, noisy processions which continued the whole day, the shops which were being closed even before the end of the afternoon, the late-night cabinet meeting, the provocative attacks at midnight—things were becoming clearer to Kundan now. The prisoners would not be 'cleared' if they could be utilized for any other work, the prison manager had said. The Principle of Banishing Suffering by the Comparative Method, which the professor had explained in detail, was at work. Kundan was gripped by a sudden spell of dismay and desperation. Knowledge, wisdom and reason were all turning to garbage before his eyes. Holding up the precious mirror of reason, he had knocked at many doors. But nobody had cared to look into it. Instead they had conspired to set themselves up as the arbitrators, unawares to Kundan, in this city which was burning.

It was Sulaiman, being used by a ruthless conspirator, who had first dropped a stone into the tranquillity of his mind. Later a group of convicts who were being used for the construction of a secret project had destroyed his peace of mind. On top of it had come Ruth's revelation that the Project itself was a sham. Now, terribly alone in a burning city, Kundan could not think of anyone who was not being used or manipulated.

For a moment it seemed to him that he understood everything. The next moment everything disappeared in a haze.

Chapter Forty-Seven

One of the things that primitive man was most obsessed with was the sound of approaching footsteps. He must have learned to recognize perfectly the animals and even the human beings following him by the sound of their footsteps. The steps told him whether it was a friend or foe, a thief or a lover. If it was an enemy, he had to decide whether to take flight or fight.

Each footstep he heard made Kundan breathless. He had no way of distinguishing one from the other as primitive man had. They were all mere footsteps to him. The security provided by society had removed that capacity for instant recognition from modern man. And in situations like the one Kundan found himself in now, his condition was worse than that of primitive man. It was difficult to accept that things like society or civilization were mere fancies now. But there was little time even to reflect on such things.

Kundan could still see the body lying in the middle of the road—if he was willing to crane his neck a little from behind the wall. Though he was taking a risk, Kundan kept sticking out his neck, less out of curiosity than out of a moral obligation or a sense of guilt. The dead man too had been frightened by the sound of the footsteps that had followed him. He was walking alone when he heard the footsteps behind him. He had tried to walk faster, and then broken into a run. The men who were following him too had broken into a run. When they closed in on him, they had pulled out their knives and stabbed him repeatedly. He fell to the ground screaming. Kundan was stunned. All he could remember afterwards was that he had run at a furious pace. When he came to his senses, he was standing in the narrow gap between two buildings. He had no idea how long he had been standing there. He was still gasping for breath.

A group of rioters passed along the street. They carried sticks and burning torches with them. One of them had a drum hanging from his neck by a band. He beat the drum and his companions sang and danced. The bloodstains on their clothes made the whole show look like a Holi procession.

The procession disappeared into the distance and silence descended on the street again. Like the roads, the houses on either side of them wore a deserted look.

Kundan turned around and surveyed the place where he stood. Rotten foodstuff, feathers, legs and heads of chickens, broken bottles, used sanitary napkins and condoms—whatever the people living in the eight floors of the building on either side thought they no longer needed had been deposited in the open space, three feet wide, which the municipal laws insisted was to be kept between the buildings. Now dead bodies could also be dumped there if necessary.

Suddenly the sound of a deafening explosion came from one of the buildings. Some shards of glass and a whole human arm landed in front of Kundan. He leaped into the air in horror and ran out into the street.

This time he ended up in a relatively better spot. The gap between the buildings was wider now, and there was not much garbage around. He stood in front of a spiral staircase which connected the rear sides of the different floors of a tall building. In desperation, Kundan went up the staircase. At every floor, the door which opened into the staircase was bolted from inside. He came down the winding cast-iron steps which unfolded under his feet like the leaves of a Japanese fan. During the process he was greeted by a sporadic clanging of pots and pans, the gurgling of running water and the smell of soap, or of pulses cooking in a kitchen. He was grazing at the peripheries of human life without being able to enter it. Exhausted and in despair, he hung on to one of the steps fanning off from the central post of the staircase.

High pitched shouts woke him up. This time they came from a house across the road. Carrying sticks and torches, a number of people were converging on it. A vehicle filled with jerrycans pulled up before the group. The rioters were fully armed and ready for action on the road while a family, helpless and beleaguered, crouched in terror inside the house.

Nobody from the houses nearby came out to help them. The reality of society appeared to have become reduced to the mere clanging of pots and pans, the gurgling of running water and the smell of soap or pulses cooking in a kitchen.

The rioters were asking the men to come out. They threatened to set fire to the house if they did not. The situation inside was not difficult to visualize. The men getting ready to go out and sacrifice themselves for the others, the women pulling them back and pleading that they would die with them, children hiding under bedsteads and behind doors and shelves, screaming invocations to God, and ultimately, the whole lot of them, fathers, mothers, husbands, wives, brothers, sisters and children clinging to one another to make a solid, human mass.

No one came out of the beleaguered house, neither the men nor the women. Invoking their gods, and to the accompaniment of deafening shouts and beating of drums, the rioters broke open the front door of the house and rushed inside. The screams of the people inside were drowned in the clamour. What followed was a drill which the rioters appeared to have perfected by repeated practice during the course of the day. The male members of the family were dragged out one by one from the building. The rioters split themselves into small groups, each dealing with one victim. With the swiftness and efficiency of soldiers, they threw the victims on the ground, clubbed them with sticks, poured kerosene over their bodies and torched them. The victims wriggled and convulsed for some time and then quietly settled down for a crude cremation, without the luxury of firewood.

When it appeared that the rioters had finished their job, one of them came out of the building jubilantly holding a boy of six or seven years over his head. In a fit of celebration, they surrounded him. This time they did not follow the standard drill. One of them opened the boy's mouth with his hands, while another poured kerosene into it. A third struck a match and lighted the boy like a torch. The boy ran for a few feet like a burning matchstick and then collapsed. As the women ran after the boy, wailing and beating their chests, the rioters moved on, shouting victory to their gods and their leaders.

When everything was over and only the spectacle of burning bodies and wailing women remained on the road, windows and doors of the houses started opening one after the other. Faces and human figures appeared in those rectangles like framed pictures. Kundan had never in his life hated anybody as he did these people who stood at the doors and windows. But then, he too was one of them.

Kundan climbed down the stairs and emerged on to the road. He walked along the middle of the deserted road. The footsteps approaching menacingly, the drums and the shouts and the invocation to gods did not frighten him now. Fear had died in him.

Kundan saw the ravages of the riot everywhere. Buildings were burning. Half-burned human bodies were smouldering. From an upturned car came the feeble groan of a man and a stream of blood. The flames from a burning fuel station made a furnace of the road. Two naked bodies, one of a man and the other of a woman, lay on the road. The genitals of the man had been cut off and placed on the woman's face.

At the head of the road, Kundan saw a small group of people who were watching a dump of human bodies, partly burned or badly mutilated. None of the onlookers said anything. They were just watching the scene. Kundan wondered what those strange twists and furrows on their faces meant. It could not be shock, distress or disgust, he was certain. Why did they come out to witness the last scene of the ghastly drama? As Kundan stared at the crowd, it suddenly dawned on him like a revelation. They were experiencing a strange sense of satisfaction. Not the satisfaction that some men, women and children were dead. No, they had nothing against the victims. It was the satisfaction that they themselves were not dead, that they had survived the holocaust. Yes, it was the gratification of survival, plain survival. The desire to survive at any cost that had prompted them to remain in their houses with the doors tightly shut while their neighbours were being butchered. It was the same desire for survival that had made the custodians of law, the jailers, the prisoners who willingly agreed to play the role of pawns, the labour officers and the self-proclaimed intellectuals look the other way when less fortunate human beings were done to death. It was the same desire for survival that sucked out all moisture and spread the desert sands into every individual, making him turn shamelessly and helplessly into himself.

A few steps ahead, Kundan saw another body with a deep gash on its neck. It was a man of middle age. The trousers the man wore and the soil around were soaked in blood. A handkerchief with a knot, which he must have taken out of his pocket just before he was attacked, was still clutched in his right hand. What did he want to remind himself of when he tied the knot on the handkerchief? Something he had promised to buy his child? To buy a kilogram of oil at the market? Or to tell an interesting piece of news to his wife on reaching home? Whatever it had been, it had already turned into plain carbon and hydrogen in his brain. No one could decipher it now. But the knot on the handkerchief had survived! Kundan saw the handkerchief turning into a human face and the knot into a pair of crooked lips grinning at all those who had survived the riots.

Chapter Forty-Eight

Kundan could not take his eyes off the thing. Not that he was surprised to see it there, for he had identified the prisoners who were involved in the attack. It was only natural that one of them had dropped something that belonged to him. The problem was how this piece of evidence was going to help him, and how futile that too might turn out to be. A sense of futility was creeping into him as he sat looking at it like a child staring at a toy.

The curtain of darkness was coming down on an eventful day, a day which had seen the snuffing out of several lives and hundreds of innocent human beings flung into an uncertain future which was worse than death. Many others might have crossed the portals of sanity, never to return. Kundan could not recollect the faces of the victims whom he had seen lying on the road that day. There were too many to be remembered. He knew that the events of the day had transformed him completely. Yet the reluctance to accept that something had snapped in him took him to the scene of the previous day's violence. There was no point in looking for evidence in a world where reason had no place in the scheme of things and everything was done in cold blood. But a sense of guilt, which he could not shake off, drew him to the corner of the street where the gruesome murder had been enacted. Those prisoners had been under his charge, and he too had used them for work, which, though he did not know it then, was not only inhuman, but also fraudulent. The reward they got for that was an extended lease of life. What had the Sarkar offered them for the task they had just accomplished? A ticket to life from certain death?

As he walked up to the corner, half in a trance, Kundan found what he was looking for—a prisoner's brass badge with a number engraved on it. It had been lying on the road with the sun shining on it. But the city had gone blind and it was left to Kundan to pick it up.

It was a strange equation: a poor, helpless Kundan against a huge, dumb city and a metal badge between the two.

Chapter Forty-Nine

The whole incident lasted less than an hour.

Kundan went into the office of the daily reputed for its bold and forthright views and its brilliant exposures and went directly to the cabin of its renowned editor. Sitting down in a chair across his desk, Kundan produced the metal badge from his pocket and placed it before the editor. He launched into his story without any preface. The editor listened with rapt attention, his eyes fixed on Kundan's face.

'You mean to say that some of those who provoked yesterday's riots were convicts on the death row?' the editor asked Kundan rhetorically when he had finished his account. 'Just as I suspected. It means that the Sarkar is directly involved. Wonderful! Nobody can reject the evidence you have produced.'

He picked up the metal badge and toyed with it, running his fingers on its smooth edges. He smiled at it like a doting grandfather smiling at his grandchild.

'I take all responsibility for this,' Kundan brought back the editor's attention from the badge. 'I am ready to testify as a witness and face the consequences.'

'You have certainly surpassed any investigative journalist in your remarkable feat!' the editor beamed at Kundan.

'It is not just the riots, sir,' Kundan continued, encouraged by the wholesome praise. 'I was at the defence project at Rambhagarh for some time. I can prove that the whole project is a fraud. It is just a cover-up operation to bury the illegal transfer of huge amounts of public money into private hands. In fact, no defence installations are being built at the Project.'

'Extremely interesting! Wonderful, I should say. We would certainly carry the story. But, Mr Kundan, you should give me a few minutes. Let me call our political correspondent.'

As they waited for the political correspondent to arrive, they talked over a cup of tea about the political situation and about Kundan's background, interests and plans.

At last the correspondent arrived. But he had undergone a metamorphosis to become the prison manger Kundan had gone to see a few days before!

The prison manager was accompanied by a police officer and two armed guards who took up position on either side of Kundan. The manager lowered himself leisurely into a chair and turned to Kundan.

'From the first day you came to me, Mr Kundan, Mr Runaway-Labour-Officer, Mr What-not, I have been tightening the rope around you. While I played with the long rope I unwound, you thought you were being smart. Now you would like to organize a jailbreak, wouldn't you?'

'Yes, if that is how you want it.' Kundan to his own amazement was unruffled by the prison manager's truculent remarks. 'Yes, I thought I could organize a jailbreak and free the prisoners.' Kundan's eyes swept the faces of the prison manager, the police officer and the guards. 'But prisoners like you seem to enjoy your captivity. You have sold your souls to the sand.'

Both the manager and the editor ignored Kundan, like all those other officers who had chosen to ignore him ever since he joined the Project.

'Here is the report,' the manager handed the editor a folder. 'You can verify the photograph for yourself. He ran away from one of the most sensitive defence projects in the country with a set of classified documents. Our men have already traced out the foreign agencies which received them from him. I have not been idle during the last few days, you know.'

Kundan realized that it was not rage, but pity for this foolish old man that overwhelmed him. He should have known how ridiculous his assertions would sound to Kundan who was now his prisoner. Here was another Yogeshwar, a man who locked up a group of helpless old men, women and children, a mere cog in the wheel who got up in the middle of the night, and without even washing his face, took up a register to note down and strike off numbers and names, all for a miserly promotion which was by no means assured. He had had no qualms about letting loose a bunch of convicts on death row to plague the city. But he could show off his power only to his prisoners. It was his servitude, not his intelligence or efficiency, that his masters appreciated.

'Forgive me, Mr Kundan,' the editor turned to Kundan. 'The riots were, of course, terrible. Our paper has vividly and graphically brought out every detail about them. I am an inveterate critic of the Sarkar. But we never compromise on matters of security of the country. If there is no security, if our borders are not safe, what is the meaning of the word "freedom"? Of what use are our civic rights? What would our lives be worth?'

'Freedom sans security! Wah! What a wonderful headline for a spy story!' The prison manager was overwhelmed by the editor's turn of phrase.

But the editor did not seem to relish the effusive praise. 'Mr Manager, don't you ever dare to suggest headlines for our stories. Ours is not a government gazette.'

'Okay, okay. If you want to have the right to design

your headlines, have it your own way. We grant you that. But please don't claim that the stories you print are also your creations! That will get you into trouble.'

'I see. So you want to claim the fatherhood of all the news we gather.' The editor's face reddened, his lips quivered and his voice rose. 'All news is made by the people and we gather it. What the government mills churn out is not news, but the excrement of intoxicating power, monsters released to prey on the people!'

The manager remained calm but unrelenting. 'Come on, Mr Editor. Why news, even history is made by governments. Whatever happens is made to happen by the governments of the world. You newsmen are just a bunch of clerks who merely write about it!'

Kundan watched with horror as the hostilities between the press and the Sarkar escalated into a battle between the transitive verb and the intransitive verb, each side holding resolutely to its position without yielding an inch. If grammar was so intoxicating, who would care for human feelings, agony and suffering?

Grammar and rhetoric gushed forth from the eight columns of the newspapers before Kundan's eyes. Large captions covering three or four columns designed by the news editors dammed the flow and diverted it into channels to quench the thirst of the public.

Column after column, well lined and channelized, the turbulent and frothy stories of treason would now be carried featuring spies like Kundan, backed up by photocopies of documents (no longer classified!), relating to the Rambhagarh Defence Installations which were passed on to foreign governments, along with bold analyses of the midnight attacks by terrorists and militants which provoked the people to retaliate with riots. Rivers of transitives and intransitives, deluges of adjectives and adverbs . . .

Like two finite verbs, the guards who stood on either side of Kundan closed in on him and handcuffed him.

Kundan could not recollect afterwards how long his incarceration lasted. Perhaps only a year. For it was winter again when he came out, with the roads frozen stiff like the limbs of the dead, and the trees naked without their leaves.

Chapter Fifty

Things were coming full circle. The rules of acquisition and maintenance of prisoner assets which the prison manager had divulged to him, and the worldly wisdom he himself had acquired during the last few months, told Kundan that this was the end of everything. The prospects of him being sent to the Rambhagarh Project as a prisoner condemned to death for espionage, and of Jaswant, now promoted to the post of labour officer, identifying him and taking him over from the warder of the jail he was lodged in, now appeared to Kundan as a distinct possibility. Whatever lay in wait for him, it was a journey to be completed alone with no chance of protesting, not to speak of deliverance, without even an illusion of martyrdom to dream of. Compared to the total irrelevance he was reduced to, the torture and suffering that awaited him in his cell were inconsequential.

The jail was a massive stone structure built in a style which could be Greek, Roman, Gothic or Islamic, depending upon the taste of the observer. To Kundan it was a giant tomb in which memories of the past and hopes for the future were buried together. The prisoners were destined to live in a perpetual present.

The routine began for Kundan quite soon after entering the prison complex. After going through the processes of registration, photography, fingerprinting and recording of his height, weight and identification marks, he was led into a room which the guards called the 'games room'. It was a large room, big enough for indoor games or jogging. But it was a different game that Kundan had to submit himself to. Three of the guards fell upon him and began to kick him vigorously. For a moment, he could not make out what was happening. Then he realized that they were playing football with his body. The game went on for some time and the floor was soon wet and sticky with his blood. When the game ended, he found it difficult to identify the parts of his body which gave him pain.

The first day's torture was only a game. There was no interrogation accompanying it. But there were no games on the second day. Instead, a volley of questions, interspersed with bouts of filthy abuse, were hurled at him. Kundan did not have answers to any of the questions. He knew none of the people his interrogators asked him about. He had never heard of the places or events they described.

In spite of the rage on their faces, Kundan had a feeling that they were not serious about eliciting answers from him. Perhaps they were merely acting out a script they had written, or which had been given to them, a routine like the game of football the guards played with his body. What then was the torture for?

As the days passed, Kundan was able to figure out a rationale for the torture too. It was a punishment, part of the prison curriculum. The problem with him was that he insisted on a conventional reason for everything. For instance, that a trial had to precede punishment. Yet punishment came by itself. So did pain. What seemed unusual or objectionable to him was but common and natural. When a needle pierced the most sensitive parts of his body, when the burning end of a cigarette was applied to them, when he was lifted by his hair, when all these were done meticulously and systematically, he had groaned and screamed like anyone else in his place would have done. He was becoming a law-abiding citizen, one who abided by a code which violated all known laws.

If atrocities or mayhem of unparalleled degrees could be let loose on the innocent population of a city, why should he, who had at least been arrested and given a number and a uniform, seek reasons for his torture?

Rational minds should know that a big un-reason which neutralizes all reason lurks behind everything, under our chairs, below the bed and under our feet. Those who demand precision, wanting to measure everything to the millimetre and milligram should know that the ground on which they stand is floating on top of a huge mass of molten lava. Those who pin their hopes on revolutions and believe that history unfolds itself to the tune of certain pre-determined forces must not forget for a moment that they stand at the target-lines of warheads that can wipe them out along with their theories in a fraction of a second.

Once Kundan overheard an official giving instructions to the guards. In fact, Kundan did not overhear it. He just happened to be present at the scene. The prison officials never hesitated to give instructions to the guards about the treatment to be given to the prisoners when the prisoners themselves were present. 'You need not have scruples of any kind when you deal with this stuff,' the official was saying. 'Things like rules or evidence have no relevance in their case. They have no rights. The constitution guarantees rights only to citizens. Citizens are those who obey the laws of the Sarkar. They have to become citizens first to earn their rights. Till then . . .'

The guards scrupulously carried out the remedial measures required to make citizens out of prisoners. Sometimes they continued their sessions for long spells without a break. Sometimes they were held less frequently, just once or twice a week. Between the sessions, Kundan lay down and dreamed about the forms of torture they would try out on him in the next session. Hoards of lice, bugs and mosquitoes wove patterns on the dark fabric of agony into which dreams and reality had merged. Kundan lost count of days, weeks, months and seasons—all that was reckoned, welcomed or regretted in the world outside his cell.

Chapter Fifty-One

The poet, while describing inferno, wrote:

> There is no greater sorrow
> Than to recall in misery
> The time when we were happy

It might be more appropriate to call the time in the past consoling, rather than happy. Suffering underlies everything. The question is whether it is bearable. When it becomes unbearable, it is disconcerting to think of the times when it was bearable.

Can suffering be made bearable by logical reasoning or by arguing with oneself? Can a sufferer find solace in the vast terrain of philosophy? Think of the unbounded sky, the innumerable stars, endless time, black holes, the ever-expanding universe, the Big Bang . . . what is this trifling life of ours over which we sit and cry? But for a man in agony, it matters little whether the universe began with a big bang or was in a steady state. It is not his powers of reasoning, but the presence of other human beings that comforts a man in suffering. If they too are afflicted by the same sorrow, so much the better.

It was the presence of Ruth that Kundan longed for. However sternly the poet warned him of the inferno to which these memories would lead him, Kundan's mind went back again and again to the days he spent with her in that small house in the desert.

Why did she come seeking him to that forlorn desert town where he was holed up? Perhaps she too had needed him. Kundan did not know whether he would ever be able to give back to her the solace she had given him then. Where could she be now? Was she too sitting cooped up in a prison cell? A charge of espionage could easily be slapped on her too. And unlike Kundan, she might really be in possession of some dangerous documents.

Kundan's imagination ran amok. Ruth had been moving in a jungle where predators abounded. Where there were no predators, there were 'rioters'. Anyone could kill anyone in a riot, with no questions asked. Individual killings were murders, but not massacres in riots. Riots were like the interregnums in the tribal society Ruth had told Kundan about, when a dead chief was yet to be replaced by a successor. All notions of accountability disappeared in riots. Even the count of the dead was a casual affair. The massive amounts of money the Sarkar spends in conducting censuses, classifying people according to their gender, age, language, religion, occupation and income are laid waste by the rioters. The profound analyses and projections made by demographers and social scientists are blown away like leaves in a storm and deposited on roads, in rivers and in the pages of newspapers.

Civilization was accountability, Ruth had once told Kundan who had countered it by saying that it was mere accounting. And they had had a good laugh over that.

The Sarkar does take a headcount after a riot. Occasionally a headcount is taken even when there are no riots, like a miser counting his coins. The count is taken with perfect equanimity, in cold blood, and recorded meticulously in columns and tables. You never know under how many heads you are accounted for: as a man, as one in the late forties, as a tall or short man, as a member of the middle-income group, as a spy, as a lawyer, as a prisoner . . .

Chapter Fifty-Two

A lawyer and a prisoner—Kundan could clearly see himself belonging to these two categories.

Perhaps that was why the jail official's instructions he overheard refused to leave his mind. Kundan did not know why he described them as 'overheard'. Overhearing was not the same as eavesdropping. On second thoughts, it occurred to Kundan that overhearing meant hearing something not addressed to the hearer, but which had implications for him. The official's instructions were certainly not meant for the prisoners to hear, which meant that they did not appear to him as normal human beings capable of hearing and understanding what he said. More than what the official actually said, it was his attitude of total indifference towards the prisoners, which amounted to an insult of their intelligence, that revolted Kundan. No man generally has second thoughts about kissing his wife in the presence of a pet dog. It is said that in ancient Egypt, ladies of the court stripped and changed their clothes in the presence of the eunuchs and slaves who guarded their chambers.

Kundan, the lawyer, could never understand why some people were looked down on like animals, or locked up in cells, or made to slave for others. But Kundan, the prisoner, who had trudged the weary path from the desert understood it only too well.

A group of human beings become a community when they exist cohesively, when each of them relates to the others. But within every community exists a counter-community which violates this principle of cohesion. In certain circumstances, this counter-community thrives and grows large enough to take over the whole community. We have a certain idea of the State as an institution which suppresses all such counter-communities, an upholder of established values and a dispenser of justice. But such a State, more often than not, exists only in our dreams. Instead, what we have is a counter-State propped up by a counter-community which has usurped the community's functions.

In times when cultivated land formed the geographic and symbolic nucleus of society, all those who did not participate in its regulated activities—bandits, outlaws, aboriginals, and also hermits who relinquished the pleasures of the world—were pushed out into the forests and wastelands that lay beyond the strip of arable land. Thus was born the poromboke on the geographical, economic and cultural peripheries of the society. Down the ages and across cultures, these poromboke people were variously labelled as barbarians, pagans, bushmen or external proletariat. It was considered the right of the established society to raid and subjugate these marginal people whenever it was convenient to them.

The nucleuses of cultivable land later joined together to form kingdoms and empires. Statecraft and division of labour became more sophisticated. Castes or guilds took on different functions., Those who had no such positions assigned to them were again placed on the peripheries: chandalas and mlechhas, heretics and Jews.

As the poromboke grew, its nature changed. As the number of the banished multiplied, it became impossible to confine them to the peripheries. The poromboke began encroaching into the pale of society. Instead of banishing or killing the outlaws, it became the practice for the Sarkar to enslave them and make them work for it. The prisoners of war worked the fields and mines in chains.

The poromboke groups now dotted the society—villages of the excommunicated, colonies of lepers, ghettos of Jews. With the spread of civilization, the democratization of the political system and the advent of competitive economic activities, the dividing line between the external and internal marginalization disappeared, along with the identity of the poromboke as a distinct geographical area outside the pale of society. Wars, famines, earthquakes, religious and ethnic conflicts and revolutions evicted men from their habitats and turned them into vagrants, bandits and finally into prisoners and slaves. Later, new categories like the unemployed and the lumpen appeared. The marginal people, now swollen into a large mass, filled the footpaths, railway stations, slums, the recruiting centres for development projects and the private armies of political parties. The spread of the ideology of the market hastened the process and practically the whole population was threatened with marginalization and the whole society was on the brink of being turned into a poromboke. Like a spider at the centre of its web, a small, omnipotent nucleus calling itself the Sarkar or the market extracted its sustenance from the massive poromboke which surrounded it, bleeding it white in the process.

The castrati who sang in the opera houses of medieval European cities had the unenviable fate of being ridiculed by the same people whom they entertained and raised into ecstasy through their music. Bought from the market at a very young age and emasculated by castration and trimming of their vocal cords, these unfortunate human beings developed unusually long arms and legs, large breasts, rounded hips and a shrill voice which made them look like buffoons. Society, while it enjoyed their performances, refused to accept them as human beings. Even the church excommunicated them.

A society which sneered at such unfortunate human beings was sneering at itself. The music which raised it to ecstatic heights came from incised vocal cords and the chastity of its women was preserved by castrated men. Its todays were erected by prisoners whose tomorrows were mortgaged. Its processions of liberty passed through streets, on either side of which hung the bodies of slaves. It consummated its *yaga* of unity and integrity by pouring kerosene into the mouths of children and setting them on fire.

In the little sermon the jail official delivered to the guards, Kundan heard the notes of a fiddle played by a monarch against the backdrop of a burning city. In his own silence, he heard the unsung ballads of the eunuchs who sacrificed their lives in order to protect the chastity of the ladies of the court. But between the ecstasy of the fiddle's notes and the silent oblivion of impotence, where was he to locate the professor's long discourse on human proclivities?

Chapter Fifty-Three

A prisoner in the dark dungeon of his cell, in fact, has a large number of visitors: the jail superintendent, the warder, the torturer, the doctor, the attendant, the sweeper, the priest, and journalists and reformers of various shades. The prisoner was at their disposal. They supervised, questioned, tortured, healed, fed, cleaned, preached, studied, or just gazed at him. The torturer was only one of the visitors, and as emotionless and disinterested as the rest.

One day Kundan saw a torturer spinning a prisoner, hanging him upside down on a rope, in one direction, and then releasing him to unspin in the other. The spinning man threw up the contents of his stomach and the centrifugal force of his motion scattered the emissions all over the floor and the walls of the cell. Unmindful of what was happening, and with an air of having accomplished his task, the torturer went out and sat chatting with his colleagues in the next room. He was in an exuberant mood that day. A son had been born to him and he was celebrating the event by distributing sweets to his colleagues.

This man, like most people, loved his wife and child.

After smashing a prisoner's head at the jail, he would go home and play with his children. He would crawl on all fours, letting his little child ride on his back. Making sure that his children's eyes were turned, he would pinch his wife's cheeks on the sly.

A torturer sold a portion of himself everyday to buy provisions for his family, a smile on his wife's lips and the lisping chatter of his little child. He was satisfied with the bargain he made. He had no sense of loss, no regret, no pricks of conscience. In fact, when he stopped to reflect on it, it might even make him proud of his cleverness in clinching the deal.

Was not Sulaiman happy with the bargain he had struck? 'Don't send me back, saheb, my wife and children will starve to death,' he had pleaded with Kundan. 'Who can fight the Sarkar, saheb? Let it go,' Gulshan had dissuaded Kundan from investigating the soldiers' outrageous behaviour. Gulshan and his girl sought peace and stability in life by letting criminals go unpunished. It was quite possible that the man whom the torturer had hung upside down and spun like a top would say after everything was over, 'Don't untie me, brother . . .'

The professor had also made a trade-off in his own way. Everybody was making trade-offs. And they all seemed to be happy about it too. Everyone did his job coolly and diligently without embarrassment and without embarrassing anybody. Every trade-off they made with the Sarkar was as simple as handing out currency notes for a dress, a chunk of fish or a bottle of liquor. Here the currency handed over was the little moisture left in them when everything else was drying up, the tiny particles of water that bound one human being to the other and made society a cohesive and organic entity.

Chapter Fifty-Four

Kundan was ill throughout the summer. He had recurring bouts of fever, diarrhoea and vomiting which made him so weak and exhausted that he could not even sit up. The frequent, unannounced discharges from his body had one positive result. On such occasions, he was taken out of the cell into the veranda. The veranda looked down into a small yard, which though closed on all sides by high walls, had its little fragment of earth and sky.

It rained intermittently and grass grew thickly in the yard. The eggs of insects which had been waiting under the soil for months hatched, and the new entrants to the world of the living rejoiced by crawling, running, hopping and flying. On the edges of the gutter, in the corners of the veranda, in the midst of the green moss growing on the red bricks, millipedes hatched from their eggs. Hundreds of them, and each with hundred legs! They squirmed and wriggled, one over the other, forming little heaps. Birds that flitted above the yard swooped down on them and swallowed them at one go.

Millions of eggs laid by the insects are destroyed by

heat, frost or moisture. Many of the young larvae, in their search for food and shelter, lost their way and eventually succumbed to hunger and fatigue. Among those which survived, many fell victims to predators. When the hazards are taken into account, it was indeed a marvel that these creatures survived at all.

Though not in danger of being eaten up by birds and reptiles, there was an element of fortuitousness in the turns and twists of human life too. If the measurements and identification marks of Sulaiman had agreed with what the warder read out from the list in his hand on that fateful evening on the railway platform, Kundan would still have been performing the duties of the labour officer at Rambhagarh Project earnestly and diligently. Undisturbed by doubts and questions, he would have been sitting on the terrace of his rented house sipping a glass of beer and watching the skyline of the town studded with the turrets of the havelis which became clear and hazy by turns.

The dissenting identification marks on Sulaiman's body would have now been eaten up by worms and microbes, and Pasupati's dossier would have quietly moved into the archives of the Project. Perhaps Amala's face too would have passed into memory. Kundan, on the other hand, was transformed into a mere physical identity, a body which emptied its bowels and spewed its stomach on the veranda, disturbing the little millipedes at play.

The fortuitous encounter with the arithmetic of weights and heights at the railway station set Kundan on the impossible errand of saving the life of a man called Sulaiman. But Sulaiman, not waiting for his saviour, found his salvation under a steel girder. Kundan then extended his mission to the entire lot of prisoners. But the prisoners exchanged their halter, in a secret deal with the Sarkar, for stabbing and burning to death thousands of people in a riot. Feeling no remorse for it, congratulating themselves on the bargain, they moved about merrily through the streets like free birds.

Kundan wondered whether all these had been just incidental. He too had perhaps managed to stay alive like the insects, avoiding the perils of heat, frost and moisture, escaping the stalking predators. But was the life of an insect too totally fortuitous?

One of the questions that Kundan had asked himself when he arrived in the desert for the first time was about the desert people's attitude towards their environment. Were they engaged in a valiant battle against adversity, or were they completely resigned to their fate? What aided the sultana in her battle against one set of circumstances was her compromise with another. Kundan did not know whether her actions, in their totality, could be termed propitiousness or combat. What was the difference between revolt and surrender? There was a time when at the end of each battle, not only the people, the army of the vanquished king, but also his courtiers and his queens lined up to greet the triumphant king with garlands in their hands and smiles and flattery on their lips. For them, one king was as good as another. They were neither surrendering nor revolting, but merely surviving. They had no choice.

For the people of the desert, their sovereigns were like the geography and the climate of their habitat—eternal and beyond repair or redemption. As Kundan ploughed his lonely furrow through the desert, he was confronted by events and circumstances he had never met before. As he sliced through the molten mass of humanity thrust before him and moulded the chunks into individuals with names, characters and identification marks, he disturbed the serene tranquility of the desert. He asked himself the old question: suppose man's circumstances were not as incorrigible or eternal like geography or climate?

A no man's land between two contradicting situations, one entirely hopeless like the desert, and the other full of hope like a fertile tract of land, can be conceived of. Between the two, there is an area which is not altogether ruled by considerations of existence or survival. The question is where, at what line of demarcation the arguments of survival give way to those of decisive human action. But if it is discovered that even beyond what is recognized as this borderline, fatalism and surrender prevail instead of the will to act, it means that the march of the desert has begun, that it has started eating into the fertile, green belt.

The survival of insects cannot perhaps be attributed solely to the fact that they lay eggs in millions. Luck may not be the only factor that takes a larvae through the various stages of its growth till it becomes a full-grown insect capable of laying eggs. And it may not just be a stroke of misfortune that the little moisture left in human beings are drying up and the pleasant notes that mediate between them are drowned in the harsh monotone of grains of sand rubbing against one another.

Chapter Fifty-Five

With the end of summer, Kundan recovered his health. Like his fellow prisoners, he began waiting for winter to set in. It was usual for the prisoners to wait for winter in summer, and for summer in winter. Their dreams traversed the distance in time between the respite from mosquitoes and bugs and the relief from the chilling cold inside the dark cells.

One day in mid-autumn, the warder took the prisoners out. He allowed them to walk in the yard between the long barracks, and to bask in the sun. The prisoners enjoyed this unusual generosity like a feast. They touched and stroked the leaves that the trees had begun to shed and the new blades of grass which had sprouted after the rains. They puffed their nostrils to take in the gentle breeze and wandered about the yard at will. The restrictions of space did not bother them. Their fear was about how long the unexpected liberty would last.

The pain of torture, which had resumed immediately after he became fit for it, was still disturbing Kundan. He stretched his limbs and massaged them as he walked. There was a wide, deep gutter which cut across the middle of the yard. Kundan stood on the edge of the gutter, watching the water that flowed through it, which though stinking and black attracted him like a river.

Suddenly somebody hit him from behind. He fell flat on his face on the ground. Before he could figure out what had happened, he was lifted by the collar of his shirt and hit again. This time it was on the pit of his stomach and he screamed. He had struck against something hard and his lips were bleeding. When he raised his head, he saw the assailant looking down at him. It was one of the prisoners. A short, stout man with a big flat face. Kundan did not remember seeing him before, but the man was staring at him contemptuously, as if he had just settled scores with him. He muttered something under his breath and spat on Kundan's face. Not satisfied with what he had done, he kicked Kundan violently and sent him rolling into the gutter. Before he could climb out of the gutter, he had gulped a couple of mouthfuls of the filthy water flowing in it.

Kundan sat on the edge of the gutter and tried to make some sense out of the incident. The prisoner who attacked him was now through with his job. He walked away nonchalantly. None of the prisoners remained on the scene; they had not thought it necessary to interfere. The scene had just been reflected on their retinas and then vanished like a film sequence on the screen.

But unlike them, the prisoner who attacked him was by no means disinterested. He had intruded rudely into Kundan's solitude who was clueless as to the motive behind the attack. He did not appear to have gone out of his senses. Perhaps he had mistaken Kundan for somebody else. Or their paths might have crossed sometime in the past. It was quite possible that he had been a worker in a factory where Kundan had been the labour officer, or a Pioneer at the Rambhagarh Project. Kundan could not have been the villain of the piece. But it was not necessary to be a villain to hurt somebody. In a society where each individual looks out only for himself, anyone could be an enemy, for everybody is a potential obstacle to the fulfilment of the individual's self-interest. So nobody could help his hands being dirtied, being accomplices or betrayers in this great game of self-obsession. The difference between guilt and innocence became a mere illusion.

Kundan rested his head on his knees and wiped the tears from his eyes. He bore no ill-will towards the man who had assaulted him. If he harboured any feeling towards him, it was gratitude. Gratitude for shattering his solitude, his insulation from his fellow beings.

Chapter Fifty-Six

It was winter again. The days became shorter and the prisoners shivered even during the day. They huddled together for warmth. Though the mosquitoes and cockroaches had retreated, bugs and rats still pursued them relentlessly.

As for Kundan, another welcome change which came with the advent of winter was that the torture sessions became less frequent. The vigour with which his torturers used to handle him had also abated. There were no more questions about his comrades or their diabolic plans to sell the country to the enemy. However, as a matter of routine, the torturers still appeared occasionally, and in a totally disinterested manner thrashed the underside of his feet or pushed a pin or two into his flesh and went away. Sometimes they were too lazy to do even that, and would just urinate on his head and leave the cell.

The torture sessions ended abruptly. He was left alone for a month. Then, on a cloudy, drizzling day, he was released into the wide open spaces of the world outside the prison.

Chapter Fifty-Seven

In the busy thoroughfares of the city one occasionally spotted a camel, an elephant or a horse with a rider on its back moving sluggishly, or at a trot in the midst of speeding vehicles and hastening pedestrians. The rider, more often than not, chose the lane meant for vehicles rather than the one set apart for pedestrians. The camel rider whom Kundan saw approaching the traffic junction had done exactly that. On the signal lights were instructions for both vehicles and pedestrians. Which set would the camel rider follow, Kundan wondered, for he had to choose one of the two, if he wanted to move ahead.

Kundan did not know where to pick up the thread of his life again. Though the thoughts that rode his mind resembled these camels or elephants, Kundan did not want to consider himself different from the others, nor that, unlike them, he had to tread the untrodden path.

With his degree in labour law, he could still manage to make a living by working in some factory. Or he could put on a lawyer's gown with some success. But he had not made up his mind yet. The money he had in his pocket when he was arrested had been returned to him when he was released. He was also fortunate to retrieve his belongings from the hotel he was staying in when he was arrested. Since he could pull on for some time with that, he was not in a hurry.

The prison manager was of the view that if a prisoner who was arrested on mistaken assumptions or false charges was let off, he would turn out to be a security risk. Why then had he been released? He had been arrested as a spy and was given the treatment which was considered appropriate for such a person. Newspapers, including the one which had fought spiritedly for its right to select the captions for the news provided by the Sarkar, must have published his photograph and biographical sketches. Still he was let off.

Pondering over the matter, Kundan soon came up with the answer. The security risk about which the manager was so exercised did not exist now. The Sarkar was now confident that no amount of allegations, no shocking exposures could cause the slightest damage to it, let alone overthrow it. Kundan could now, perhaps, walk into the offices of any of the dailies in the city and narrate the story of his detention, the false charges that were framed against him and the brutal torture he was subjected to. Today, the dailies may even spread them out voluminously on their pages, sparing none of the horrifying details. The stories would move the readers to tears. But nothing more would happen.

Kundan's incarceration started at the beginning of a winter and ended at the beginning of the next. The question that was being hotly debated at the professor's house then was whether the government would fall. Perhaps it did not and the riots propped it up. Or it fell and was replaced by another. Whatever might have happened during the last twelve months—riots, elections, war—they had changed nothing. If they had done anything, it was to strengthen the Sarkar, for the Sarkar, or whatever name was given to it, seemed to be constantly accumulating strength.

It was a burning and ravaged city that Kundan had left behind when he was arrested. Dark columns of smoke rose everywhere and corpses littered the streets. People were killing their neighbours and singing songs of victory. A sandstorm was blowing through the city burying men and all that they used to hold high at some time. But today the city was smiling again. People had turned out in their colourful woollens to bask in the sun. A thick green carpet of grass had spread over the lawns in the traffic islands. Dahlia, dianthus, salvia and anturhnum greeted the passers-by from the road-side gardens. Children playing and riding bicycles were enjoying themselves. By all accounts, the city seemed to have forgotten the holocaust that laid it waste just a year ago. It had shaken off its stupor, had a refreshing bath, put on new clothes and come out with a welcoming smile to greet the brief respite before the next round of riots, massacres, or even a war. A whole group of people distinguished by its caste, religion, language or political affiliation, perhaps a whole generation, may lie dead to rot under the sun. The child tripping gaily on the lawn may become a mass of flesh charred beyond recognition by tomorrow. The girl in the corner whispering to her boyfriend had not thought of the possibility of her body lying torn and bleeding under the same tree she leaned against. The family coming out of the shopping plaza with heavy bags could not see the vultures who fastened their greedy eyes on them from the top of the tall monuments across the road.

They were all kept on a long leash by the Sarkar. The difference between them and the prisoners was only in the length of the rope given to them by the Sarkar. The young men discussing a film or play they had seen, the child sucking its thumb and looking wide-eyed at the world around it, the old man working in the garden—they were all sentenced to death and were living on borrowed time.

Soldiers in battledress stood behind the sandbag shelters

erected on the sidewalks, with machine-guns fixed on them. Police vans with red lights revolving on the top patrolled the streets, the wireless sets in the officers' hands humming, crackling and beeping. Behind ten-foot-high iron gates, Alsatian dogs, their tongues hanging out, kept watch the whole night to pounce upon intruders. Chowkidars, wrapped in large overcoats and trudging in down-at-heel boots, blew their whistles and banged their sticks on the echoing walls in the small hours of the day.

The assault they were awaiting with dread was yet to materialize.

Through the haze of the misty dawn the people who had formed a long queue before the milk booth looked like pilgrims at a shrine. They shivered in the cold, and shifted their weight uneasily from one foot to the other, sticking out their necks and swaying from side to side when they became too restless. When a man, taking advantage of the mist, tried to sneak into the queue, some of the people in the queue pounced on him. There were angry shouts and battle cries, till someone dragged the intruder away. The pilgrims resumed their patient progress to the shrine.

In the crowded bus, a man clutching on to the iron bar under the roof kept losing his balance and falling on Kundan. When the bus swerved at turnings and the man's face and hands brushed against his body, Kundan noticed he was running a high temperature.

A woman with a child on her shoulder, indifferent to the biting cold and the chilling wind, was trying to sell newspapers, which the drizzle had almost turned into pulp, at a traffic junction. She moved from one car to another, tapping vainly on the closed glass shutters. Her body was wrapped in a cotton sari which revealed that she did not even have a blouse under it. The child, naked but for the end of the sari which was pulled over its body, cried incessantly. As she waved the papers in her hand, she turned to console the child. *Don't cry, my dear, you know your mother has nothing to give you.* The child, as if it could understand her helplessness, stopped crying and lay quietly on her shoulder.

Kundan removed the shawl he had wrapped over his coat and covered the mother and child with it. The child opened its eyes for a moment. The mother just lowered her eyes after a grateful glance at Kundan. He watched them disappearing into the crowd.

At Rambhagarh, a year before, Kundan and Ruth had watched in silence a group of old men, women and children, a column of defeated humanity, moving out of the town, across the desert into their villages. The tap of their shoes and sandals on the cobbled streets of the town still rang in Kundan's ears. Here, in this sprawling city, the defeated mothers and children made no sound as they retreated, for they wore nothing on their feet even in the freezing cold. As Kundan was leaving Rambhagarh for good, on another cold night, a door in the street suddenly opened and Suku appeared at it. She greeted him, and then bid him farewell with a broad smile.

Kundan's eyes wandered over the countless doors of the endless houses on either side of the road. Was Ruth standing at one of them? Where would she be now? Lying buried under the sands of the desert, killed by a bullet from the rifle of a policeman or a Pasupati? Squatting in a prison cell staring listlessly at the iron bars? All fancies. Reality was a piece of white paper; blank, like the mind of a prisoner coming out of the torture chamber.

Ruth was missing. Amala was missing. Bhola too. And like them many more.

Yet, from the emptiness, like a cloud in a clear sky, like a sudden shower, like words out of pursed lips, like a wink in motionless eyes, Ruth would emerge from a door. That was one thing that made the missing different from the dead—a possibility, however slender, of coming back. What people called hope, what poor Suku held tightly to her heart for years . . .

Ruth may return. Amala too, with her eyes that took

you to unknown worlds. Bhola, with the fire within him. Suku's brother, after mustering courage. All these missing ones, perhaps even the professor with his incisive intellect regained.

The mother and child who walked away shivering in the cold may come back.

The old men, women and children who had returned to their villages after abandoning their siege of Rambhagarh may return.

Everybody who went back defeated may return . . .

The cities may again be inhabited.

The aquifers may still get recharged underneath our society, and springs may sprout again to restore the moisture that binds man with man. The harsh grinding sound which grains of sand make when rubbed together, might become a thing of the past.

Perhaps all this will happen . . . but then, perhaps they may not . . .

Meanwhile, tomorrow too, taking advantage of the mist, somebody may try to sneak into the middle of the queue before the milk booth. Others may push him out. An altercation, a fight, or even a murder may follow.

The man who protested loudly against the intruder in the queue was conscious of his rights. He was a small rebel. But his eyes were fixed on the counter, and a litre of milk was all that he had in his mind, not the abstractions of right and wrong, not even the problems of water, electricity and the rising prices of vegetables and cereals that he had to face when he returned home from the booth. He unsheathed his sword to protect his litre of milk. Would he take up cudgels for his wife and children, for his neighbour, for his fellow human beings upon whom injustice fell like rain?

The question remains unanswered—like the other questions about closed doors, missing men and abandoned cities. Like all the other questions yet to be identified.

READ MORE IN PENGUIN

In every corner of the world, on every subject under the sun, Penguin represents quality and variety—the very best in publishing today.

For complete information about books available from Penguin—including Puffins, Penguin Classics and Arkana—and how to order them, write to us at the appropriate address below. Please note that for copyright reasons the selection of books varies from country to country.

In India: Please write to *Penguin Books India Pvt. Ltd. 210 Chiranjiv Tower, Nehru Place, New Delhi, 110019*

In the United Kingdom: Please write to *Dept JC, Penguin Books Ltd. Bath Road, Harmondsworth, West Drayton, Middlesex, UB7 ODA. UK*

In the United States: Please write to *Penguin USA Inc., 375 Hudson Street, New York, NY 10014*

In Canada: Please write to *Penguin Books Canada Ltd. 10 Alcorn Avenue, Suite 300, Toronto, Ontario M4V 3B2*

In Australia: Please write to *Penguin Books Australia Ltd. 487, Maroondah Highway, Ring Wood, Victoria 3134*

In New Zealand: Please write to *Penguin Books (NZ) Ltd. Private Bag, Takapuna, Auckland 9*

In the Netherlands: Please write to *Penguin Books Netherlands B.V., Keizersgracht 231 NL-1016 DV Amsterdom*

In Germany : Please write to *Penguin Books Deutschland GmbH, Metzlerstrasse 26, 60595 Frankfurt am Main, Germany*

In Spain: Please write to *Penguin Books S.A., Bravo Murillo, 19-1'B, E-28015 Madrid, Spain*

In Italy: Please write to *Penguin Italia s.r.l., Via Felice Casati 20, 1-20104 Milano*

In France: Please write to *Penguin France S.A., 17 rue Lejeune, F-31000 Toulouse*

In Japan: Please write to *Penguin Books Japan. Ishikiribashi Building, 2-5-4, Suido, Tokyo 112*

In Greece: Please write to *Penguin Hellas Ltd, dimocritou 3, GR-106 71 Athens*

In South Africa: Please write to *Longman Penguin Books Southern Africa (Pty) Ltd, Private Bag X08, Bertsham 2013*